ANCIENT
DESTINY

VOL 2: ESCAPE FROM THE EARTH

ISBN-13   Paperback   978-1-964100-99-9
           eBook   978-1-964100-98-2

ANCIENT DESTINY

VOL 2: ESCAPE FROM THE EARTH

ALBERT LYNN CLARK

BOOKS
BY ALBERT CLARK FICTION

The Price of Peace (1987, 2012)

Ancient Destiny (Volume I) (2012)

Ancient Destiny (Volume II) coming soon
Non-Fiction

Computer Supported Network
Analysis System (1981)

CSNAS

Guide to Acquisition Logistics (1985)

Logistics Support Analysis

Various US Air Force Manuals

DEDICATION

vii

To my wife, Carolyn Clark who humored me
when I spent hours at the computer writing,
searching the internet, reading my email,

CONTENTS

ACKNOWLEDGMENTS

Thank you to the education I received. Thank you to all the science fiction authors out there. Thank you for my 33 first cousins who spent days and weeks discussing strange things about science, possible futures, and sharing their books.

PART ONE

PLANNING

1

BACKGROUND IN SCIENCE

The history of Earth is not quite what is in the history books. First there was Mars. The Martians discovered a large interstellar body that was going to impact Mars as a catastrophic life ending event. In response they built spaceships more advanced than what we have today and evacuated tens of thousands to Earth.

There is a Rift Valley on Mars 5,000 kilometers long or about 3,000 miles long that appears to have been formed by an interstellar impact. If it was, it would have been sufficient to end life on Mars and blow away its atmosphere. What little remains of Martian atmosphere are similar to our own, but very very thin.

Phase two of this history was our history of Atlantis. Our history treats it as both a far fetched and possibly true story by Plato, and an ancient city-state that was destroyed by a volcano. Many scientists believe that Atlantis actually existed. Some said it was outside the Pillars of Hercules, some said it was in the Mediterranean.

Some scientists actually name the Greek Island of Santorini as Atlantis. I have been there and have the photos. Today it has a village on a high cliff you can reach from the sea by donkey, walk, or take cable cars to the top. From the top you can see a large bay curving away from the village with a sometimes smoking remnant of a volcano at the distant point of the crescent shaped bay. There are frequently several cruise ships and other boats in the bay. The story goes that the volcano exploded, destroying Atlantis and just leaving the volcano and the crescent shaped bay remaining.

The stories say that Atlantis had crystals on the mountain peaks that sent out power for airships to roam the earth. Descriptions of the actual city-state depict Atlantis as a great city with advanced technology with multiple circular canals around the city.

One story of Atlantis describes an army of 10,000 Atlanteans easily beating back hundreds of thousands of Arabs in Northern Africa and southern Europe. Every battle is a monumental victory with thousands of defenders dying with almost no losses on the Atlantean side. However, when Egypt and Greece were about to be overrun, the Atlanteans received word that something bad was happening in Atlantis and they all retreated home just before Atlantis was destroyed and forever lost. Does this mean that humans were on Earth when the Martians came and established Atlantis? Does this mean that maybe colonies from Atlantis were attempting to rebel against Atlantis rule?

Or, was Plato simply describing a fictional Utopia that never existed. Plato said he was reading ancient documents. History says that 200 years after Plato, the Greeks built the library of Alexandria to hold all the great documents of the world, but the library was destroyed and all the documents lost in a fire in 48 B.C. when Caesar decided to burn his fleet to prevent Achilles from communicating by sea. The burning of the library was accidentally caused by the burning of the fleet. That is only one story. Some say it was destroyed by Christians against paganism. Some say it was the Moslems around 900 A.D. I think we can assume the library existed. Did it hold the history of Atlantis? Did it contain the science that Atlantis had? We'll never know.

There is a whole area of pseudo science called Forbidden Archeology where there is evidence of very advanced, very old societies predating Egypt. There is the brass mechanical computer attributed to ancient Greece. It was found in the Mediterranean and encrusted. X- Rays reveal multiple gears to compute. Just get on the internet and search for "forbidden archeology". There is a coin discovered that appears to be 200,000 years old. Far before Egypt, but do your own looking at forbidden archeology.

Don't forget that sometimes archeology is spelled archaeology.

All of the above is evidence that at least some of the story could be true.

Just a note in my own history. When I started in first grade in grade school I was reading Popular Science and Popular Mechanics magazines and many novels while the other first graders were learning "See Tom Run". I was taught that all airplanes had to have propellers and my teachers and classmates could not understand when I was building clay model jet aircraft while they had propellers on their clay airplanes. I was told I was wrong. I was taught that nothing could exist above the speed of sound, but I knew that Chuck Yeager had done just that in 1947 when I was only 3 years old. I read all about it when I was in first grade, so by the second grade I was arguing that Chuck Yeager had already done it and survived. I was taught that E=MC2. At the speed of light all material is changed to energy. Recently I have read that scientists have evidence that some particles have exceeded the speed of light. Star Trek has used Warp Drive for multiples of the speed of light.

2

REVIEW OF VOLUME ONE

Volume one starts right in with the SHIP. The SHIP was left behind by this very advanced Martian or Atlantean civilization when they escaped our solar system for somewhere in interstellar space. Just like they escaped Mars before its destruction which left behind the Rift Valley and a weak atmosphere, Atlantis was destroyed centuries later. They could not evacuate the entire population. In the event that humans survived on Earth after the cataclysm, they left the ship behind to educate humans and advance science so that once again, some humanity would evacuate Earth in advance of the same rock that destroyed their civilization on Mars. But this time it was aimed at Earth. This final disaster was predicted for thousands of years from the time Atlantis was destroyed.

SHIP was their most advanced interstellar spaceship. It had capabilities far beyond Earth in the 21st century. It was built from materials that we would have a hard time understanding. It used energy that we would say is impossible, just like splitting the atom used to be impossible. It had artificial intelligence we are just starting to understand and does not exist in our current science.

SHIP orbits Earth, but cannot be seen on radar or through telescopes. The only real evidence we currently have is that sometimes, astronomers have seen an object temporarily flashing across their telescopes. It has the capability of changing its image to blend with the background just like the military is experimenting with a coating that makes objects disappear into the background. There are people that can paint themselves to appear like what they are standing in front of and cannot be seen until they move.

While SHIP can observe anyone and anywhere on Earth, SHIP can only focus on a few at any one time. Its software told it to pick one person at a time, bring that person to the SHIP and give him knowledge to advance science. There are outstanding scientists throughout history that were far ahead of their time. They were limited in what they could do because Earth science had to start over as cavemen after the destruction of Atlantis and a loss of all its science. The energy beamed from Atlantis powered all of the aircraft, ships at sea, communications, computers, and most of the science. When Atlantis was destroyed the science disappeared into the dust after a few thousand years. Archeologists discovered some left over artifacts that survived but seemed out of place. There were historical references to advanced technology, but not the technology. So scientists like Aristotle could only do so much with the existing technology. They could advance that technology, but only so far. Centuries after Aristotle, Tesla attempted to beam power, just like Atlantis did. You can read about Tesla whenever you want by going on the internet or reading other hardcopy books.

Volume Two starts with SHIP choosing the most recent and the last chosen scientist. Time is running out before the interstellar body comes back to the solar system again destroying Earth just like it had Mars tens of thousands of years before.

Craig was a freshman at the University of Oklahoma when chosen by SHIP. He was highly intelligent, but not technically a genius. Maybe 150 IQ, but with a lot to learn. He was teleported to SHIP and educated in certain facts by a brainwave system that implanted information in his brain. The human brain, while more complex and capable than the best computer in the early twenty-first century could not hold all the information collected by SHIP over eons. To supplement his new learning, SHIP could telepathically communicate with Craig on anything he needed to know at the moment. It was not like a discussion that Craig had to listen to.

If Craig were asked to solve the most complex mathematical equation ever developed, the answer would just appear in his mind. It was not as if Craig could work this math problem at warp speed, it was that Craig knew the answer. He knew the answer came from SHIP because he would have had to spend weeks or months solving the problem. Plus, the knowledge inserted into his mind by SHIP was an overview of many technologies and theories.

Craig used this learned knowledge and with telepathic answers from SHIP he convinced the professors at the University of Oklahoma that he should be granted a nearly instant PhD. This added to the credibility of what Craig needed to do to save humanity. While they might not listen to a college freshman, they would pay more attention to a Dr. Craig Decker that had multiple PhDs at age 19.

Craig achieved this by being able to answer any question a panel of professors could ask and solve complex problems instantly. In addition, he gave several of the professors extremely advanced knowledge far beyond what the professors thought possible. He gave them a new metal that was basically indestructible but feather light. Craig had called it impervium. He gave them a cure for many cancers and AIDS. He gave them aerodynamics that far exceeded what they thought was possible. They had no idea where his knowledge came from, but they awarded multiple doctors degrees based on these facts and that he knew more than they ever thought they would know in their lifetimes.

Mankind had no knowledge, other than what he told them, of the disaster coming. Science knew of the Rift Valley on Mars and had already postulated that it blew away the atmosphere on Mars. Science had proved the existence of ice and therefore water on Mars.

The university, industry, and eventually the US government started committing money and science on developing the science that Craig provided. It is one thing to know how to make a new super metal; it is another thing to build an interstellar spaceship with it. With the light weight and new aerodynamics existing rocket engines could get it into space, but if you add a thousand people per ship with their food and supplies to build a new civilization, they could not launch without a new source of power. The alternative would be launching the empty ship, then transport everything to the new ship with shuttles.

It would take 40 years at the speed of light to get to another star. How would you get to an earth-like planet 400 light years away? You would have to have broken the light speed barrier. SHIP had that capability, but its drive was beyond the capability of Earth to build, therefore a new simpler form of interstellar ship would have to be developed. The rest of Volume Two is Craig's effort to get human-kind to another solar system and settling it for a new home for humankind.

3

CHANGED EXPECTATIONS

Dawn said, "There is too much for the two of us to do. We need more help. Are you sure the ship cannot take on a larger crew? There is plenty of room for a few more."

"I agree that we could use more help, but Ship said that I could only bring a wife on board with me. No one else. Isn't that right, Ship?"

"Actually, I said wives on board. There are seven chairs at the dining room table. The people of Atlantis had many wives. There is only one captain and only one captain's chair, but there are six side chairs. You and Dawn have already come to the conclusion that women make better space travelers. It is also important to have more women to build the population when colonizing new worlds."

Dawn broke the ensuing silence, "Craig. We did come to that conclusion ourselves. We just did not apply it to ourselves. What is our personal mission besides advancing science?"

"We have to find planets for the colony or colonies."

"Then we need a zoologist, a botanist, a geologist to tell us about minerals available, and an archeologist if we keep coming across the remains of Atlantis, and what?"

"An outdoorsman, er a woman. Someone that can lead an expedition on a strange planet. A survivalist type.

"Didn't you tell me you had researched other women before choosing me? I think you better see who is available."

"But we are married and I can't marry more than one nor do I want to."

"Craig, legal marriage is an Earth law. Ship has its own definition. If I remember, you chose me out of necessity. Well, this is necessary too. You don't really have a choice. We have to accelerate progress, find new planets to go to. You told me how you were attracted to some of the other women and chose me because I had a unique background is astral navigation which was critical. You married me because I wanted to be married if we were going to live together for the years to prepare. Well, things change. Now you need quantity not a single choice."

"We know that a human mind, as great as it is, is only capable of becoming an expert in one or two areas. You have the cursory knowledge from many areas and have SHIP to provide you detailed answers, but as SHIP has said, computers cannot come up with new ideas, only regurgitate existing information in its memory and learn new information after humans invent the ideas. Therefore, we need to come up with an inventory of the experts we need on the SHIP. SHIP can educate those extra passengers with everything SHIP knows of single concepts, like Astral Navigation, but the human mind would go into overload if it was swamped with everything there is to know. We can only assimilate a certain amount of knowledge at a time. As we learn at a normal human pace, we can fit it into our background and see how it fits. For example, if I were to have SHIP give me all the knowledge it has in geology it would probably make me nutty as a fruitcake trying to decide what is astral navigation and what is geology. How do they fit together? True, studying geology or learning it hands on over ten years would allow me the time to integrate or segregate the information into two piles and keep me sane. We know from SHIP that previous SHIP captains have attempted too much on their own and gone crazy losing the political help they needed on Earth to make things happen."

Craig replied, "Okay, I see the point. We need to come up with a list of the experts we need on SHIP, and have the SHIP train them in their area of interest, then learn the rest on their own. We know from SHIP that SHIP was prepared to take on a total of six women plus the male captain, me. According to SHIP this was because that was decreed by our Atlantean ancestors. I wonder if it is hard and fast and why if it is mandatory."

SHIP provided, "Seven is a special number that has been inserted into your culture. In your history there are the Seven Kings of Rome, Seven Emperors of Rome, Seven Hills of Constantinople, Seven Hills of Rome, Seven Liberal Arts, Seven Sages of the Bamboo Grove-China, Seven Sages of Greece, Seven Wonders of the Ancient World. The number seven is throughout your Bible and just in Christianity, but also Hinduism, Judaism, and Islam. The stories of Atlantis say there were seven islands. There are seven continents, though technically Europe and Asia are connected as one land mass."

Dawn provided, "I suspect it is because anytime humans are attempting to colonize a new planet, they want more females to have more children at a faster pace than one child at a time from one woman. The Mormons encouraged polygamy when they first moved to Utah because they wanted to increase their population fast. After they were established the Mormon Church decreed one wife per husband. The Catholic Church has always encouraged women against any birth control so they would produce the maximum number of Catholics. Early American Pioneers wanted big families to help with the farm. The Atlanteans that came from Mars were still trying to populate a whole planet with their own. That had gone on for thousands of years before Atlantis failed. Maybe it was not that way on Mars. Maybe Mars had a sustainable population whereas Earth had a lot of empty land waiting for humanity to inhabit it."

"Alright, Dawn, I get the point. Until we have totally established a sustainable population on a new planet we need to have multiple women per man to assure the survival of our new planet. Now, how do we, I, convince other women to join in polygamy?

"Craig, we are becoming known on Earth, our mission will soon become an earth wide mission, I would imagine it will not be long and people will be trying to buy their way off the planet by any means at hand, murder, money, or whatever. I don't think it will take much convincing. You are already famous, your knowledge is legion. You need to get on with it. Remember, we got married on Earth because I insisted on it, but that was before you were famous. I married you because I believed in the idea, I knew you were not a bad person, and I thought that just maybe this whole thing was legit. I wanted the respectability of marriage to live together. I did not really realize that Earth was in jeopardy of being destroyed soon. If I knew then what I know now, marriage would not really have been as issue."

"Okay, Dawn; let's summarize what we need to do and then how to go about it."

Craig had SHIP provide a personal computer that Craig was familiar with and a large screen monitor to show the lists he was going to make. He sat at the computer while he and Dawn made a list of the technologies and science that did not yet exist on Earth.

4

WHAT THE COLONY SHIPS WOULD CARRY

SHIP had the advantage of storing everything at the subatomic level. If you needed food, SHIP would take the subatomic matter to build molecules to build the exact food you were thinking of. If you wanted Maine lobster, it was delivered cooked as the best possible Maine lobster to match your expectations. There was no point in having a closet full of clothing. All you had to do was have an idea of what you might want to wear and there it was. If you changed your mind the clothing would change. The colony ships would not have this capability so if you wanted clothing; it had to be on the colony ship. If you wanted food it had to be dehydrated, frozen, or grown in hydroponics or something.

1. Construction of massive colony ships to move humans and their life support to another planet.

    a. The impervium was easily fabricated, but it was not just making the skyscraper sized ship, it was installing floors, doors, and stores of spare food, bedding and clothing that would wear out much sooner than the ship.

    b. A way to use the impervium in its initial form before curing that they could use to weld parts together for the floors and doors.

2. A list of what life support would be needed for the trip and the establishment of colonies on another planet with unknown resources.

    a. Food and water for the trip and for the initial colony. Food for the colony would come later.

    b. Clothing, bedding, soap, water recycling equipment and methods to be able to reuse the on board water over and over.

c.   Oxygen for the trip. You could not have thousands on a ship breathing the same air without some way to break down the CO2 back into Carbon that could be used to produce food and oxygen to breath. SHIP could provide that easily. Recycling the air from oxygen to carbon dioxide and back to oxygen would be easy.

  i.   SHIP would provide the technology to use waste like left over carbon from the air supply and human waste to produce food acceptable to eat.

  ii.   There would still have to be a supply of material for the food. It would chemically have to be more than just eating carbon. Meat and plants have a much more elaborate chemical composition than just carbon.

d.   Power equipment to build buildings, roads, and factories at the new planet. The new equipment could be made out of the impervium to make it almost indestructible and feather weight. Almost everything would be in kit form to save space.

i. A light weight bulldozer would not work, but could be made with the impervium to have compartments to fill with dirt or rock to make it heavy enough to do the dirt work necessary in construction.

ii. The engines made of the impervium would have to be fueled either with fuels on the new planets or be rechargeable from the ship's power supply. They would have to have oil because even the impervium would generate heat with internal friction. It might not hurt the metal or wear out the engine, but friction is friction.

iii. New battery technology as the current state of the art would not provide sufficient power for a long enough period of time. That is one reason electric cars and even hybrids had not replaced gasoline engines on Earth.

e. Hand tools for assembly of equipment and repair of equipment. Again made with the impervium to last for centuries, but things could work loose with time, stress, and vibrations. Since the equipment would be shipped as parts, hand tools would be used for assembly with bolts and nuts made from the impervium, but nuts can work their way loose over time.

3. A method of getting the above into orbit.

a. Just build the ship on earth and rocket it into space then shuttle the people and supplies in smaller rocket powered ships. The ship would not have to be empty, but neither could it be fully loaded with the existing rocket power on Earth.

b. The shuttles would be easily built with the new indestructible metal and conventional rocket engines. If manufacturing got behind ballistic missile rocket engines could be used. We bet that countries will forget about war when the evacuation gets closer.

4. Faster than light drive for their colony ships with the fuel to travel for light years at faster than the speed of light. SHIP provided the answer. Whereas SHIP converted matter directly to energy to use gravity and anti-gravity drive to pull itself toward one star while repelling another this was too far beyond Earth technology.

    a. The colony ships would use nuclear particle accelerators and anti-matter and dark energy collected from space to produce faster than light travel for extended months or years.

    b. Once landed on the new planet the ships could no longer gather anti-matter from space, but would have to rely strictly on nuclear power. Over time, nuclear fuel would have to be found, mined, and refined to supply the nuclear reactors. The impervium eliminated the need for extensive shielding. A tenth of an inch could protect against any radiation and smaller rocks in space. At faster than light speed Einstein's theory of relativity takes over. This theory is that as mass approaches the speed of light it becomes infinite. When it is infinite, a planet could pass through the ship like cosmic rays pass through our bodies every day. While infinite is undefined, imagine a ship the larger than the empire state building expanding to many times the size of our solar system. The passengers inside the ship would be like a fly on an airline traveling at 500 miles per hour. The fly can fly around just like in any room not knowing it is traveling 500 miles per hour.

c. The passengers in SHIP felt no acceleration due to the controlled gravity, but the colony ships would not have anti-gravity drive. The passengers in the colony ships would be subjected to acceleration. While humans could withstand twelve gees in special couches/chairs, they could not stand two gees for an extended period of time. Therefore, to accelerate up to speed, the colony ships would have to spend part of every day at nine gees, and then the rest of the time at something just over 1 gee. This would be inconvenient and uncomfortable but no different than any air force fighter pilot. The short period of acceleration along with the gradual acceleration would take weeks to exceed the speed of light. Once above the speed of light the particles from the accelerator would also be of infinite size and therefore much more powerful. During the flight they would have to be careful that their exhaust were directed away from asteroids and other small bodies or they would accelerate them in the opposite direction potentially becoming dangerous objects that could damage other planets. They would be moving at thousands of miles per hour similar to asteroids that came close to Earth in the past. Not knowing where life in the universe was might mean endangering life with their exhaust. On the other hand the amount of fuel used would be very small in comparison to the fuel on the ship. The nuclear fuel could last for years in the flight if necessary and many years on the new planet.

5. The other major obstacle would be for SHIP and his crew to find suitable habitable planets for the colony ships, preferably before take-off. By knowing the destination:

a. The flight could be planned out in advance to keep the exhaust from the colony ship from hitting too many bodies in space that in turn would become projectiles in their wake.

b. The flight could be planned for the minimum travel time to the new planets which would keep the use of materials like food to a minimum in flight.

c. Where it might take weeks or months to get up to speed the slowing back down for landing on the new planet would take an equal amount of time. The same routine would be computed, nine gees for short times and slightly above 1 gee the rest of the time followed by zero gee before landing.

6. After landing on the new planet, the ship would be permanently there for eternity or until it eventually turned to dust after a few thousand years.

7. New long lasting equipment that can do the job until the new colony can build their own factories on the new planet.

   a. In addition to the construction equipment, they would need transportation to explore their new surroundings. Helicopters, motorbikes, jeep type vehicles that would have electric power assuming they could develop better batteries. SHIP confirmed that this could happen.

   b. Their kitted special vehicles would be manufactured of the new metal called Impervium, but would be shipped in parts to be assembled after arrival on planet.

   c. Initially all vehicles would be battery powered by the nuclear power plant on the ship.

   d. Parts to build petroleum fueled engines would also be shipped. At some point the nuclear power plant would die and electricity may have to be generated with petroleum fuels. These fuels might come from oil wells and refineries or they might be alcohol from crops. However, using food crops for alcohol would not make sense. However, it was only a theory that petroleum could be found on the new planet.

e.   They would not want to continue to live in the cramped confines of the ship, but would want to build their own buildings, hopefully with materials found on their new planet. Maybe tree type vegetation for cabins, and so on. While close to the ship they could hook up to the nuclear power plant for years, but eventually would need other sources of power for cooking, heating, and cooling. Ships would have to carry tons of copper wire or transmit electricity like Tesla attempted, or find a light weight conductor.

f.   Food would be critical. Hopefully, planets could be found with earth-like flora and fauna to eat, make new clothing, and build buildings. Any planet they went to would have to have something for food and would have to have a climate where they could grow their own.

    i.   The colony ships would have to carry seeds and plantings for earth plants assuming soil and climate were compatible.

    ii.   The colony ships would carry a limited number of livestock to breed upon landing. This meant carrying livestock food along and conversion of livestock waste into foodstuffs.

    iii.   The colony ship would have huge refrigeration areas only partially heated by the nuclear reactor, but using the near absolute zero of space for cooling. The ship would have cooking equipment, but villages outside the ship on a new planet would need to be able to assemble their own refrigerators, clothes washers, cooking equipment.

g.   Even pharmaceuticals would have to be manufactured on planet before ship supplies ran out. Since crew selection would be extensive, they would not expect to use many pharmaceuticals enroot and they should not be bringing earth diseases with them. It might take some research to develop new pharmaceuticals.

h.   Miscellaneous equipment would include tents, ropes, and axes, for exploration and yes, guns and ammunition for protection against animals that might be a threat to humans.

8.   They had to find crews for the colony ships.

a.   The crews would be composed of 6 women for every man because women ate less, were better at being cooped up in a ship for an unknown period of time.

b.   To colonize a new planet and make it successful it would require a rapid increase in population after landing the ships on a new planet. This meant more women to men in order to have more children in less time than the normal couple relationship.

c.   Men were going to be required for their superior muscle power and generally better mechanical aptitude. Not that women could not build, but if came to building log cabins on the new planet, the muscle power would be important immediately. Plus, artificial insemination was iffy. Eventually, the population would equal out to men and women so they might as well start with some number of men.

d. Women would initially outnumber the men by 6 to 1 based on the SHIP's history of thousands of years of Martian and Atlantean history of colonization of new planets. This number, seven, was born out by Earth history as a special number. Had that number been planed by SHIP over millennia?

e. The selection criteria would be based on intelligence first and physical fitness second. The intelligence was largely based on education and IQ tests. Physical fitness included family history of having healthy children, no history of cancer or heart disease, or even arthritis. Coming from a family that had a history of long life was critical. Men and women would be tested for fertility.

f.   Training of the crew would have to start immediately.

    i.   Survival techniques.

    ii.   Construction techniques.

    iii.   Agriculture

    iv.   Medical, some would be slightly older medical doctors with the training to treat anything. These older doctors would be primarily women and would not be expected to have as large a family as the other women. Even with an intrinsically healthy crew, there would be broken bones and other injuries after they arrived at the new planet. Everyone would get some medical training in order to treat injuries on the spot prior to getting to one of the doctors. On a strange planet there could be unrecognized poisons, diseases, and hazards not seen by humans.

    v.   This would be a monumental job and would require one

member of the crew to spend extensive time on this job.

9. Talents for the colony.

  a. Medical is covered above.
  b. Agriculture-farming will be very important
  c. Construction, masons, architects, carpentry, lumberjacks assuming they had tree like plants to cut and build with.
  d. Resources - Water, sewage, oil refining, mining, smelting, foundry, castings.
  e. Technology - electronics, computer repair, electronics manufacturing, power generation, nuclear power.
  f. Mechanics - Electric motor and internal combustion engine repair, vehicle repair, small engine repair (especially chain saws, and so on.)
  g. Medical - Surgeon, female, radiology, bio-chemistry, pharmacologist, virologists, veterinarian, dentist, psychiatry.
  h. Arts - music, sewing, cooking.

10. Inventions needed.

a. Compact nuclear reactor to be enclosed in thin walls of the impervium at the back of the ship.

b. Faster than light drive – antimatter ram jet where antimatter is sucked in from the near vacuum of space and accelerated by the nuclear reactor to provide a rocket like thrust of particles.

c. Better batteries that can hold far more power for far longer than the best batteries available today. They also need to be lighter weight. That is why electric cars and hybrids today are not practical except for short distances like a super golf cart. On the new planet we will need to potentially travel twelve hours by helicopter on battery power. Smaller versions of this battery will be used for power hand tools from wrenches to chain saws, drills, and so on.

d. Mining and drilling equipment made with the impervium to take advantage of raw materials on the new planet.

    e.   Material to make factories for creating the impervium, replacement parts for those lost.

Dawn and Craig with help from SHIP came up with a list of what they needed in a crew for SHIP.

1. A geologist to identify minerals on the new planet. Will there be good stone for building? What about limestone for cement? What about deposits of metals and oil? Are there geological hazards like volcanic activity?
2. A survivalist to lead explorations on a new planet. SHIP can analyze a planet by flying by, but actually being there and seeing and testing might be critical
3. A chemist and mathematician, statistician, and so on. The chemist will help develop new batteries, help produce artificial food, make chemical fuels, help develop new pharmaceuticals and to help Dawn calculate requirements of all types.
4. Dawn is the astronomer and astral navigation specialist that will plot the courses to the new home planet or planets. This is an area that not even SHIP has extensive experience in. SHIP, with its gravitation

based propulsion can just go without concern for exhaust. Its relative small size and gravitational pull is not going to upset the existing location of interstellar bodies. SHIP requires a person to tell it what direction to go. It will remember where it has been and how to get back, but SHIP has never been further than Mars.

5.   A botanist to identify plants on the new planet when they found one.

6.   A zoologist to identify animal life on the new planet. A veterinarian with a zoologist background would be ideal as the veterinarian would help select breeding animals from Earth and then getting herds going on the new planet.

7.   Craig is a generalist with some skills in all areas but not specialized. Intense training in one skill might overload his brain so he has to stay in a helping mode to his crew. As the Captain and the selected one, SHIP could telepathically transmit thoughts directly to Craig almost as if they were his only memory whenever he needed an answer. SHIP could not do this except with the selected Captain.

PART TWO

THE CREW
THE FAMILY

5

RECRUITING THE CREW

"Craig, you know what you have to do now. Fill out the SHIP's crew. While you are doing that I will be working on telling the world the time limit we have and start the process of explaining the colony ships and what we have to do now. You can check back regularly."

The SHIP verbally spoke to both of them, "Dawn, you have been to and from the ship often enough now that you are a full fledged crew member committed to the mission. I can now provide the teleportation to and from Earth complete with your wardrobe and any small things you would like to take. I can watch after you and teleport you back here if you are in danger. I can read your mind just like I can tune in on anyone's thoughts and if you ask to be teleported it will happen immediately. However, I can only telepathically transmit ideas with my captain, Craig."

"That solves a major issue. Craig, I will ask SHIP to contact you whenever I need your personal help. You need to go out on your own now and recruit your other wives."

"That just doesn't sound moral. I never wanted more than one wife. SHIP, are you sure I can't just have you teleport them here and recruit them as I would a regular crew?"

"It doesn't work that way, Craig. Dawn is correct, you have to seduce them, convince them, or whatever to have sex with you to consummate the relationship. Until they become as fully committed as Dawn is they can only be teleported without clothing, the first time has to be during the sex act. If and when they become as committed as Dawn, then I will be able to teleport them at their will complete with whatever small things they want to take with them."

"Dawn, are you sure about this?"

"Yes, Craig. I told you, we were never truly in love and the official marriage was largely for my parents since they knew we would be living together some place. Things have changed now. We need more crew members. SHIP was constructed for one Captain and six wives. Official marriage in the eyes of man has nothing to do with it. They don't have to be in love with you or you with them. We are talking about manning thousand person colony ships with a six to one ratio of female to male. We have to do the same on SHIP. SHIP, take me to the US President now, wherever he is. If he and his visitors see me appear out of thin air, that might be more convincing then my words. Just keep me safe. Have fun, Craig, enjoy it. This is a lifelong adventure."

Dawn disappeared to appear in the Oval Office while the President, the secretaries of defense and state were discussing an international issue. There was silence until Dawn spoke, "Excuse me Mr. President and gentlemen, for just dropping in on you. You know Craig Decker already. I am wife number one and I have come with bad news and a plan."

6

GEOLOGIST PETROCHEMICAL ENGINEER

Craig went to Dawn's friend, Jill first. Jill was Dawn's best friend. Craig had already met and considered her before deciding Dawn was his sole mate. Jill had appeared to be all in favor of it, so she should be an easy addition to SHIP's crew. Jill knew Dawn had already joined with Craig and she already knew the mission was legit. Craig was famous and Dawn was getting famous.

Jill was a duel major, petrochemical engineering and Geology which sort of fit together. Geology was important to recognize soils and rocks that might contain easily mineable minerals, building materials, and petroleum. Petrochemical engineering would be helpful in setting up refineries.

Mining radioactive material to fuel their nuclear power plant is dangerous. Refining radioactive material is difficult and dangerous. Handling the refined material is dangerous. Once in the reactor, it is fairly safe. Finding suitable uranium oar might be difficult. Portable nuclear power is difficult. How can they provide transportation all around a new planet using nuclear powered aircraft and vehicles? Battery power will always be limited in range. Will uranium exist on a new planet?

Petroleum, on the other hand, is much easier to find. Any planet that had millennia of plant life probably has oil that can be safely drilled, handled, refined, and used far more safely than uranium. Petroleum is easy to transport and would be far cheaper to carry extra fuel or set up fueling stations than to try to transport batteries, set up nuclear powered charging stations. Some would object to the pollution from burning fossil fuels on the new planet, but it is still the most practical fuel for a whole planet. Maybe after a thousand years on the new planet, they will find a new pollution free fuel that will replace oil.

Jill was easy to find. Craig just went to her sorority room at the University of Oklahoma. She was at her desk studying. "Jill, Craig here."

"Craig? Is Dawn okay?"

"Absolutely, she dropped in on the U.S. President. But Dawn has pointed out and insisted that we need help in our mission to save humankind."

"You know I will do anything to help." "You don't know what I will be asking?"

"It doesn't matter. There can be no higher requirement. But what can I do?"

"We need to have a geologist as a member of our inner team." "I am just a student."

"We can eliminate your lack of training and make you the most knowledgeable geologist alive today."

"Yeah, right."

"No, you think I could provide the world the inventions I have so far with what I learned in school? Schools did not have that knowledge and I had no earthly way of just inventing things like indestructible metals or cures for cancer."

"Okay, let's assume you are telling the truth. Why would I object to that?

"I am asking you to give up any other future you may have imagined and become a member of my inner circle with Dawn for many years into the future, maybe the rest of your life."

"Okay, now it's more complicated. What about marriage and family? What about my existing family of mother, father, cousins, and so on?"

"I'm going to tell you something Dawn and I have known for awhile now, but will soon tell the world. You can't tell anyone until it is released. Earth as we know it will be destroyed soon. There is a large asteroid, moon, small planet, whatever, coming for Earth. Dawn and I have been working to advance science very quickly for an evacuation of a small set of humans to a new planet. Only a few thousand out of billions will survive. If you come with us, you will survive, but chances are that no one in your extended family will survive."

"Craig. Are you serious?"

"Yes, that is what Dawn is telling the President as we speak." "Okay, why would I refuse to join the team?"

"Because you will have to join in a polygamist relationship with me, Dawn, and eventually 4 other women. You would have to trust me to have sex with me and then be prepared for a totally life changing experience."

"Craig. I am not promiscuous, but I am not a virgin. There is no such sexual experience to be life changing. Besides, you are not exactly being romantic about this. I know that Dawn and you are changing the world now, but if you think I will just hop into bed with you, you are mistaken. Yes, I have teased you in the past before you married Dawn, but that was teasing. I don't really know you."

"You're right. I approached this as a business deal, not very romantic. How about we set a date for tomorrow at 7 PM and I will take you out to dinner and we can start over."

"How about I talk with Dawn and make sure you are not lying? If she confirms your story I'll go on a date with you tomorrow and we can talk about such things as your family history, what kind of music you like, and personal things. You are asking a lot."

"Okay, Jil. I'm sorry I approached it this way. With your teasing when we first met I thought you would jump at the opportunity."

"I'm sorry too, Craig. I should not have led you on when we first met. I'm still attracted to you, but let's face it, that was a very different seduction routine. I hope Dawn confirms your story."

"See you tomorrow." Craig disappeared back to SHIP. Dawn was already there.

"That went well. I shouldn't have but I used the screens on SHIP to look in on you. I'll go see Jill tomorrow morning."

"How did your visit to the President go?"

"About as well as your visit with Jill. You need to drop in on him tomorrow with some facts and figures and convincing arguments to get him to believe you. The President was with the secretaries of defense and state. They are not dummies. We are talking about the dissolution of the United States of America and every other country on earth. We are talking about killing billions of humans. Not something you can easily convince people of. Jill is easy in comparison."

"Okay, let's regroup. We went about this backwards. At least SHIP is now allowing you nearly full status with the capability of teleportation, communication back to SHIP, and SHIP's protection. SHIP will be watching out for you and teleport you back here if there is any immediate threat to you."

"Craig, something else happened."

"That is scary, what?"

"I thought it had been a long time since I went to a dentist so I asked SHIP to teleport me to my regular dentist in Norman and SHIP sort of refused."

"What? Why would SHIP do that?"

"SHIP teleported me back here and then told me to check my teeth in the mirror."

"And?"

"I no longer have any fillings." "Excuse me."

"SHIP then explained that every time we are teleported SHIP corrects any health issues we might have."

"Are you saying, your fillings were replaced by healthy teeth?"

"Yes, but that is only the start. You didn't listen to what I said. I said SHIP corrects any health issue. I questioned SHIP more on this and SHIP confirmed that every time we are teleported SHIP will not only correct previous injuries and diseases we might have picked up, but also corrects genetic defects we might not even know about."

"Wow! SHIP, is that true?"

Dawn answered instead of SHIP, "Included in genetic defects is aging. Every time SHIP teleports us, SHIP disintegrates our bodies and uses particles at our destination to reassemble our bodies perfectly. By perfectly, that includes changing our age back to the point we were first teleported."

"In other words, it is not my imagination that I still feel 19 years old."

SHIP broke in verbally so both Dawn and Craig could hear, "Not exactly. Women hit their peak physical mental age earlier than men and can vary from 19 to 24 years old. Men, on the other hand, reach the perfect age from 24 to 27 years old. Craig, I correct anything wrong with you, but you will continue to age until you reach at least 24. Dawn, your perfect age will be around 21. However, mentally, there is no real age limit. Mental fitness is how much your brain learns and remembers. The human brain can do things computers like me cannot do. Every time you look across a room you use a fraction of a second to absorb gigabytes of data. You see colors, shapes, and identify most of the objects, the size of the room all within that fraction of a second. The difference is size. Only a small part of your brain stores data. I use the whole SHIP to store data. Much of your brain is used to keep it running: your heart beating, your muscles, your senses including touch. More of your brain is being used for processing data. That is an area where the human brain is so much faster and better than a computer. However, due to the small area of your brain for storing data, the more data you put in, the harder it is to recall data. That is why humans must either be a generalist that can forget 80% of everything or a specialist where you remember 80% of a narrow field while never totally understanding or remembering all the other things."

"Craig, you are the generalist. You can process a lot of data and remember tidbits of lots of specialties, but you also forget a lot of things. No one ever totally forgets anything, but bringing that memory out of your databank gets harder as you cram more data in over a lifetime."

"Dawn, your specialty is astral navigation which requires you to know mathematics and astronomy. As we travel away from your solar system you will be using the math to compute the journey back and will be learning more astronomy than any other earthman. The older you get the more you will be learning. At some point other memories may replace what you will be learning in the next few years, but your memories are still specialized."

"Not to worry. You will never have Alzheimer's, but as you crowd in more data, other data will be shuffled to the back of your memory and will be hard to pull back out. It is sort of like having a computer index the data. What is used most often is quicker to access. What has not been used for years will take longer to find…if you can ever find it. On the other hand, with my ship wide memory capacity, I can pull up those memories and repeat them back to you when your memory is too jumbled."

"While your bodies will remain ultimately healthy and eventually reach a peak at an early age, your mind will never shrivel and you can continue to learn forever using my memory banks to refresh forgotten facts."

"Dawn, let's get some sleep now. Tomorrow, I will visit the President with data telepathically from SHIP and you can go visit your old sorority sister, Jill."

The next morning they started over, but with Craig teleporting in to the President and Dawn to Jill.

"Jill, when is your next class?"

"Dawn! You startled me. Ah, my next class is in two hours. I assume you are here to talk about Craig. Are you two not getting along?"

"No, we are getting along great considering the situation. I made the initial decision that we need more help. I am forbidden to tell you everything except that everything Craig told you was true."

"Is Craig making you do this? Is he not the kind person we thought"

"No this whole thing was my idea and I had to argue with Craig to get him to agree. Craig is a much better person than we imagined. Yes, he young, but he is also doing everything he can to save Earth."

"Do you mean about he and I having sex in order to join the team?"

"You will understand afterwards. Earth is running out of time.

There is too much to do in too short a time. Craig was not kidding." "Did you just materialize in the room like Craig has?"

"Yes, and I think eventually you will be able to also in time."

"I like Jim, but I can't just have sex on command. I am not that kind of girl."

"I can't explain until afterward and you will be amazed at what you learn afterward. You will technically become one of Craig's six wives."

"Excuusssee ME?" Did you say I would become one of Craig's SIX wives?"

"Yes, technically, but not legally in terms of human law, but, yes, Jim needs six wives to help him save humankind and we don't have much time. I went to see the President yesterday and they did not believe me so Craig is there now. I guess I can tell you now, but you can't tell anyone until it becomes public."

"So?"

"Earth is going to be destroyed in a little over two years. In that time we have to explore outer space to find habitable planets, that's where you come in. We need someone to identify the geology and identify potential natural resources."

"Dawn, I am just getting started on my education. I can't be the expert to verify a new planet."

"If you cooperate with Craig, by next week you will know more than any geologist on Earth. You will also know everything you need to know in geology and petrochemical engineering. Craig has a … a … a machine of learning … that will teach you everything you need to know. Craig has access to equipment you cannot imagine that you will also have access to. Craig used this, ah, learning method, to get his multiple PhDs in only a few weeks."

"We cannot do it with just Craig and I. We also have to teach others to build interstellar faster than light space ships. We have to select what people will travel into space and what billions will die here on Earth in a little over two years. The odds are Craig and I will be the only people you know that will survive and only if you agree to join us in this effort.

"Dawn. You're serious. Two years to melt down? What about my parents and the rest of my family?"

"Craig says you two have a date at 7 tonight. Do what you have to, but agree with him and do it. Within the hour you will understand what I cannot tell you. By next week you will know the truth of what is happening."

"Okay Dawn. I believe you and I will go along with it. It is not like I have not had sex before, just very few times and I was usually sorry. Maybe this time it will be better. Don't tell Craig, I want to string him along."

At the same time, Craig teleported into a cabinet meeting with the President. The President had met Craig before, but appearing out of nowhere was a shock to most of the cabinet members.

"Mr. President. I hope you will forgive me for popping in, but this is knowledge perfect for haviing your cabinet with you." The security officers, recovering from the shock of his appearance, started to move toward Craig.

The President stopped them, "As you were gentlemen. I have met Craig like this before. What is it now?"

"I have firm information that two years from April a large interstellar body the size of a small moon will impact Earth destroying all or most all life here. What I have done so far was aimed at pushing our technology toward a partial evacuation to space. I just found out the time frame is a couple of years less than expected. If I may, I will take over your projection screens and tell you most of what I know and what needs to be done."

The screens around the room came on showing the lists that Dawn and Craig had developed on SHIP. He walked the group through all the lists, one list per screen.

"What is there that we can believe." came from the labor secretary.

"The lists are the best we can make. We have two years to launch our ships into space."

"But nothing can travel faster than light."

"Not true. When I was in grade school my teachers said nothing could exist beyond the speed of sound, but fighter jets today routinely go over up to three times the speed of sound. The moon missions exceed 25,000 miles per hour. Some of space probes have gone far faster. The impervium was critical because it is necessary for long range space flight. We still need to develop the engines to provide the faster than light travel."

"How are we going to sell sending six women to every man on this mission?"

"I went through that. There are even more reasons for that number. I am talking about building as many ships as we can and putting a thousand or more people on each ship."

"Where are they going?"

"Another issue. I don't know yet. We have to do some quick exploration of near space to find one or more suitable planets. I have traveled to the moon and Mars using technology beyond what I am asking the United States to build. Let's assume that every country will want to build colony ships if we can get them to believe in the necessity. I need the full cooperation of the U.S. Government to persuade the world to work together on this mission."

The President stood, "Craig. You have already given the world several major advancements. You have brought a temporary peace to the Middle East. You have dramatically cut into the drug world. I tend to believe you, but what you are asking is monumental. Can you come back on Monday at 8 A.M. to this room after we have had a chance to discuss all of this and to confer with our scientists?

"Of course, Mr. President. Tell me what proof you need that I could possibly provide and I will attempt to convince all of you. Here is a phone you can call me on at any time to provide me with your requirement to prove the truth. We are pressed for time with only two years to go. Wait, I have an idea, we have a space probe near Uranus. It takes a long time for a television picture to arrive back here on Earth. At 7 A.M. Monday I will put a sign in plain English in front of its camera and I will report back here for the meeting at 8 A.M. I think that would convince everyone that faster than light travel is possible." With that Craig disappeared from the room and went back to SHIP. Dawn was already there. She had watched his presentation on one of SHIP's television monitors with sound.

"Can you do it?"

"SHIP suggested it telepathically. That should convince them. SHIP will take me there Monday morning. I will then use the small shuttle to appear in front of the camera with a sign in the window. I will then go back to SHIP and come back here on time. That way they will see the shuttle they have seen before, but still will not see SHIP."

Dawn queried SHIP, "That right SHIP?" "No problem."

Craig made reservations for the best suite at the Embassy Suites in Norman, Oklahoma. His favorite all time restaurant was El Chico's in the Sooner

Fashion Mall in Norman. It was not fancy, but it was great Tex-Mex food and the apple pie with cinnamon ice cream and rum sauce was the best desert he had ever had. Not only that but to add just a little romanticism, it required two people to share it, too much for one. "I hope Jill likes Mexican food."

"Yes, but that is not expensive or classy.

"No, but I thought it would be a good way to let your hair down and just be yourself at El Chico's."

"Good choice. We eat there anytime we are shopping in the mall, or at least we used to when Jill and I were still living in the sorority house. I think you just need to sit down and talk about each other without expecting anything immediately. You don't wear a suit to El Chico's but wear something nice. Impress her with that Dodge Viper convertible you had that one time."

"Okay. I think when I saw Jill yesterday, I was so wrapped up in the mission that I forgot who I was. I don't blame Jill for telling me to get out. It may not be love and marriage, but neither is it a business deal. We are talking about a potential lifetime together. Actually, according to SHIP, it might be far longer than a normal lifetime."

"Craig, I am not sure I believe in living forever. It was nice to have my fillings replaced by healthy teeth, but keep in mind that SHIP has fired some its captains."

SHIP spoke, "Actually, it was usually because my previous captains left me. They were so interested in their own fame that they quit working toward the mission. They used me for new inventions to their time frame. Many times they tried to jump too far ahead in technology in one leap and Earth simply could not possibly succeed. Then there were a few that simply insisted on dumping too much information from me into their own brain and overloaded their brain and went crazy.

Some refused to follow the simple rules and tried to bring girls here just to impress the girls with no thought to mission, and I could not let them. Some wanted to bring other people here just to study me, and that was not the mission. As long as you keep the mission first and foremost I think we may have a long time together. When you went after peace in the Middle East and then cut into the illegal drug trade I was afraid I had picked wrong. Those are inconsequential compared to the disaster coming."

"Okay, SHIP. Right now I can see no reason that we cannot keep on this mission for a long long time.

"Craig, do you want my help in picking what you will wear tonight?"

"I want to be myself with Jill. Why don't you let me choose and then get your approval?"

"Okay, better get with it. You cannot just make your car appear at her house. You have to get the car materialized away from anyone that will see it happen and then drive to her house below the speed limit."

At six PM the Dodge Viper with Craig in the driver's seat materialized down in Washington Township south of Norman in an area of woods away from view of anyone that might see it appear. He started the car and sedately drove across the bridge over the South Canadian River into Norman and then to the sorority house arriving ten minutes early. He saw the curtains part in what would be the living room and some girls looking out trying not to be seen. He got out and walked up to the door to the sorority house and rang the bell. A girl he had never seen before opened the door. There were several girls sitting in the living room apparently waiting for him to arrive.

Jill came down the stairs dressed in a skimpy red dress. Her auburn hair was done up on the top of her head accentuating her long neck. She wore long hoop earrings, again accentuating her neck. She wore no other jewelry. The top of the dress was low cut showing some cleavage. Her shoes were low red heels with no back, a little band just behind her toes but with long leather straps going around her ankles to hold them on. With the shortness of the dress and the complex straps on the shoes, it accentuated her long smooth legs. The dress was casual, not a formal cocktail dress. She was making her grand entrance while the other girls looked on. It was not a dressy dress, but walking through the mall would definitely attract attention from every man in the place.

Craig was wearing black slacks with a red polo shirt and black slip- on dress shoes. By chance or maybe by SHIP the red matched both the Viper and her dress. He suspected that SHIP knew what she was planning to wear. His hair was more like a long military style haircut. He stood near the door and waited for Jill to eventually get to him standing there feeling uncomfortable.

Jill came up to him, gave him a peck on the cheek and put an arm through his, "Shall we go?"

Craig was still embarrassed. Jill really was a beautiful young woman and she was dressed seductively. He immediately felt inadequate for such a beauty, but he recovered, "Yes. I hope you are not expecting some fancy restaurant."

With that they walked out the door arm in arm to his red convertible that matched both his shirt and her dress. The girls from the living room were now crowding the picture window watching them.

"I thought we would just go to El Chico."

"El Chico is fine. I love their food, but I am surprised you didn't plan on some wine and cheese type place with the waiters having a white towel over the arm of their tucks.

"That would not be me. That would be me putting on airs. You were right; we need to get to know each other a whole lot better. Tonight, I will try to be up front with you. The only things I did that are not really me are this car and not wearing blue jeans."

"Okay, then, let's go. I think we are being stared at."

Craig started the Viper and slowly pulled up the street toward Lindsay Street. When they arrived at the mall they had to loop around twice before they found a convenient parking space. Craig kept looking at Jill's long legs stretched out in the Viper with her short dress riding up. It was most distracting.

On the way there Craig said, "You are very beautiful. I was almost stunned when I saw you coming down the stairs."

"I wanted you to see me dressed up for a change. Maybe it was too much?"

"No. Perfect. I can't imagine any woman looking much better. I always thought you attractive, but I just never pictured you looking this good. If you meant to impress, you certainly did."

"I don't go out much so I guess you saw the lookyloos in the living room. They knew I was going on a special date tonight so they just had to watch. I was hoping you would drive the Viper. Is this your car?"

"Yes and no. I guess I own it, but, no, it is not my only car." "Are you wealthy?"

"Yes and no. Hopefully you will understand more after we get to know each other better. You know that I have become kind of famous the past couple of years. I have not gotten money from my inventions and scientific breakthroughs. That is not what this is about. Let's just say I have legal access to just about anything I want without being rich."

They were in the mall, but there was the standard line at El Chico. "So, Craig, where did you go to high school?"

"Enid. You?"

"Norman North. Are you in a fraternity?"

"No. Tell me about being in high school." They were standing close beside each other, still arm in arm. Craig tried not to, but kept looking down her dress every time he looked at her, then came up to her face. Her face was also beautiful. Even her skin had a reddish glow to it. Maybe from her dress and his shirt, but it looked natural, not reflected."

"I played the piccolo in the orchestra. I took all the honor courses I could. My senior year, I took mainly college courses at the Oklahoma City Community College. I wanted to graduate with my class but could not see enrolling in video productions or student newspaper and had already finished all my requirements."

"I was a baritone-bass in the mixed chorus at Enid and was a defensive center line backer on the football team until I got hurt in practice. As freshman, I thought I was a pretty good football player, but after getting hurt, I spent most of the time on the bench."

"Did you woo all the girls?"

"Not really. When it came to the big dances like homecoming, or the May Fete, I was the date of the queen of whatever, but it was more because I was a safe date. No one would get upset by her going with me and she did not have to worry about me taking it too seriously. I was more a friend to the in crowd of girls. I wasn't really in their financial class. It was kind of interesting driving my 7 year old car to pick up my dates from the biggest mansions in town and then taking the girls home at the earliest they could get leave the celebrations."

"When I tried actual dates with girls from my own financial class they seemed like they only wanted to make out. I was not ready for hot sex and potential pregnancy at that time. It wasn't until I came to college that I understood that most of the high school girls just wanted to get married right after high school and were willing to trap a husband that might have a future. As a top student, I had a future in their eyes, I guess. How about you?"

"I started dating in junior high and through most of high school. I was not looking for a husband or to get pregnant so kept it straight. Most guys did not ask me out twice when I didn't have sex on the first date. When I was a junior, I met a college boy over the summer that I thought I was in love with and lost my virginity. When school started again, I never heard from him again. Since then I have been concentrating on my studies. The only dates were basically required by the sorority. I met the frat boys at the party and came home early by myself."

They were called in to a booth that Craig had requested. The small talk continued. Jill sat opposite Craig so they had to talk across the table. To be heard they leaned across the table to keep people from hearing at other tables. As Jill leaned forward, Craig noted that Jill was wearing no bra and it was all he could do to look at her lovely face. The conversation drifted between personal likes and dislikes and to the mission and the future.

They both liked classical and oldies but goodies rock music. They both read mystery books. Jill was Methodist while Craig was Episcopal. Eventually they got to the dessert.

"I have never had the desert. It looks fattening. It is delicious. I see what you mean by sharing it. It is almost too much for just two of us." Every time Jill reached to get another spoonful, Craig got an eyeful.

Eventually, they finished, Craig put the money and a generous tip on the table. As they walked back to the car, Craig said, "So we can continue our talk, I have a room at the Embassy Suites where we can talk in private. I would like to tell you more about the mission."

"Let's go. I can't just take you back to my sorority room and I don't think you even have a place here at the University since you are no longer attending classes and I do not see you or Dawn around campus."

Craig just asked for the keycard to his reserved room and they took the elevator. Craig then got more serious into the discussion. "Earth will cease to exist as we know it two years from April. There is an interstellar body that is on course to hit Earth. It is too large to try to blow it up with nukes. There is no such thing as hiding in a bunker. The only humans that will survive have to be off the planet." "As in where?"

"Hopefully another planet. You know that I have been trying for a major space program. What you don't know is that we need to explore space and find another earthlike planet."

"That would require faster than light travel."

"Yes, and I am going to prove it to the President and his cabinet on Monday. I will demonstrate faster than light travel by appearing on a camera on a deep space probe and less than an hour later teleporting into the cabinet room."

"So why do you need me?"

"To prepare for the space colony right now I need you to design a new refinery kit that can be carried along and built on the new planet. Then I need a geologist during the exploration to help find a planet with the mineral resources for this colony. Then I will need you to help the colonists mine or drill for the minerals and refine them."

"Craig, I still have at least two years for my bachelors and that would not make me knowledgeable enough for this. You said you need help right now."

"I do need the help right now. This sounds like a lie but if you will agree to be one of my wives, by the end of the week you will know more about your specialties than any human alive."

"Let's take a shower together while I think about this."

Craig was surprised by the sudden turn in her attention, but he had been on the verge of arousal since she came down the stairs, on the drive to El Chico, sitting across from her at El Chico, and checking into the room. It was only with the serious discussion that he had calmed down. Jill was standing with her hand out to him. He got up and she pulled him closer, pulled his shirt off over his head, undid his belt… after the sensual shower … Jill led him to the bed flipped back the covers … shortly thereafter they came together … and they were on SHIP. Talk about breaking the mood for Jill.

"Craig, where are we? What happened?"

"Welcome to the ship that we call SHIP. This is where Dawn and I have been living. SHIP now considers you my wife." They floated down to be standing on the floor, once again, Jill was dressed as she had been in the sorority before this started and Craig was in blue jeans with a t-shirt.

"Did I or am I dreaming? One minute we were having good sex and suddenly I am dressed and standing here looking out a window to outer space. Look, there is the earth coming into view."

"I could not tell you about SHIP until you agreed to become a wife in SHIP's thinking. Let me show you around." They walked through the dining room with an elegant formal table with one head chair and six side chairs into the living room. Dawn was watching a wall size digital movie.

"Hi, Jill. I see you agreed. You haven't seen or learned anything yet. Wait until tomorrow."

"Dawn! Are you sure you are all right with sharing Craig as just one of his wives?"

"Yes, I'm all right with it. We'll talk more after you have gotten some training tomorrow. Right now, just pretend I am not here and go on with your tour. You and Craig use the bedroom you just came from after the tour. It will take Craig longer than me to adjust. He really is a prude, but he will adapt."

The walls of the living area except for the television screen were open to space, a bright sparkling space you could not see from the polluted Earth. From there Jill followed Craig into the control room. He showed her the learning device and explained how tomorrow she would sit in it and lower the hood over her head and then become the greatest geologist and petrochemical engineer in modern Earth history.

Jill was overwhelmed. It was past 11 P.M., "So what do we do now? Go the bedroom and pick up where we left off?"

When Craig and Jill returned to the bedroom it was totally different. It was smaller and more cozy. Craig discovered that SHIP now had two bedrooms and the master bedroom was now decorated the way Jill would have done it herself. "Craig, it's beautiful. How did it happen?"

"SHIP read you mind and decorated it for you. If Dawn were here, it would be for her. If I were alone it would be decorated for me. It continues changing. This is the first time I have seen it this way. I like it."

The next morning Dawn, Jill, and Craig had breakfast in the dining room served by SHIP. What they really wanted did not have to be ordered, it just appeared perfectly to their liking. Dawn and Craig had gotten used to it, but Jill was amazed. After breakfast, both Dawn and Craig took Jill to the learning machine. A few hours later, Jill emerged with a whole new understanding.

"Wow! That is amazing. I learned things about geology and petrochemical engineering that I don't think anyone else knows. I also understand the mission and its importance to the world. SHIP convinced me how it has to remain a secret forever, the learning system has to remain secret, and the importance of my mission. SHIP also told me about how you still need to add more women to the crew and why they must be women. How are you taking this Craig?"

"I don't think I have a choice. Intellectually, I understand why, but I never wanted more than one woman. Now I have to spread myself over a harem."

"SHIP explained about the colony needing six women per man to expand the population, but what about us, the crew?"

Dawn jumped in, "We learned something recently, SHIP repairs any genetic damage, any fillings in your mouth, any left over trace of injuries, and something I am not sure is good. Every time we teleport, SHIP returns us perfect again. By that, I mean that we will only age until we hit our individual physical peak and then we will return to that peak physical age every time we teleport. That includes never having old age dementia of any kind. So, our child-bearing years are extended out until we decide it's time to have children, and forever after, no matter how many children we have. In the meantime, SHIP will not let us get pregnant. If we happen to get pregnant on Earth, it will be corrected when we teleport without our even knowing. I guess, when the time is right we would be unlimited in the number of children we could produce."

Jill joked, "Sort of like Adam and Eve, and Eve, and Eve, and Eve, and Eve, and Eve?" Six women and one man reproducing forever???"

SHIP said, "That is it, but until you have secured new colonies and completed the mission, pregnancy cannot be allowed. You will have to have your children in the colonies and then leave them behind if you want to return here. There is no room for children here on the ship."

"Jill, until you have been teleported more times, I cannot teleport you alone. You must be with Craig and without clothing. Dawn has done it enough times she can tell me when and where without Craig. It takes a long time before I can so specifically identify your molecular structure. I know Craig's molecular structure and all of Craig's possessions are made by me and I have learned Dawn's. When you teleport with Craig, I identify Craig and since he is holding you, I can teleport you safely. If I were to try to teleport you without Craig, I might get a little fly DNA mixed in like in the movie, "The Fly". Same thing teleporting you with clothing. It would be fatal to teleport a button inside your internal organs."

Jill interjected, "I will be perfectly happy to teleport with Craig rather than have that kind of mistake. Do computers make jokes?"

"Now, Craig, your number one mission is to complete the crew. You need four more members. Jill, Craig will take you down to the College of Engineering at the University of Oklahoma and you can now start the design and building of portable refineries, drilling rigs that be assembled on site, and so on. Craig will explain since they know him, but once they start listening to you, you can easily overwhelm them with your new knowledge. Jill, be alone in your sorority room at 5 P.M. and as soon as it is convenient I will teleport Craig there then you can come back here together. Craig, try to get alone at that time so I can teleport you to Jill."

7

BOTANIST

Dawn would spend the day spend with NASA discussing colony selection. She also went over all the supply lists for the colonies. Invariably they came up with existing equipment made with existing metal, not the impervium. She opened up the discussion of building a supersize colony ship of the impervium and the problems of getting a fully loaded ship into orbit.

Craig called together the engineers already working on the project. These were no longer just University of Oklahoma engineers. There were other schools that had better labs in different areas, but Craig had focused here because this was his school. Many of the projects were taken back to other universities and private companies more suited to different phases of different projects. He was well known and everyone of them was eager to learn and do, limited only by federal funding.

Craig told them he was hoping to get the backing of the government and unlimited funding. They had a lot of funding, but, in these dire circumstances, they needed unlimited funding with no consideration of cost. Money would be worthless soon.

Craig introduced them to Jill, "Jill is the project manager for a new project. If we get a colony on a new planet we will need to be able to mine and drill for natural resources. First order of business is a portable kit for a refinery for petroleum products. This will be made from the impervium which will last for hundreds of years and is impervious to heat and almost any impact. I want you to treat Jill as if she knows more about the subject than all of you put together, which she most assuredly does. However, she and I cannot build this thing without you. Knowing how to build a skyscraper is nice, but doing it alone is impossible. This refinery has to be as small as possible producing only a few hundred barrels a day of refined petroleum products, but expandable when more metal is available."

"Jill, if you will take over now, I have to be working on another project. Gentlemen, until next time. Ask Jill anything about the subject and she will know answers you may never have heard of before. Don't try to test her answers, she will be right and we do not have time to waste. I need her on other projects soon and you will be on your own to complete the project with only a few visits by Jill or myself."

Jill knew she knew more than anyone there, and was very confident. She had SHIP's design in her mind and had paper and computer copies to pass out and display on large screen monitors in the conference room. There were words of approval from many of the engineers. Where the technology was new, there were questions she had to put in simple terms, but she easily satisfied the questions.

Craig went to the restroom down the hall and teleported to Skidmore University outside Saratoga Springs, New York, and found Estera Shea walking to her next class with several other girls. Summer is short in upstate New York. Estera was wearing a plaid woolen skirt, knee socks, and a white blousy blouse. Her dark hair was silky, nearly shoulder length, and dark blond hair was nearly brown. She was five foot one inches, and slender, one hundred ten pounds. She had green eyes magnified by her eyeglasses. Her dark blond hair was straight, but with the last five inches swept into an inward facing curl toward her face. She had sharp features. Very long eyelashes and large sultry lips.

Craig had met Estera at the start of his hunt for a first mate. Estera was studying botany. SHIP had sent him to her early on. They had met in the hot baths at the park in Saratoga and Estera had helped Craig to convince her father, Representative Shea, the House Ways and Means Committee chairman to put in some good words for him.

Estera could not have anything more to do with him at that time, but things were different now. Craig caught up with the group of girls walking to their next class and Craig called out, "Estera. Remember me?"

The group stopped as Estera stopped and turned to fact him, "Craig, of course I remember you. You are quite famous now you know."

One of the girls with Estera tugged on her sleeve, "Do we get an introduction?"

"Craig, my classmates."

Craig replied, "Pleased to meet you."

Estera, "I meant introduce us not just wave us off. It's not every day we meet a world renowned genius our own age."

Estera obliged and some girls just offered their hands to shake while others put their arms around him and hugged as they were introduced. Some girls were probably less impressed, some were more reserved, and some were taking advantage of the opportunity for a hug. Craig shook hands or hugged in return.

Craig said, "Estera, can we talk?"

"Excuse us girls. Craig, walk with me." and walked in the opposite direction from which the group had been headed.

Craig caught up with a few big steps. "Estera, things are getting far more serious. I need your help again, but this time your personal help."

"I have heard the story you had back then and helped. What do you need now?"

"Something far more personal that lasts possibly forever. I have an inner team directing things and I need you to join the team."

"I have a long way to go to graduate."

"I mean now. Just like you know I can appear and disappear through teleportation, I can train you in short order to be the ultimate botanist."

"Okay, you are going to have to tell me more."

"Can you go on a date with me tonight. Let's say I come by car by your house at 5 P.M. and we go out to eat somewhere in Saratoga Springs and talk over our meal."

"You know my father. I was not allowed to date until I was twenty- one. I can ask him. Come by the house at five and we'll see. Okay."

She turned back in the direction of her next class leaving him there.

Craig realized that he had just set up a data for 5 P.M. Eastern Standard Time and was supposed to pick up Jill and take her back to SHIP at 5 P.M. Central Standard Time or only an hour later. Craig went directly to Engineering at the University of Oklahoma and watched Jill manage the engineering team for the new miniature refinery kit. At 2 P.M. he excused Jill from the group and took Jill to a motel where they undressed and teleported back to SHIP.

"Sorry I had to pull you out early, but I made a date for five Eastern Time so I had to get you back here. Assuming she cooperates better than you did when I first asked you to come with me; she may be coming to SHIP tonight. Her name is Estera Shea and her father is the chairman of the House Ways and Means Committee."

"Wow, a VIP. Doesn't hurt to be politically connected. Does she have a specialty?

"Botanist. I met her years ago and her father helped me get funding back then. He may not even let me take her out to dinner. She's had a pretty strict upbringing."

"Luck."

At 5 P.M. sharp he drove up in an antique Jaguar XKE figuring it would impress the father and Estera. He walked up to the front door, but before he could knock, Representative Shea, opened the door. "Come in Craig, or should I call you Doctor Decker now?"

"Craig is fine, the doctor degrees are honorary at best."

"Well, come in and join me in my office. I would like to talk with you about my daughter."

Craig followed him into his office. The office had one wall covered by a library of law and history books. It was all done in rich cherry wood and obviously not veneer, but solid cherry wood. The opposing wall was a large screen television built into the wall above a full bar. The wall opposite the door was leaded glass framed in cherry wood looking out on a rose garden.

"Craig, I have been briefed in on your latest visit to the President and his cabinet. I have been following your career since you first met my daughter."

"Yes sir?"

"Well I don't know about the President or his cabinet, but I believe your story and I believe you have access to technology we could only dream about. You are human from Earth aren't you?"

"Yes sir. I went to high school in a small city in Oklahoma and then the University of Oklahoma. Something happened while there and I found myself in possession of untold wonders and a disaster. I have been working since then to get at least a few humans into space before the disaster."

"I believe you. Estera said you needed her long term help. I may have leaped ahead, but I think you are asking her to join in this quest and come away with you right now. Am I right? How can she be a botanist with her meager education?"

"Yes, sir, but I was hoping to discuss it with Estera first. Just like I learned a whole lot in a short time, I can teach Estera to be a super botanist in a short time."

"Well, my daughter and I have discussed it. If she goes with you will she be among those to escape Earth?"

"Yes, sir. She will, but there are other considerations."

"I am assuming this would mean years together with you. Would she be with you or just one of the young women on the colony ships with one man for every six girls?"

"I have to be honest with you. She will be with me and five other girls, the same ratio as the colony ships, but the seven of us will be by ourselves, not on a colony ship."

"Does that mean you will be having sex, not only with my daughter, but with five other women?"

"Yes Sir. I will explain more in the future, but I cannot take another man on the crew. I need a botanist on my team who will help me identify new potential planets for the colony or colonies. I am not doing this just because I think I need multiple wives. I am not a Mormon and come from an Episcopal background where I believed in one wife for life. However, with the disaster coming, we have determined that the colonies need to start with that high proportion of women to men and I need to set the example. Women are more suited for long space trips, the boredom of being cooped up and maybe would make better pioneers. We need some men for the heavy work and for those few areas where men excel mentally. Apparently you know everything I told the President."

"Yes. Are you saying that you and six women, including my daughter will be exploring space ahead of the colony ships?"

"Yes, sir. It will be safe." Craig decided to talk around the fact of SHIP, pretending something less but coming close. Hopefully, SHIP would let him get by with alluding to SHIP.

"Are you saying that you will be taking an un-tested prototype ship out to explore?"

"No, sir. My smaller ship is much simpler because of its size. You know about the metal. My ship will be smaller and stronger. I have discussed the prototype power plant for the new colony ships, but my smaller ship will have a better power plant that just isn't suitable for the huge colony ships."

"I think that you are saying no one over thirty will be leaving Earth. I think you are also saying any-one not going into space will die in about two years when Earth is destroyed."

"Yes, sir. You have it. I hope I can convince the government that money means nothing and this effort has to be an all out effort with nothing left out."

"Okay, Craig. You have my permission to take Estera with you tonight for her life. I suspected that was why you contacted Estera. It is too early for making up the colony ships. I did not know why you wanted her, but I was right. Estera and I talked about this all afternoon. Will she be able to visit home before the final days?"

"Yes, most assuredly. I will bring her myself every few weeks to visit. Eventually, she may be able to come on her own. She will not be as busy as I and some of the other women will be. Her mission will be in finding a new planet and then actually taming that colony for ourselves. When not in space she can assist the rest of us as we will all be busy."

"I'm glad I am not saying goodbye yet. What about a wedding?" "Sorry, sir. I married Dawn a couple of years ago when this started.

It has been she and I until now. Dawn had to talk me into taking on a total of six women. We married to make her parents happy and can't break it now. As long as we have laws against bigamy, I cannot marry her, but I will treat her as a real wife. I suspect that I will be the one subordinate to the women."

"Can you go wait in your car? By the way, I like the baby blue Jag and the matching slacks and polo shirt. Trying to impress me were you? Anyway, I would like some time to talk with Estera then I will send her out.

"I'll have to admit I picked the car and clothes for you not Estera. I never expected you to approve, in fact, I was concerned you would not let me take your daughter to dinner tonight."

"I do not expect her back tonight, but please bring her to visit until time is up."

"I will, Sir."

It was thirty minutes before Estera came out. She came out slowly as if in thought then ran the final steps. "Craig. I was expected to just go to dinner with you tonight and have more time to think about this, but Daddy says I should go with you tonight and I mean go."

"We can still go downtown Saratoga for dinner. We will be back to visit your father. How much did he tell you?"

"He said Earth was coming to an end in two years and that I should go with you now to help prepare the Earth as much as possible until then. I'm still not sure what you expect of me."

"Let's discuss it over dinner. You might not want to do what is asked of you."

"Daddy said I would become one of six wives with only you as the husband, but that we would not really be legally married. We would spend the rest of our lives together."

"That about sums it up. Do you have a favorite place to eat where we can talk in private?

"How about The Wishing Well...no The Saratoga City Tavern? I feel like a drink. I just turned 21 and have never been to a bar, but I understand it has some privacy during the week. Do you need directions?"

"No, I have an internal GPS with turn by turn directions." "You are kidding."

"Sort of. Tomorrow you will understand."

When they arrived there were few people in the pub. It was only 6 P.M. They were able to find a quiet booth and the waitress was right there since they were about the only ones in the tavern.

They ordered burgers and beer. "Estera, you do realize you will be a member of my little seven member family? Only one of six women your age. Each one will have their own area of expertise except for me. I am the generalist. If you decide to go with me it will be for years and maybe for life."

"Yes, Daddy already told me. Quite a change from not being able to date to just running off with you. We hardly know each other. We met two years ago and haven't talked since. Now here you are asking me to be part of a polygamist relationship with five other women."

They talked for another hour and two more beers each, and then Craig said, "To join with me, you really have to join with me. Are you sure you are that willing to have sex with me to cement the deal?"

"Sounds crazy, but yes. It's still early. Let's go out to the hot springs to cement the deal in the water. I have always wondered about that."

They did and an hour later the Jaguar no longer existed and they were onboard SHIP just like Jill had come on board yesterday, except that now ship had three bedrooms, with one looking like Estera's bedroom in her father's mansion.

The first thing Estera said, "Something is wrong with my eyes, I can't see anything. Is this my bedroom? Oh, what happened? It's not my glasses, it's my eyes. I can see without them!"

Craig said, "You are on my ship which we call, SHIP. When we teleport to SHIP, anything wrong with you gets corrected. With Dawn, it was her fillings getting replaced by healthy teeth. With you it was your eyesight being corrected. Just think what you want to wear and the clothing will appear. Get dressed and we will go meet your sisters."

Jill and Dawn welcomed her warmly. It had been at Dawn's idea originally and Jill had been there less than 48 hours before."

Craig stayed with Estera the next date except for a quick trip with Jill to the University of Oklahoma. Estera was as amazed as any of them after her training session. She not only knew every Earth plant, but every Martian plant before Mars was destroyed. The information about Mars botany might be critical to know if they found a new planet. She knew the history of SHIP and understood completely where Craig and Dawn were going with their ideas. She also saw Jill's importance and even her own importance in the near future and why Craig needed more recruiting. She could not tell her father everything when she saw him again, but she could assure him and get more political support for the mission.

Congress and the President were out of a job shortly after the evacuation.

Dawn was doing well at NASA now that she had them seriously looking at new technology previously not considered. They refined the provisioning lists of supplies to take along and started running various computer simulations on the mix of women to men for the journey. In general, Dawn and Craig's list was holding up well, but now NASA had moved the colony project to be number one. They were all looking forward to the demonstration of faster than light travel set for Monday.

Jill was working with the engineers and oil company engineers were being donated by the big American oil companies. Jill had all the answers, but there were a lot of questions about how to actually build the needed kit.

While Estera was in training, Craig had been working with SHIP on their lists, listening in at NASA and listening to Jill and the questions being raised.

They all met at the dinner table that evening. Estera was glowing about her new knowledge. Tomorrow, Craig would take her to NASA to work with Dawn and the scientists. NASA had called in the experts at their various contractors around the country like JPL, Northrop, and Boeing. Estera would not be a big help, but it would be good training for the general mission.

Craig would take Jill to the University of Oklahoma again. "Jill, you might be prepared to spend the night in your sorority. I am going to California to try to recruit a zoologist and I may not make it back to bring you back to SHIP. Dawn, if I don't return for Estera, please get a couple of rooms there in Houston and assume that I did not make it back until late or not at all.

ZOOLOGIST

Craig was going to try to recruit Sandy Scofield. He did not think it would be too difficult. He had found her trapped on a private island trapped between cliffs and an incoming tide back when he was starting to look for a mate. To save them he had SHIP teleport them to a private island a little more hospitable. They had spent hours near a nice waterfall and had a picnic and made love. Sandy's father was a Northrop engineer who had seen Craig's inventions and work at NASA..

Sandy was at the public Redondo Beach, but not out on her private island. Maybe she had learned her lesson after Craig had to rescue her. She was by herself on a large beach towel on her stomach. Her bikini bra straps were loose by her sides and her bottom was not really covered by almost a thong swimsuit.

Craig smeared some tanning oil on her back. "Hi, Sandy."

Sandy hardly jumped at his touch. "Hi, Craig. I was hoping you would come back." With that she turned over on her side to face him while using her free hand to hold her swim top in place.

"I'm back. A lot that has happened since we met on that island."

"Depends, I haven't been with a man since then. I have wrapped myself in a duel major of zoology and pre-med with the idea of being a vet."

"You told me once that you wanted to go into space with me. You said you would like to be my wife. Are those two facts still true?"

"Yes! Most emphatically. I have been watching you in the news and I have been pumping my father as to what he has been working on at Northrop. I've been hoping you would come back for me."

"There is a lot that has not become public yet. There are some issues that could change your mind. Let me say, that, yes, I did come back for you and want to take you as a wife. Yes, the world is going to end in a couple of years. Yes, at least some will escape into space. But we need to talk somewhere private. This is about as private as it gets as far as talking. We might get arrested for more than talk, but with the surf, no one can hear." Sandy reached behind her back to tie her top in place.

"You're right. Okay, here goes. I want you as one of my wives. I need you and your talent and interest in zoology and we need a veterinarian. Don't worry about completing college. I can have you trained as the best zoologist and veterinarian on Earth in a day or two. You already know about the mission so I will say we need you to help us identify a new planet for colonies to move to. We need to find and recognize animal life on an alien planet. Once colonized we need a veterinarian to take care of the few animals we will bring with us. We will need a veterinarian to study new animals no one ever saw before. Still interested?"

"More than ever, but for clarification, did you say one of my wives?"

"Yes, I did say one of. I married a girl a couple of years ago interested in astral navigation that I knew would be necessary to guide fleets of colony ships to a new planet. At that time I did not envision more than one wife. The decision has been made that the colony ships will carry 1,000 people on each ship and each ship will have six females for every male for a whole lot of reasons. One reason is to populate a new colony because we can increase the population faster for a better chance of success. In addition, women are really more suited for long space travel than men. I will be exploring for new suitable planets with a small ship with six women and myself as the man. I have a crew of three, the astral navigation specialist, a geologist, a botanist, and hopefully now you as a zoologist. I will still need a chemist and a survivalist."

"A female survivalist? What for? Wouldn't it be easier to find a male survivalist?"

"It has to be female. If you agree to become one of my six wives, you will understand why it has to be female. Believe me, I am limited to six people to directly help me and they must all be female. Plus since the colony ships will have the same ratio and we are the leaders of the colony it is politically advantageous to have the same makeup. It will not be important until after the colony is established."

"Why a survivalist?"

"Because we may have equipment to scan for a planet, find a planet, and scan for resources and climate, but we need to set foot on the planet. The geologist must not only identify potential resources, but must determine how accessible those resources are. The botanist must identify plant life to determine if it can be consumed, made into houses, domesticated, poisonous, or would it have medicinal benefits when our pharmaceuticals that we bring run out. The zoologist, you, will identify animal life that we can eat or be eaten. Could it be domesticated like we have domesticated cows and pigs? Eventually we will need a vet to keep animals from Earth healthy. We need a chemist because we will have to manufacture our own chemicals after we get there. We need a survivalist to help protect the rest of us, identify dangers we may not see, teach us to camp, hunt, or fish safely and then teach colonists to explore the new world."

"I said I was ready. What do I have to do?"

"We have to have sex, during sex, to consummate the marriage. Legally, we will not be married, but the commitment and the act cement the relationship."

"I'm ready. Could we go back to the Pacific Island?"

"Why not. However, don't you want to talk with your father before you go with me? Depending on how things work out…well, he is too old to go on a colony ship.

"Oh. Yes, I guess I should see him, but he is in Houston."

"I can bring you back to see him in a few days, if that will be okay. Where can we go to get out of sight of people that would see us disappear?

"Let's go to those restrooms over there." They did and reappeared by the waterfall on the private South Pacific island they had been on years before. They were having sex when they transported to SHIP."

Sandy was not as surprised as the other girls had been. "I thought that you had a spaceship somewhere. Where are we exactly?"

"We're in Earth orbit, but cannot be seen on radar or by telescope. The SHIP is not that large, but can change as necessary to accommodate the full crew. He gave her the standard walk through. She had to stand in the living area looking out at space for a long time.

"Craig, this is amazing. I have only dreamed about such a thing." Eventually they completed their tour and Craig showed her the learning machine and explained what it would do the next day. "Why not now? I'm ready."

"It is early since I did not have to convince you. Okay, let's do it." It was still early afternoon Eastern Time when Sandy finished her zoology training.

Sandy came out of the training module incredulous. "Were there really all those animals roaming Mars? They were so alike but so different than our animals. Their fur! So luxurious, and the colors and hues of colors. Is that why cavemen were so hairy? Not that they were descended from apes, but they came from a cooler planet than ours?"

"Sorry, I don't know. You are our zoologist so you got the intensive training in the animal world. My training was mainly on a few scientific break throughs. Dawn got a similar training to mine except with more math because SHIP does not know that much about outside our solar system. Estera is a botanist so I guess her training in botany was as in-depth as yours was in zoology. Jill's training was in geology so I guess there was nothing so dramatic between Earth and Mars as the animals."

"You are right. The Martian animals were so different and yet basically just animals like on Earth. But I was surprised when I saw the Martians as upright ape men. It makes our own history fit better. We may have evolved from the apes, but it explains why the Cro-Magnons and Neanderthals may have co-existed for awhile and maybe interbred. The Martians were the taller Neanderthals because they evolved on a planet with less gravity than Cro-Magnons. When Atlantis was destroyed the survivors here lost their technology while humans were Cro-Magnons that never had the technology. Apparently Cro-Magnons learned from Neanderthals. There was even some interbreeding, sort of like between white man and Indians in America. It was frowned on, but genetically possible and maybe even good for humanity."

"When you man the colonies will you have a mix of races for interbreeding?"

"Let's hold that discussion for after we all get together at dinner. I need to go get the other women and bring them home. Dawn has been on SHIP for two years so SHIP allows her to teleport on her own, but I have to go get Jill and Estera."

"Does that mean you having sex with both of them every time they come and go from SHIP?"

Craig laughed, "Wait and see when you and I leave SHIP. I've got to go now."

Craig left Sandy with the SHIP providing a video on the big screen of their trip to Mars, videos of Atlantis in its glory, and explaining the mission. He went to collect Estera and Dawn first. Dawn came by herself, but Craig and Estera had to find some privacy to teleport in an embrace. Craig then teleported to Jill's sorority room where they did the same.

Dawn met Sandy first, "I thought there must be some other girl that Craig was really attracted to before picking me. I think he had a lot of doubt but my specialty and SHIP's recommendation tipped the balance to me. If there were no interstellar mission, I think it would have been you that he picked."

"I appreciate that, but he did pick you and now we will be sharing him for life. I hope that does not cause you concern."

"No, I had to talk Craig into the logic of having multiple wives. Ship even had 6 side chairs at the dining table when Craig arrived before any of this. It was inevitable. I married Craig for my parents to feel good about me going away to live together with Craig."

"What about the other girls?"

"Estera's dad is the head of the House Ways and Means Committee and knew all about Craig and what he is trying to do. He practically kicked Estera out when Craig asked her. He wanted his daughter to be off planet."

"Jill was my sorority sister and best friend. She was not all that involved with her family. They lived right there in the same town as the college and I don't think she ever went home or said goodbye when joining our little family."

About that time, Craig and Estera arrived from the direction of the bedrooms. Estera observed, "You must be Sandy. I see the walls have changed in the SHIP again to include your bedroom. I have only been on the ship for about 3 days total. Has Dawn told you my history and why I am here?"

"Yes, but only just barely. I guess we will have a long time to get to know each other better. I met Craig years ago and have been waiting for him to possibly come back for me. Dawn beat me out, but now I understand why. You beat me too."

Jill walked in, "You must be Sandy?" "Yes, and you must be Jill the geologist."

"That right. I am. I'm famished. How about we all eat dinner since we are all here and we can talk afterward."

"I am starved also. I have not eaten since breakfast and then I arrived here and had my first training session in the learning machine. It has been a lot of excitement so I was not hungry, but now that you mentioned it I'm starving."

They all went in to the dining room and juggled seats. Sandy said, "Are there reserved seats in any order?"

Dawn said, "No. It is sort of first come first seating. I suspect that has time goes by we will juggle the seating so that we can sit near the one we are currently working with. I think the only reserved seat is Craig's at the head of the table."

"But I did not see a kitchen and who is serving, or is that my job since I'm the newbie? Can someone show me the kitchen and tell me what you want?"

Estera said, "Just think about what you want and it will appear. SHIP converts matter within the ship to manufacture the best food you have ever had. We can all think of something different and it will appear in front of you."

Sandy discovered a large oblong plate with lobster and butter in front of her with the tools to tackle the lobster. Craig had steak and potatoes, and dinner was served around the table. After they all had finished, and the dishes disappeared, the conversation started. They all reported on what their day had accomplished and what was planned for tomorrow.

"So, what is my assignment tomorrow? I didn't hear any zoology assignment."

Craig said, "Your zoology assignment has not started yet. I think tomorrow you should have the learning machine tackle veterinary medicine tomorrow and just wander around the ship. Do not ask the ship to provide any other training. The most danger we are in is that we overload our minds with too much. That is why everyone is a specialist and why we must rely on the specialists rather than try to learn too much ourselves. If you overload your brain you may just go crazy and will have to be ejected from the ship and our crew. I don't think SHIP would allow you too much, but it has happened to some of my predecessors."

I have one more crew member to recruit and train. Since I do not personally know a survivalist, I will have to get recommendations from SHIP. From experience other recommendations from SHIP have not worked out because SHIP does not understand some of our prejudices, likes, and dislikes. It will probably take more than one day. Do any of you know a survivalist that might fit in?"

They all shook their heads, NO.

"Everyone try to get things as organized as possible over the next few days. I want to start exploring space for a habitable planet soon. Tomorrow is Monday and I have to demonstrate faster than light travel. Should be an exciting day for the President and his cabinet."

Dawn said, "NASA is pretty excited about your demonstration too.

After all, it is their deep space probe, so technically they will see your signal there before the White House."

"Have you seen my dad at NASA? He is Doctor Scofield, an engineer for Northrop."

"As a matter of fact, he has been a godsend. He goes along with whatever facts I put out and makes my job a lot easier by helping me get agreement by the group."

"Will you say hello for me?"

"Sure. Maybe sometime tomorrow or the next day you can join us at NASA and be with your father. We could use some advice on engineering the stable on the colony ships."

Dawn left for NASA. Craig decided Sandy would have a day off from training and took her to NASA where he had rented a hotel room to teleport to, then returned with Estera. The two girls then took a rental car to NASA.

He then went back and teleported Jill to her sorority room and returned to ship.

Craig had a mission today to fly to the deep space probe, show NASA and the President that he was there and then get back to the President by 8 A.M. SHIP took him into position near the probe. Craig was already in the one man shuttle, space-fighter, or just the small ship and SHIP piloted him in front of the camera of the space probe. He was holding a sign against the cockpit window that said, "I SAID I WOULD BE HERE".

SHIP then piloted the little ship back inside SHIP and blasted back to Earth orbit within a couple of minutes. Craig felt no acceleration inside SHIP due to its anti-gravity drive. Once in orbit he teleported to the President's cabinet room still holding the sign.

He arrived before the picture from the probe could be received by NASA and forwarded to the cabinet room.

Even though the cabinet had seen him teleport in and out the previous week it was still a shock. The security did nothing this time. The President said, "Hello Craig. We have not yet received your proof of faster than light travel." The screens lit up and the picture from the probe started scanning onto the screens around the room.

The President said, "Okay now we have it. NASA, when did the probe take the picture? Gentlemen, ladies, look at the lower left. The photo has a date time stamp of less than five minutes ago, but the signal, at the speed of light took nearly 30 minutes to arrive at NASA. I guess that proves that faster than light travel is possible."

There were nods around the room, "Craig. You have proved your point. What do you want from us?"

"I want an unlimited budget to the government agencies and universities working on this project. Money will be worthless in two years so this needs to be an all out effort, money be damned. Then I want the full backing of the U.S. Government and the personal efforts of the President and Secretary of State to convince the rest of the world to follow our lead to build colony ships. There is no us and them. There is only an all out effort to save as many humans as possible. France, Great Britain, China, Russia, everyone capable of high technology should be building their own ships. No secrets. Every colony ship should be manned and supplied just like ours and ours needs to follow the plans being drawn up at NASA as we speak."

"Quite an order. Let us discuss it. It needs to go to Congress you know?"

"Mr. President, we do not have time for debate and normal channels. If you check with Representative Shea, the chairman of the House Ways and Means Committee, I think you will find that he was convinced before today and is ready to pull every string he can find."

"Okay, I will call you when we have something to tell you."

"Thank you, Mr. President. Remember we only have two years to go into space permanently, there are no delays possible. I am doing everything I can, but money is only important right now. After two years there will be no more money and no more earthlings."

"I believe you Craig, but the President cannot act alone. I will call next week or you can contact me anytime." Craig disappeared.

The evening in SHIP was much like the previous night. Dawn came by herself and Craig made one trip for each of his other crew. What they were wearing before teleportation was usually much more than what SHIP provided after their arrival back at SHIP. In public, you dress to impress. In SHIP you dress or undress to be comfortable.

In the morning they repeated yesterday's trips to deliver the girls to there stations.

9

SURVIVALIST

"SHIP, I am looking for a survivalist who is proficient in tenting, building emergency shelters, hunting, fishing, navigating without GPS and without a compass. We need someone that can lead us in exploration on a strange planet and can help us if we get into trouble. I know you will zap us back here in an emergency, but the current one at a time could be fatal, plus we might have to start all over rather than sticking out a questionable situation. The survivalist has to meet my basic criteria of being attractive by human terms and physically fit. She has to have innate intelligence. She has to have a personality that will fit in with the rest of us here. She has to be attracted to men, not a homosexual. I don't know if you can select someone I will be attracted to and vice versa, but I think you have an idea. Can you pick one and let me view her on the screen for now.

SHIP displayed a girl in her early twenties or late teens hiking in the Colorado mountains by her-

"

self. She was wearing camouflaged shorts that came to just above mid thigh and a pale tan v-neck cotton t-shirt and high top hiking boots. She carried a walking cane in one hand and on her waist she had a large combat knife, a canteen, and some pouches. She had a bow and arrow quiver over her shoulders over a large fanny pack. For a girl, her legs and arms had well defined muscle almost like a body builder, but without the bulk that some female body builders had from steroids. She looked like the preverbal Amazon woman. Statuesque beauty in perfect physical condition, probably from years of hiking the mountains.

"Tell me about her."

"Her name is Karen Martin, she was born with an American Indian name that would translate to She Who Wanders. She is half Apache and half English. Her father was a sergeant major in the U.S. Army and her mother was from England. Both parents are still married and healthy. Karen alternates between her parents and the woods during summer. In the winter, she goes to south Texas and works as a forester. She occasionally travels to forest fires with the U.S. Forest Service. She attended two years at the University of Colorado with a 4.0 grade average and then dropped out. She is five foot eight, one hundred forty two pounds. She has black hair from her Apache father and deep blue eyes from her English mother. Her skin tone is like a permanent light tan like some Italians. Her measurements are 37, 24, 35. Her parents decided to live in Colorado after his retirement because it was cooler for her English mother. The whole family has frequent camping trips. When resting in the forest she reads science fiction and has a desire to explore new areas where no one else has gone. She is currently in the outback of a national forest with no one within 10 miles. She has a 44 magnum pistol in her fanny pack. She is an excellent shot with handguns and rifles, but prefers the bow and arrow for protection. She once fell from a cliff when the rock she was standing on split, fell 20 feet and broke her tibia. She fashioned her own splint and walked out of the forest. As soon as she could she was back out inspecting the split rock. She has dated, but has never had a steady boyfriend. As you can tell, she tends to be loner, but is gregarious in a group. She has many friends in Colorado and in the Forest Service, but no close friends. She seems to be looking for a man that likes to camp like her father. She has attempted to take men with her on her visits to the mountains or the woods in the state of Washington, but they don't last a day without wimping out. If you want a female survivalist she would be perfect. This is the first I am telling you this, but I have given you great strength. You have read about someone having super human strength and ripping a door off a truck to save the truck driver. You have that strength any time you need it, not just during an emergency. Your muscles are still yours, you mind now has the ability to control them better. Usually when someone lifts up they involuntarily let other muscles pull back down, reducing their apparent strength. I have only added toning to your muscles. Your bone density is stronger than the average because I have slightly altered the bone structure. In the event you are really in danger, I will teleport you back here and heal any minor injuries as you teleport.

"Ship, put me down ahead of her on the same trail with similar equipment to her own, but with a small crossbow and small arrows. I presume I will know how to use it?"

"You will be an expert if you decide to use the crossbow."

Craig appeared on the trail uphill from Karen Martin. He was wearing olive drab shorts, high socks, and sleeved t-shirt. He had a utility belt with fanny pack, combat knife, canteen, and a small crossbow dangling from the fanny pack. He also had a small backpack that had a small nylon two man tent and a small sleeping roll on top. He decided to just sit on a rock and wait for Karen to find him. The alternative was to startle her coming down at her, or make lots of noise to warn her. In either case, she might be cautious and hide off the trail. By just sitting and waiting, she would see him first and then have to pass by him on the way up. It wasn't long before he saw her shadow passing behind the trees along the trail.

He debated what to do when she came fully into view. If he just nodded and said hello she would probably just say hello, maybe sit and rest for a few minutes, but regardless she would leave him going on up the mountain trail. As a woodsman himself he would have to acknowledge her and be looking her way when she could clearly see him. If he just offered to continue with her, she would probably say no and if he insisted she would probably turn and go back down. Instead he decided to be bold. He leaned back against a boulder and kept his eyes almost closed.

When she came into view and near enough to hear, he spoke up without opening his eyes or shifting his reclining position, "Hello, Karen Martin."

She started to make a comeback about his knowing her name and ambushing her, but he just interrupted her, "I'm Craig Decker. You have probably heard of me. I am planning on evacuating as many humans as possible into space. You should have heard something about that already. What you don't know is that I need you in particular to join my team."

Again, she continued toward him and tried to say something. He just kept on talking, "I am going to start an interstellar exploration for a suitable planet next week and I need someone with your talents to lead on planet explorations. Are you interested in joining a very small team on a very small spaceship for a very long space journey?"

Karen had no words to that. She picked another small boulder and sat down where she could plainly see him and evaluate him as friend or foe. He remained silent, now opening his eyes from his reclining position and looking directly at her in his most non-threatening pose. She was beautiful in an exotic way with her straight black hair, tan complexion, and startlingly deep blue eyes.

Eventually she responded, "What makes you think you can do any space exploration in a week?"

"Faster than light travel. I demonstrated it to NASA and our President yesterday."

"You have a faster than light ship?" "Yes. Are you interested?"

"I'll let you know, let's hike." "Is this a test?"

"Yes. I have heard of Craig Decker, but do not know if you are he. I think while hiking and climbing. There is no point in leading you on an alien planet if you cannot keep up."

She set a blistering pace up the trail. Eventually the trail ended at a rock cliff with a water pool below. "Sometimes I go swimming here. It is very cold. I think it is fed by an underground spring by a glacier up above that cliff. Are you up for a climb?"

She started free climbing the stone face of the cliff finding a hand hold here and a foot step there, climbing like spider woman. Craig followed using the same hand holds and steps that she took. It took about thirty minutes and the view was spectacular. Sure enough there was a glacier not too far from the cliff. "Are you hot? Let's get some ice."

"Not sure how clean the ice is, but I could use a little to just cool off. I have a canteen to drink."

"That's warm water."

He held out the canteen, "No, it is cold. Try it." "Whoa! It is ice cold. How do you keep it cold?"

"It is made out of the impervium which is a near 100% insulator. It would take weeks for it to warm up to this outdoor temperature."

"That's really cool. Where can I get a canteen like that? Are they for sale?"

"Not yet, this was made for me as the inventor to give it a try. With the coming end of the world there is no point in manufacturing consumer goods. We need to do everything possible to effect an evacuation into space. That's why I need you now."

"I haven't decided to trust you yet. Who else do you need for this team of yours?"

"I need a chemist. I think I know the chemist, but I wanted to contact you first so you would have time to think it over."

"Explain this team."

"We have an astral navigation specialist, a geologist and petrochemical engineer, a botanist, and a zoologist, myself as a generalist and inventor and leader, and I need you as our survivalist and exploration leader, and lastly I will need a chemist."

"Okay what are the names and ages of your team?"

"The oldest so far is 22, the youngest 21. Their names are Dawn, Jill, Estera, and Sandy."

"Are you saying it is an all girl team except for you?"

"Yes, and all the colony ships will be manned with 6 girls to each guy. Women are smarter in some areas than men and are better adapted to prolonged space travel. Once the colonies land, the population can expand quicker with more women to men."

"Are you saying that you expect me to be part of your harem?"

"If you put it that way, yes. But I am restricted to an all female crew except for myself. You will understand more later, why I need six specialized women and myself for the mission. I need you right now. You will be learning to be the expert."

"I don't think there is anything you can teach me about the outdoors. Do you expect me to have sex with you on this expedition?"

"Yes. To join the team we must have sex. You will be considered one of my wives after that."

"Fat chance, buddy. You have impressed me climbing that rock. Maybe you are who you say you are, but if you think I am ready to have sex with you be aware of the fact that I am a black belt and know how to use knives, guns, and arrows, not to mention whatever weapon comes to hand."

"I'm here to recruit you and convince you, not to attack you. You can rest easy on that."

"Okay, I'll race you to the bottom of the cliff."

"I don't think racing down the cliff is a very good idea."

"Chicken. Deal's off for sure." Karen started going hand over hand down the cliff.

SHIP told Craig to just jump off the cliff. He did, he disappeared in flight only to reappear on the ground below the cliff. SHIP had teleported him in mid flight to place him at the bottom. He called out, "Waiting!"

Karen looked down, saw him at the bottom and promptly lost her grip and started falling. Craig caught her in his arms. "How?" "How did you get down so fast and how could you catch me? I am no lightweight and I fell a good twenty feet. No one is that strong."

"Have I convinced you to join my crew?"

"Still thinking. How did you jump down from that high without any injury and how could you catch me without breaking anything?"

"You will understand within 24 hours of agreeing to join the team and having sex with me."

"Yeah, right. I did not plan on meeting your or spending the time climbing the cliff today and it is getting late. I think maybe we should spend the night here."

"That's fine with me, but you have to give me awhile alone in the woods before we set up camp."

"I'll set up my own camp while you are out in the woods. You can set up your own camp when you return. If you think I am afraid of being alone with or without you out here, you are wrong. I routinely sleep in the mountains alone."

"Okay, you set up camp now and I will be back within the hour." Craig walked off out of sight in the heavy timber and brush and teleported to bring Sandy, then Estera, and finally Jill back to SHIP. He filled them in on his day and said he would be back when he could. If he did not make it back by morning, Dawn could go on to NASA and the other three girls would have to stay on SHIP until he returned. He then teleported back to the woods and walked out to see Karen. She had built a lean-to out of branches and a bed of pine branches. She had a small fire going in a rock pit she had made. She appeared to be taking a nap in her shelter.

Without looking at him she said, "Hi Craig. Potty time? You have any energy bars in that fanny pack or do you need some of mine?"

"No thanks, watch this." He pulled off the small tent package and pressed a button, it unfolded and set itself up as a nice two man mountain tent. He pulled a small package out of his fanny pack and it became a camp chair, then another package made a second camp chair. A third package became a table between the two chairs.

"Care to have a seat for dinner?" Her eyes were wide and she was leaning on an elbow watching the show.

"I only have four energy bars and we need to save two for breakfast tomorrow morning, but yes, I will have a seat. Do you have more cold water in that canteen?"

As they both sat in their opposing chairs on opposite sides of the table she had two energy bars in hand when two complete meals with a bottle of opened wine appeared on the table. Karen fell backwards off her chair. "My god! Where did that come from?"

"I think you were thinking some rainbow trout in an almond gravy with fresh carrots would be what you wanted. I am having an Angus hamburger and fries. I know the burger doesn't go with 1972 Mosel ice wine, but I can drink Mosel ice wine with anything and it should go nicely with fish."

"Okay! I will sign on, but first I want to eat. Is this real china?"

"Yes, it is Lenox china, and no we don't have to wash it. It will disappear after our meal."

"This trout is delicious. Where did it come from? Did you fish it out of the pool when I wasn't looking and use mirrors to make it appear?"

"Actually, all the food came from raw atoms and assembled into food we would like by telepathically reading our minds for what we really wanted to eat."

"Whatever."

"What do you know about me that you picked me for your crew?" "I know everything.

You were recommended as a female survivalist that will fit into my little family of scientists and explorers. I know you are half Apache and half British from your parents. I know you had a 4.0 your first two years in college and then just quit. I do not know why."

"I quit because the professors were trying to brainwash me without really teaching anything I wanted to know. I want to be a guide in South America, Africa," She winked, "an alien planet, and college was wasting my time."

As it got cold they moved into the Craig's tent which was very comfortable. "Are you a little concerned about a bear clawing into the tent?"

"No. One time when I was camping in a National Park in California, I thought there was a dog sniffing at my head through the tent. I swatted its nose and it ran away. The next morning everyone was talking about the bear that went running down through the campground from my campsite. It knocked over tents and caused a lot of damage. The rangers were everywhere calming people and looking for bears. I just packed up my tent and left. However, this tent is bear proof. I suppose a bear could attack hard enough to pull up the tent spikes and knock the tent around, but it will not collapse unless I am ready for it to. It is made out of the metal. We have found out how to make it flexible, then strong, like now, then fold it up small again."

"Are you saying I could not cut my way out with my knife?"

She tried and could not scratch it. They stayed in the tent and talked for a couple more hours. At 2 A.M. they were on the SHIP and she was a crew member.

Once Karen got over the shock of finding herself on SHIP she inspected the master bedroom that was now rustic with Navaho rugs on the walls and beamed ceilings. She then inspected herself and said, "Where did my Indian tattoos go?"

Craig said, "SHIP makes you as perfect as you can be. It corrects old broken bones, changes any fillings to healthy teeth, removes scars, corrects eyesight, and apparently removes tattoos. If you think of what clothing you want it will appear immediately, if you change your mind new clothing will appear."

"Where does it come from? SHIP makes it from subatomic materials that make up the ship. If you think, cotton, it will be indistinguishable from cotton. You think deerskin, no one would be able to tell the difference except yours will be perfect without blemish."

"Okay, what now?"

"How about breakfast with the rest of the family?"

They all ate breakfast together and spent an hour getting acquainted, then Drew went to NASA again. Craig took Jill and Estera to Jill's room in the sorority (two trips). Sandy stayed with Karen and Craig in SHIP. Karen had her training. Then while Karen and Craig talked about what she had learned, Sandy took her veterinarian training in the training module.

"That training was amazing. Not all of the training will directly work, like living off the land on Mars, since Mars is no longer habitable. However, that gave me a taste of surviving on an alien planet. Some of the animals were interesting. I think we should take along a big game gun on any alien planet."

When Sandy finished her training, Craig had to go get Jill and Estera and then Dawn came home to SHIP and they and Sandy spent hours getting to know Karen and Karen to know them. Craig decided they could all work well together. SHIP had reached the limit of its growth with five small bedrooms and one larger master bedroom that would change its décor as different girls joined Craig.

SHIP made a pass over the Sahara Desert to suck up some sand to replenish its subatomic structure.

The next day, Craig took Karen to NASA, then Sandy to NASA where she met up with her dad. In fact, it was agreed that Sandy would spend the night with her dad in a hotel and meet Dawn at NASA the next day. Craig took Jill and Estera to the sorority room for them to work with the engineers meeting at the University of Oklahoma. They agreed to spend the night there at the sorority so that Craig could work on getting the last member of their team.

10

CHEMIST

Craig had met the cheerleader, Shelby Denton, two years earlier just like he had everyone but Karen Martin, the survivalist, but Shelby had never seen him. He had remained invisible during their visit in her room. He had teleported in uninvited and pestered her. She had felt him and talked with him, but was never really sure whether she was awake or not. However, Craig had always admired her as a cheerleader. She had such a perfect body. She was a chemistry major which he needed. She had said back then that she would like to explore space.

She had brown hair and brown eyes. She was five foot three inches. She was neither skinny nor overweight at all. She was slightly taller than the other cheerleaders. Apparently, small size goes with all there pyramid routines and being tossed in the air by the male cheerleaders. She was not busty, but everything seemed to fit perfectly. He had always admired how straight her legs were compared to the sometimes bowlegged cheerleaders. She seemed prim and proper even though doing all the right motions exactly like the other cheerleaders. While some could kick their legs high and appeared to be showing how sexy they were, she kicked higher with exact timing and still seemed ladylike.

Craig knew from his visit to her room two years earlier that she was a big Star Trek fan and read science fiction. She had said she wanted to explore space if there was someway to exceed the speed of light. Their discussion had been interesting. She thought he might be an alien come to abduct her, but did not seem afraid. Craig was more uncomfortable than she appeared to be even though Craig was the one that invaded her space. He had kept telling her she was dreaming and finally left to go visit Jill who was much more outgoing.

They needed a chemistry major on their team. She had no boyfriend when he had met her before. The photograph in her room turned out to be her brother. Rather than invade her bedroom in invisible mode, he caught up with her on the sidewalk coming from a cheerleader practice held on Owen Field. The football field was still called Owen Field even though the 87,000 seat stadium was called The Gaylord Family Stadium. She was wearing an older cheerleading outfit versus her current new game outfit. That consisted of a halter top and very short tennis type skirt.

"Shelby, mind if I walk with you?" "Suit yourself. I can't stop you." "Can I carry some of your books?" "No need, I have them."

"Have you read "Lucifer's Hammer by Larry Niven?" "Yes, that is an old book, but it was good."

She was all but ignoring him but Craig continued on, "What are the odds of something like that but worse happening."

"Depends on who you talk to."

"Have you been following the engineering efforts on campus?" "Not really. I just know it has taken all the attention away from everything else on campus. The extra news media around here is getting in the way of everything. Every hotel is full of engineers and visiting professors. Have you read this afternoon student newspaper?"

"No. What about it?"

"Well, I know that there is some big effort to build monster spaceships, maybe here in the state. These ships are supposedly colony ships to take a bunch of humans to some unknown place off planet because of something like Lucifer's Hammer on its way to hit earth."

"You sound like you don't believe it."

"Not sure. I wish I had more information on when this is supposed to happen. Is this next year or 100 years in the future? Is this just a big media event to raise taxes?"

"What was in the student newspaper?"

"It claimed that they were going to select crews for these spaceships soon and that there would be six girls for every man and the ages would be from 18 to 25."

"That was not supposed to be released yet." "What makes you say that?"

"Do you know the name Craig Decker?" "Who doesn't? Do you know him?"

"Do you remember telling me that you would love to explore space and would be willing to go on a mission like you were just telling me about?"

"No, I never told…are you? Are you Craig Decker? Did you sneak into my room one night?

"Yes to all the above." She stopped and really looked at him for the first time.

"Why are you here talking with me?"

"Because someone has to go into space ahead of the colony ships. In two years Earth will cease to support life because there is a large interstellar body headed for Earth. There is a faster than light ship that will be leaving within days or least weeks to search for a new planet. I am its captain and we are one member short of having our crew. We need a chemist. We can make you the world's expert on chemistry in hours so don't tell me you don't have your bachelors. Are you interested?"

"Of course. What I told you in my room a couple of years ago still stands, I would love the adventure if it is true."

"Okay, you know I can disappear or appear anywhere. It is by teleportation to and from the ship. My crew is just like the student newspaper reported. Six women to one man. Because we will be living together for probably years, you will be wife number six if you choose to go."

"What kind of proof can you give me that you are telling the truth?

Can I see your ship?"

"You cannot see the ship unless you join the crew by becoming one of my wives. Of course I'm not talking about legal marriage, but you will understand if you agree to all the conditions and join the crew. What proof can I give you? Have you heard about the female University of Oklahoma student that is leading the engineering effort here on campus?"

"I have heard about her. Are you saying she is a member of your crew?

"She is the geologist and petrochemical engineer on the crew. For the past several days they have been trying to develop a compact kit for drilling and then refining oil on the new planet. We don't know if we will find uranium on the new planet. It is dangerous to mine and refine for nuclear fuel, but we know any planet that will support life has to have a long history of plant life which hopefully means oil and oil is easy to drill for and refine in comparison. So, a collapsible kit that can be transported compactly and then assembled on planet after arrival. Today, she has another crew member with her. Both crew members were trained after joining the crew. The other crew members are at NASA in Houston. We need a sixth woman, a chemist?"

"Okay, one item of proof would be if you can get past all the security and have this expert confirm she is a crew member and one of your five wives."

"Let's go." Craig walked over to engineering past all the security that just passed them through without question. The news media surrounding the engineering building recognized Craig and security had to keep them back while Shelby and Craig passed through and into the building. SHIP telepathically told Craig where to find Jill and he led Shelby to her. Jill and Estera saw him and ran to him giving him a hug, "What are you doing here? Is this our chemist?"

"Not yet. I am trying to convince her."

Estera said, "My father is the chairman of the House Ways and Means Committee and he practically ordered me to accept Craig's invitation. If we never get a colony ship off the earth, our crew will be okay."

Jill added, "My parents don't really know what is going on except that I am happy and famous in my own right. I was just another student here until a few days ago and now look what I am doing. We need a chemist. Don't worry about a degree. Degrees will be meaningless in a couple of years."

Shelby replied, "Well Craig, how do I sign up?"

"Not here." He winked at Jill and Estera. "Shall we go elsewhere to discuss the deal?"

The engineers and professors had stopped to watch the exchange. They couldn't hear what was going on, but they could see the family reunion nature of the meeting.

Craig took Shelby into a restroom on another floor and had SHIP teleport them to Jill's sorority room. "Where are we? How did we get here?"

"This is Jill's sorority room on the OU campus. We teleported here."

"But on Star Trek they slowly dematerialized and then slowly materialized at their destination. One minute we were in a women's restroom in the engineering building and suddenly we were here?"

"This is not Star Trek. It is nearly instantaneous. Remember what I told you earlier. You will become not only the seventh member and last member of the crew, but the last of my six wives. We have to have sex to transport to my ship. Ship gives us new clothing when we arrive either on location or on the ship, but that initial trip has to be made during the act of becoming my physical wife. You will understand tomorrow if you decide to do it today."

"My one sexual experience was when I thought I was in love and he went off and left me crying in a hotel room never to be seen again. I am not so sure about the sex thing, but I am willing to try if you are."

Craig started slowly kissing and undressing her there in Jill's room. Shelby cooperated by removing Craig's shirt, then loosening his belt and jeans. It was awkward, but an hour later, they were onboard SHIP.

Shelby didn't notice immediately, "That was more like I have read about sex. I think those years ago in the motel room I was rap… Where are we?"

"We are on the ship. You are the final member of the crew. Just think about what you want to wear and it will be there." Her new cheerleading outfit was laying on the foot of the bed.

"But this is how I would decorate a master bedroom if I had a master bedroom."

"Then it will look like this anytime you are in here. The SHIP is not large. Each girl has their own small bedroom decorated however they think they want it when they are not with me in the master bedroom. The master bedroom changes with whoever is here. Get dressed and I will show you the rest of SHIP."

"Why do say SHIP instead of THE ship?"

"You will know after your training, but SHIP is intelligent and older than our modern civilization."

"Excuse me?"

"Just wait until your training tomorrow." Like all of them she stared for a long time out the windows into space and watched the earth go past and saw the moon rising past the earth. Craig had only seen that a few times, "Pretty amazing isn't it?"

"That's the understatement of the year."

He showed her around the SHIP and then Craig decided she was comfortable enough to be left alone while he retrieved the rest of the women.

SHIP said, "Welcome Shelby. Craig is going to leave you with me for awhile while he retrieves the rest of his wives. Let me entertain you with a little historical video of what I know of history. You can just get comfortable on one of the sofas there. If you need anything to eat or drink just ask?" SHIP read her mind and a margarita over ice with ice on the rim appeared on the coffee table in front of her.

"I will be in and out once for each of four girls, but Dawn has been with me long enough that SHIP teleports her when she wants. She will probably be the first to show up back here at the ship. I may be short one girl tonight because Sandy will be staying with her father tonight. When the rest of us are all here, SHIP will serve us our dinner. We all eat together in the dining room."

Tentatively, Shelby said, "Okay. I am so overwhelmed that I am almost dizzy right now and watching the video should relax me. I have so many questions I would not know where to start?"

"You can either wait and ask the group over dinner, or just ask SHIP at any time. SHIP has knowledge predating modern man and everything learned by modern man. I'll be back in and out and back in to stay in an hour or two. The rest of my crew has not been with me long enough for SHIP to confidently teleport them alone yet."

The crew for SHIP was complete. The first colony ship was in final design with most of the issues worked out such as welding section pieces together by using uncured super metal on cured super metal. Once joined, within twenty-four hours it was permanent with the two welded pieces now as one with no sign of a weld. They had worked out how to put in doors and air locks and everything about the colony ships themselves except money to actually build one. The missing technology was the faster than light drive. Engineers, professors, and students around the country were trying to figure out how to build plans provided by Craig from the ship. There were years of work remaining on the ship.

The portable kit drilling and refinery were nearing completion. Estera's father had been trying to convince the House to provide unlimited funding.

Craig and his crew decided it was time for at least a week long search for a suitable planet.

PART THREE

EXPLORATIONS

11

FIRST EXPORATION

Craig and family crew took the day off to discuss their upcoming voyage into outer space to other solar systems. This was an area that even SHIP did not have experience. "SHIP, why don't you start off and tell us your capabilities for exploration."

SHIP started by saying "NASA has a telescope called Kepler. It has been searching for planets. As of December 2011 it had discovered 1,094 new exoplanet candidates, pushing the spacecraft's total so far to 2,326, including ten candidate Earth-size worlds orbiting in the habitable zones of their parent stars. One called Kepler 22b is six hundred light years from earth. It is 15% closer to its sun, but the sun is cooler than our sun so the temperature might be the same. It is 2.4 times the size of Earth. If the makeup of the planet is that same gravity as Earth then gravity would be several times higher making it uninhabitable, but Earth is about as dense as cast iron making it a very solid planet with a strong gravity for its size." A planet without a molten core of iron would not have as much gravity even though the same size as Earth. A somewhat larger planet with more topsoil and less rock might have the same gravity. The mission requires that we find a planet with nearly the same gravity as Earth with similar temperatures, topsoil similar, and with sufficient minerals to support a modern civilization."

"Faster-than-Light-travel or FaTL that is spelled with all capital letters and a little a. It is pronounced Fatal, which it is not. My Martian ancestors settled on that acronym meaning it was to be used when their planet was facing a fatal event. I will list my capabilities on the view screen or TV so you can see them and consider them.

1. FaTL speed multiple times faster than light. Once I exceed the speed of light small planet could pass through my passengers with no more notice than you have felt cosmic rays passing through you throughout you life. Einstein's Theory of Relativity says that as mass approaches the speed of light mass becomes infinite. Not only mass, but size. In relation to my weight on Earth there will be no change, but my total size will exceed this solar system. I will still need to avoid stars as they could do some amount of damage.

It would not be fatal for me as I could quickly repair a hole, but depending on where you were hit, it could kill one of you. An extremely large star could kill all my passengers and require me several years to repair myself.

2. I can see with my sensors millions of miles and analyze objects as to size and general content. Even though traveling faster than light I will use the reference to light years as the only measurement of distance in my vocabulary. I can see and analyze objects out to at least 100 light years depending on objects that may overlap in my line of sight. If a planet is behind a star at 50 light years, I might not see it. Based on my sensors my top speed between galaxies might exceed 1000 light years per hour. In the Milky Way galaxy my speed will probably be limited to 50 light years per hour to be able to avoid impacting stars.

3. I can see planets out to hundreds of light years from here, but I can only analyze rough temperatures, atmosphere make-up, rotation speed. I could not tell whether it has natural resources or life. I could spot a potential planet any where within 50 light years. If I were to maintain 50 light years per hour I would have only two hours to

scan it for content, life, or potential to support humans. This would only give me a probability of a planet that could support life. To determine whether it was safe for a human exploration, I would have to slow down to orbit speed and make several orbits to map out the planet, thoroughly analyze the atmosphere, general plant life, and evidence of animal life. It would take you to teleport to actually get samples and see for yourself. I can analyze samples and have more data to compare to than exists on Earth.

4.   I can provide some shelters and weapons to help keep you safe, but so far Craig and Dawn are the only ones I cold teleport out of danger. That would leave Karen, Jill, Estera, Shelby, and Sandy in danger. The tent that Craig used with Karen would protect from a bear of Colorado size, but a Kodiak or Polar Bear might be able to toss it far enough to injure the parties within. The tent is paper thin. It would protect against a 50 caliber bullet or fragmentation grenade or any Earth animals teeth or claws, but not against a volcano or a 100 ton rock falling 100 feet. I can provide any human weapons you want. It might be good to materialize an armored

personnel carrier for your exploration. I could make one in the maintenance bay in place of the shuttle plane and teleport it to the surface. It would give you some land speed and a place of shelter while on the planet.

5. I can provide ship's food or any other supplies while on the surface. I cannot analyze whether a particular unknown plant is edible without having a sample here on board and a few minutes to break it down.

Dawn asked, "With the thousands of years you have been here, you must have found a lot of potential planets. Would you recommend a course?"

"I would recommend trying along our current spiral of the Milky Way. As you know, a galaxy is a spiral that has sparse arms at the outer part of the galaxy. There is empty space between the arms of a galaxy. As you go straight toward the center, you will have stars in a band then a huge gap then another band of starts thicker than the first, then a smaller huge gap to the next thicker band of stars. As you get halfway to the center of the galaxy the arms become almost continuous with very little empty space. The starlight at night would eliminate the need for streetlights. As you got closer to the center, it would never get dark and presumably life could not exist due to natural radiation from the compact stars."

Dawn said, "Therefore our own spiral would be most likely to have an earthlike planet?"

"Yes."

Craig asked, "For a ship without anti-gravity you would have to limit acceleration to keep from hurting the passengers. Tell me if I am wrong. One light year equals about 10 trillion miles. If the ship could average 1.4 gees of acceleration for one year we are talking about around 1200 light years distance traveled. Is that correct?"

"However, earthlings are used to one gravity. A constant 1.4 gravities would be too much to start; maybe 1.2 gravities or gees of acceleration with short pre-scheduled bursts would be more practical. If it were known that we were going to a planet with a larger mass than Earth we might want to build up the constant to 1.4 gees to strengthen the people to live at a higher gravity."

Estera asked, "Humans have been discovering planets for the ten years or so. In what direction?"

"No set direction."

"How many that humans have identified could support human life?" "About 50 could support some life, but only possibly one that could support human life.

Craig asked the group, "I think that all of our projects could run for a week without our help so we could take off tomorrow for an initial exploration. I think we should take the direction of our spiral of the galaxy but toward galaxy center. Does anyone disagree for any reason?"

"We want to maintain speed. And travel outward for three days and return in three days. That will leave us one day in case we find something interesting. We need to break up into two 12 hour shifts. Three of us will stay in the control room and three can do whatever to relax and get some rest. That is not to say that only four can be in control, but we should have two at least at all times. I will not pull a specific shift and you can call on me anytime there is any question."

They all went through their daily routines with their research groups telling the research groups they would have to work on their own70% They met back early, made last minute plans, went to bed. At 0600 Eastern Standard Earth Time, they told SHIP to take them straight down the galactic spiral as Earth. The planets blurred and within seconds the Sun was a star in the distance behind them and other stars growing brighter and dimmer. SHIP would be side scanning for 50 light years side to side for potential planets. SHIP would note potential planets along the way. If they happened on one that seemed especially good they would slow and enter orbit. If it still looked good they would teleport down to the best locations on the planet to really look it over and take actual samples back to SHIP.

The entire crew/family lined up to watch out the windows as SHIP accelerated out of the solar system. It only took seconds. Where we picture a ship acceleration in the flat plain of the solar system, a quicker way out is at a 90 degree angle to that plain. Why fly between planets in the plain of the solar system? Behind them they could see our solar system with its planets as a vertical image behind them. SHIP said, "Due to our small size the attraction and repulsion of my anti-gravity drive should have no impact on the objects in our solar system, but we could hit an asteroid and knock it out of orbit. It is better to just go at a 90 degree angle rather than go through the asteroid belt and dodge planets and moons. Your earthly ships needed to slingshot around one object or another to gain the momentum needed to go further faster. I don't."

Craig replied, "I had not thought about that. If we wanted to travel from one galaxy to another rather than travel through the thick part of the galaxy we should just go the shortest distance which is 90 degrees from the plain of the galaxy."

"That is correct. There is also the curvature of space. When we exceed the speed of light we simply cut across the lines of space. Basically we don't exist as we take this shortcut across space. When we slow down to below the speed of light we reenter the curvature lines of space where we exist again."

They all stayed standing watching the stars get larger than smaller as they traveled between them at the incredible FaTL speed. SHIP said, "I have found that most of the time I can travel faster than anticipated between stars. There is so much empty space. Remember, even the Martians or Atlanteans as you call them, had not done much travel outside the solar system when they manufactured me so this is new to me also."

"I am scanning 50 light years to each side looking for potential planets as we travel. So far I have found a number of planets but they were too close or too far from the relative size of their suns or they were gas giants."

The family relaxed after the first hour, with everyone finding a place to sit. The two that were assigned to the control room took seats to watch in real time and listen to the running description of SHIP. Some of the others sat in the living area watching out the windows and watching the TV screen that SHIP was projecting and some eventually went to their rooms to rest until they were on duty. Craig was in telepathic communication with SHIP.

12

PANGAEA

That evening earth time, SHIP slowed to orbit a planet. The family felt no deceleration but the stars apparent motion stopped and one sun was stationery. SHIP announced, "I veered off our straight course because only 10 light years off course I found a likely planet. It is the right distance from its sun support human life. It has an atmosphere similar to Earth except that it is low in carbon dioxide and slightly higher in oxygen. Nitrogen is in similar concentration to Earth and there are similar concentrations of the other Earth gases. My sensors are indicating extensive plant life, fresh water rivers and lakes, and it has salty seas, slightly less salty than earth."

Everyone heard SHIP's announcement all around SHIP. Everyone was standing at monitors in the control room or standing at the windows in the living area. SHIP said, "I am going to make several orbits of the planet at different angles to survey the whole planet for life, water, measure ice as the poles, determine its rotation, and look for animal life."

They orbited for 10 hours before most members of the crew decided to try to sleep before an on planet exploration. After a total of 16 hours of orbiting, SHIP announced, "This planet appears to be very earthlike, but you will need to look at several areas and take samples for me to analyze."

"What I have found in my orbits is that the planet is very stable with only a slight tilt, which means no radically different seasons. There will be mild winters and slightly warmer summers. The equator will remain hot year round and the polar ice caps will remain ice with very little melting. The rest of the planet varies from cold near the poles and getting warmer near the equator. Comparing it to Earth means that being North like Kansas it would get down to lows of 15 to 20 degrees Fahrenheit in the winters and up to 90-97 in the summer season versus Earth Kansas varies from slightly below zero to 105 in the summer. In other words very earthlike climate."

The geological makeup is one large irregular continent with 70% salt water ocean covering the rest. Similar to what Earth was like geologically millions of years ago. The largest continent three hundred million years ago on Earth was called Pangaea which would be an app name for this planet to define it from others we may find. Most of the forest is near the coast, the mountains, and along the rivers and streams. Much of the interior between rivers and natural lakes is grassy plain or at the equator dead desert with very little plant life. It has a magnetic field that I think we should refer to as North like Earth North. The magnetic north is actually much closer to its true pole so very little magnetic correction will be necessary.

There is a range of mountains that starts on the east side of the continent and runs north to south for sixty percent of the length. One thing different from this description is that east of the mountain range at the equator is a jungle as dense as the rain forest in Brazil. West of the mountains all the way to the west coast of the continent is desert near the equator. This is because the planet turns in the opposite direction of Earth. The morning sun rise will appear in the west and set in the east. This makes for prevailing winds and the jet streams to come from the east. This explains the jungle east of the mountain range. Moisture from the ocean comes on shore and is mostly blocked by the mountains making the east side very wet and the west side very dry. The mountain range at the equator ranges to 20,000 feet and tapers off both north and south to rolling hills. There are smaller ranges of low mountains and large hills here and there throughout the planet. The planet has slightly more dense than Earth. The size difference would not make the difference in gravity, but the gravity is 1.1 times that of earth. A day is twenty-two Earth hours. It will take four hundred days to go around its sun once so the year will be four hundred days long. There is no moon and therefore almost no tides."

"I have picked a clearing in the coastal forest for your first expedition."

Karen, the survivalist, asked, "What do you recommend we take for protection.?"

SHIP replied, "I have found animal life in the forests, but cannot determine what. There are large animals on the plains that appear to be similar to Earth's cattle. These plains creatures weigh in at between 400 and 1000 pounds. On one orbit, some smaller creatures attacked and killed one of the plains creatures, but I did not identify them as either Martian or Earthly. I recommend that you, Karen, take a forty caliber hunting rifle with a twenty shot magazine. Craig, you take a similar rifle with a ten shot magazine and an attached forty millimeter grenade launcher, just in case. All of the family should carry forty caliber Heckler and Koch P2000's except Dawn and Estera should carry Sig Sauer P250 Compact 40's which are a little lighter weight. I will provide each member with a kit of scientific equipment and sample containers for each specialty, Botany, Zoology, Geology, and Chemical. You will be able to do some testing on your own, but I request samples of everything you test on your own and a larger sample of everything not identified. Craig and Karen will have air samplers to make sure that there are no poisonous gases or spores or other biological things in the air that could be harmful. Dawn, as the astral navigation specialist I suggest that you work with me here onboard to help me determine a logical course back to Earth that could be taken from Earth to here with consideration of the colony ships exhaust plume and harm it could cause."

Craig had to make one trip per each of the five girls to get all down to the surface. He took Karen first as the one most likely to protect herself while alone on the planet. SHIP provided her a full camouflage suit with long legs and sleeves, gloves, heavy hiking boots, and belts with extra ammunition clips two combat knives, her rifle and handgun.

Moments later it was Estera's turn with her Botany equipment and compact 40 caliber handgun with similar clothing, but only two ammo clips and one combat knife. She had a pack and belt pouches for testing and samples. She had to dress on planet while Craig kept watch for wild animals.

Then it was Sandy's turn with similar equipment, but also with a incredibly advanced and small digital camera with 100 power stabilized zoom capable of video transmission direct to SHIP that was now hovering stationery 200 miles above them. She was to take continuous video of both plant life and any animals from insects to elephants that they saw.

Next was Shelby the chemist. She could also sample the air, the soil, some plant life, water and test them for chemical content. She would take samples of all back to SHIP.

Finally, Jill arrived, she was equipped with a small folding shovel, pick axes, and a small powered drill for core samples up to four feet deep, and a large backpack for soil and rock samples. Craig was able to stay on planet after Jill arrived. Craig's was equipped similar to Karen.

He was not one of the experts so he would back up Karen for protection they hoped would be unnecessary.

The total process of teleporting, getting their clothing and equipment on took over half of an hour. Going back to SHIP would be take less than half that because they could strip off clothing and equipment quicker than putting it on.

Once they were assembled and their equipment arranged how they wanted, they looked around at their surroundings. SHIP had set them down in a large clearing circled with what were trees, although not what the kind they were familiar with. It was looking like this would be Estera's day.

"These trees look like a mixture of oak and maple trees. They are quite large with substantial trunks and limbs, but the leaves on the oak like trees are spear shaped and on the maple like trees they are perfectly round. I'll collect some leaves in the sample bags."

Karen warned, "Let me approach the tree line first. If there are animals nearby they will either be afraid of us or be looking at us as a source of food."

Karen unsnapped the strap on her handgun, and held her rifle at the ready as she approached the tree line. Everyone held their positions and their breath as she did so. Craig had his rifle aimed near her, just in case. Karen stood a few feet from the trees and just listened moving her rifle side to side and up into the trees. It was exceedingly quiet. Finally she called out, "I'm going to step into the trees just a few feet to make sure it's safe."

"Nothing moved at my loud voice, so here goes." Karen cautiously stepped into the trees. There was not much underbrush became of the thick canopy. She went in 2 feet past the nearest tree trunk, looked around and up; then 5 feet into the trees and finally she kept going until she was out of sight.

"Karen, that's far enough for now, I can't see you to provide cover.

Come on back out and let Estera join you at the tree line for her samples. Jill, take some surface and core drill samples. Shelby, why don't you do a quick chemical test of the surface soil to just get a rough idea of chemicals in the soil."

Estera asked Karen, "Can I get a small limb and a cutting from the trunk?"

"Don't see why not."

"The small limb broke like an Earth tree. See how I had to twist it around to get it loose. The sample I cut with my knife cut just like I would expect an Earth tree to cut. Now let me cut into the bark of the trunk of this maple like tree. Look, a little sap is coming out."

Karen admonished, "Don't touch the sap. For all we know it is an acid that could eat through your gloves. Stab your knife into the ground to clean off the sap before putting it back in its scabbard. Take a sap sample to Shelby and let's go back to the others in the center of the clearing."

As they walked back to the group, Estera collected some flower and grass samples from the clearing. They then reversed the process of teleportation to get back to the ship with Karen going last.

SHIP reported, "I transported no debris from the surface except those in the sample containers. I detected no unknown virus or bacteria in any of you. Next time we do this I should teleport Karen individually and let her stay there under observation for an hour or so and then teleport her back her to check for anomalies before transporting the rest of you. You might notice I said only Karen. Without other humans around and being overly critical about transporting each of you back, I have now analyzed your molecular content such that I can transport each of you like I have been doing with Dawn for weeks now. You are all full fledged members of my and Craig's family. That also provides me with the capability of teleporting any and all of you back here in case of emergency. At this time it is teleporting you one at a time unless you are with Craig. Craig and Dawn are the only ones I am confident in teleporting with clothing and equipment."

"I have teleported all your equipment separately. Your equipment is part of my molecular makeup, but the samples were teleported intact to my analyzers. I will analyze them one at a time and give you a report on the video when each is completed."

They all ate around the dining table. The excitement of finding and walking, however briefly, on an alien planet had made them all very hungry. As they finished their individually prepared lunches, SHIP was ready to start the analysis videos.

"I have found that what you said looked like an oak tree, is indeed basically an oak tree. You should be able to burn it for heat, lumber it for building. The maple like tree is for all intents and purposes a sugar maple. The sap analyzes like maple sap."

Estera said, "That was my assessment of the trees also. Except the bark seemed unnaturally smooth. The maple was smooth, not unlike a birch tree but darker with bumps. The oak had furrows, but not as deep as an Earth oak tree."

Shelby added, "My chemical analysis showed no difference between an Earth tree and these."

SHIP, "I have analyzed the grass and flowers which Earth would call weeds. The grass is *Triticale* similar to wheat before it was bred for its grain in the Middle East. I found nothing harmful to humans and should be good food for grazing animals."

Jill joined in, "My analysis of the dirt is dirt. Even the core sample was good undisturbed natural top soil even 3 feet deep."

SHIP, "Coincides with my analysis, however there is animal life in your soil sample. There were some trace of insects that live in the dirt like crickets, ants, and a worm like creature that processes the dirt like an earthworm. However, they were very small and not poisonous; you could eat them if you wanted."

That got faces from everyone. Craig said, "What about another exploration point. How about some close in images of the animals you saw on the plains?"

The view screen showed some bovine creatures like the American buffalo, but with horns more like a water buffalo. They were not shaggy, but had short hair with a tuft on the tail for swatting bugs. Their feet looked peculiar, but they could not really tell what they were like because their feet were covered by hair.

Karen asked, "Should be maybe go to the plains and shoot one of them to look a little closer and see if they are edible?"

Dawn spoke up and said, "Is that what we going to do landing on a new planet is to start killing the wildlife?"

Craig interjected, "Karen is right. By the time the colonists get here they will have been eating frozen, manufactured and dehydrated food on the ship. Depending on how long the colony ships take to get here, the food may be down to only months of supplies and the colonists will be tired of dehydrated, manufactured and frozen foods. This is definitely not like the food we get on SHIP. Their food is like calling Tang the same as fresh orange juice. It can be palatable, but not the same. There will not be enough domestic animals on board to have a herd for food for several years. That is one criterion for a habitable planet. It is not just about trees for building, ores and oil for resources, it is also about food. We can plant wheat and corn and have a crop the next year if the planet cooperates. Fruit trees will take years to bear fruit so we need to find edible plant life also, preferably nutritious fruits. SHIP, what do you say?"

"I cannot make decisions like that. In principle that would appear to be important, but natural minerals are important too. However, I do not want to split up the family. I suggest that Karen and Craig go alone to the plains, shoot a bovine, cut out some skin and muscle to be analyzed here and return. Do not get too close, the bovines should not be spooked by you since they have never seen humans, but they have wicked looking horns. I can teleport one at a time back here. I suggest that Craig and Karen separate keeping each other under cover of their rifles and Karen be the one to shoot one of the animals. If the animal falls and nothing bad happens then you can take your time. Karen, even when stalking the animal keep watch on Craig. I will try to keep both of you safe. If you see Craig disappear, back off on your hunt and prepare to be teleported back. Craig, the same goes for you, but I can teleport you back fully dressed and equipped."

Karen asked, "What is the temperature in Fahrenheit on the plains?" "It varies from 50 to 100 degrees depending on location."

"If the animals appear to be the same, I would prefer 80 degrees. I can go with minimal clothes and only my weapons which I can toss down in case of trouble and be teleported back immediately. SHIP, can you provide me with deerskin loincloth and bra that would be identical to tanned deerskin including smell? I would also like to take a bow and quiver of arrows like I had on Earth. That way I can kill one without spooking the rest with a gun shot."

"Of course."

Karen and Craig were teleported down while the rest of the family watched on the view screens with strong telephoto lenses. SHIP provided a fringed loincloth and bra which Karen put on and with her dark hair, ruddy skin, and rifle with only a loincloth, a belt with a knife, handgun, ammo clips and her bow and arrows looked like a modernly equipped aboriginal female warrior. Craig was teleported about seventy- five yards to her right. They were both five hundred yards from the edge of the herd or about one third of a mile and downwind. Karen moved forward very slowly to not spook the herd. Craig stayed seventy-five yards to her right and further from the herd. There were maybe two hundred animals in the herd. When Karen got down to one hundred fifty yards or one and a half football fields, she slowly aimed her arrow. One twang and the animal keeled over dead with an arrow in its heart. At almost the same time, Craig saw movement in the grass beyond Karen. It was some large animal rushing in Karen's direction. Craig, fired his gun past Karen toward the animal, whatever it was. It jumped straight up apparently wounded but not killed. Karen swung toward it and fired her rifle again while it was still mid-jump. The buffalo herd stampeded away. There was other movement in the tall grass, but away from Karen toward a copse of trees near a stream. Karen and Craig both circled around, their rifles ready to fire again, but it seemed they were alone. The herd of grazing animals were milling around at least a mile off now.

SHIP communicated with Craig telepathically. "Sorry, I was zoomed in so close to you and Karen watching for danger from the herd, that I did not see a large cat like creature stalking Karen. I was spending more time looking for your safety as my captain. I have widened my view looking for any movement from anything within a thousand yards of your positions."

"Karen, SHIP says we are all clear now, but keep on the alert. SHIP says that second animal we shot was some form of large cat. Let's go see it first because it was a predator stalking you as you stalked the herd."

Karen waited for Craig to come to her and the walked together scanning for themselves for any threats. When they got to the animal they discovered it was some form of lion size cat and that Craig had put his shot in the front leg and Karen had made a head shot nearly between its eyes.

"Nice shot. I picked well when I picked you as our human protector."

"Not too bad yourself. You had to shoot within a foot of me to hit the cat that was mainly hidden in the grass. You had a lousy target. You saved my life, and when the cat jumped in the air I had a clear shot without having to worry about shooting anything else and no grass so I could see it clearly."

"Thanks. Let's take a close look. It has short hair like a lioness with no mane, but it was a male. It is tan like the color of the dried wheat like grass. Perfect camouflage for this plain. It and the others with it must have been stalking the herd when you came into view. It decided to go after you as easier to bring down than a buffalo size animal. The rest of the pride of lions or whatever they are ran after my shot wounded this one."

Karen was squatting down next to the cat, "This is no lion. It is larger than an Earth lion, but look at these paws or are they hands. The toes look almost like fingers as if they belonged to a guerilla instead of a cat. The shape of the rear legs are like a cat, so it cannot stand upright like an ape, but it looks like this cat can climb with its hand type front legs. It has some wicked teeth like a saber tooth tiger. Its claws are too fat for climbing trees so if it climbs it has to do so by gripping the tree limbs. However, the claws would definitely slaughter another animal."

"Let me take some extensive pictures. I have the sample bags in my backpack. Let's cut off a hand or paw or whatever to study back on SHIP. SHIP can analyze the meat on the paw to determine more about the cat. NO. I have gloves; don't touch it with your bare skin."

Karen said, "Let's go see our buffalo. Can you tell SHIP to send me some sample bags and some gloves. You did not show me much about knowing how to butcher an animal when cutting off a lion paw. Apparently SHIP is inexperienced and could not give you that knowledge." A pack and gloves appeared next to her. Karen grabbed the pack and pulled on the gloves. She hooked the pack to her utility belt which held her deerskin loincloth. Craig gave her a head start to again cover her just in case and then followed her to the buffalo. SHIP told Craig, "I am not zooming in on the two of you this time. I am holding back to look at the big picture. Craig thought back to SHIP, "The team was picked by the two of us and trained by you. You must trust them with the close in work while you watch out for us."

Craig admired Karen's nearly bare back side. He wondered how long before SHIP would be able to teleport her fully clothed like Dawn. It was sometimes inconvenient but teleporting in an embrace was something no red blooded young man would reject. Karen reached the buffalo and was waiting for Craig. He got his mind back on business and hurried to her side.

"I think I will skin an area on its hip and then cut out a hunk of muscle to see if it would be as meat."

"You know better than I. Go to it. I'm still keeping watch. I think I can hear the cats over in that distant line of trees. I think they had planned on getting this buffalo and are upset that we are taking it ourselves. SHIP, send me one of those digital video cameras. I think after we send the samples back to you, Karen and I should back off in another direction and see if the rest of the cats will go after the remains of this buffalo. Sound okay with you Karen?"

"That's fine but lets go over to that little hill where we can look down on the surrounding grass and down on the dead buffalo so we could see something approaching better. Before we go, look at this."

Craig looked at what she was holding, "That is not a hoof, it is more of a paw. It has three pads instead of a hoof. Isn't that like a prehistoric horse?"

"Ask SHIP or Sandy. They should know. Take some video for SHIP to show the family. See, the paw even has vestigial nails. Maybe in another millennia they will form into hooves."

They waited twenty minutes watching the buffalo then SHIP alerted Craig to infrared signatures moving toward the edge of the trees. Craig zoomed in with the camera and could plainly see the "lions", for lack of a better name, moving through the grass. Karen kept swiveling around to make sure nothing was stalking them while watching the lions. The lions came out slowly and seemed to look in the direction of the two humans and continued to the dead buffalo which they started eating. Craig kept filming.

SHIP changed the order of things. "Since I can teleport you as is and you are not in immediate danger, let me teleport Karen first. With no other humans around on this planet, I am able to teleport her alone."

"Karen, SHIP is going to teleport you as soon as you dump your equipment and then me." Karen took off her utility belt and handed Craig her belt and her rifle. SHIP teleported her. One minute later, Craig was teleported back to SHIP.

"That was a little too exciting." Dawn said, "I hope it was worth it."

SHIP replied, "I have analyzed the meat from the buffalo. It is similar to American buffalo; low in cholesterol and high in protein. I detect no poisons or parasites in the meat. If they are all this healthy you will have a ready supply of high quality protein without importing cattle on the colony ship. There are an estimated 500 million of these Pangaea buffalo on this continent. There is also a smaller grazing animal that appears to be a cross between a pig and a sheep. It roots in the ground, but has long hair. It acts like a pig, but stays away from mud unlike a pig. There are another 300 million of them on this continent. We might want to go hunting for one of them to test next."

"The Pageant lion is like a lion except it does have hands. It may be far more intelligent than the Earth lion. Hands mean that it can grip things and might be able to climb and potentially use tools. Since they might hunt humans we will have to study them from afar to see what threat they might be."

"We now know there are animals to support a human population and we found one dangerous animal. We need to look further."

Craig interjected, "I suggest we call a rest break for a few hours. Then we need to get a look at mineral resources. It is fine to have animals to eat and wood to build and heat houses and cook the meat, but to support a modern civilization we will need metals and energy. SHIP, while we rest, please look for two locations. One is an area likely to have oil and the second is geology where we might find metal ore near the surface where we can get some samples. If you need more areas to search, you need more areas. Why can't you just teleport samples to test?

"To teleport I have to know the total molecular makeup of the object. I spend years searching for a captain. When Craig decided to bring a wife on board, I had centuries of experience in humans. As you know, at first I even had to teleport them with Craig. The first time had to be during sex. Now after weeks and with no other humans to interfere, I am able to teleport any of you alone, but still not with your clothing and equipment. Hopefully, I will be able to do better like I do with Dawn. I can teleport anything I make or any common human items. Everything on this planet is unknown until you bring me a sample to analyze. I could teleport a Pangaea oak or maple tree, or buffalo except they are too large to fit nicely, but I am not familiar enough with the Pangaea lion as I only have a foot."

Sandy asked, "Why not transport a dead Pangaea lion here where you can analyze it?"

"I do not have enough data on it. That is why you must collect samples for me. I must learn its total molecular structure from samples. I have learned most of your structure. I know the structure of your equipment and clothing that I make here. I have learned every object from Earth or Mars, but we are on an alien planet. As you get samples and put them in the sample containers I provide I can teleport that container and whatever is in it. I then analyze the contents down below the atom level and could now teleport that sample here."

Sandy responded, "In other words to teleport a whole lion we would have to cut up a lion small enough to put in the sample containers and then teleport those parts one at a time? Why not provide a container large enough to put in a whole lion?"

"Why would I want to learn out how to teleport lions?"

"So you can analyze the whole lion to be able to tell us all about it." "I could, if that is what you want."

"I think it would be more important to transport a whole Pangaea buffalo since we will be considering using all of it. I'll let you know, SHIP."

Craig asked, "Will you be able to identify bacteria or viruses that could be harmful?"

"I can only identify that which was on Mars or Earth, but I can identify the fact that there are an unknown bacteria or virus. Thus far, nothing."

"Karen, are you up to another expedition today?"

"Absolutely, I am so amped up I would welcome it. I have always wanted to hunt in the nude like my ancient ancestors did. Clothing can introduce smells that animals can identify with. As long as it is just us, I like doing it in the minimal deerskin clothing with just my weapons. Where to now?"

"Ship, why don't we go find a source for metal ore?" "What kind, gold, iron, tin?"

"Is there an area with any of those basically on the ground? We can't go mining with a shovel and a drill?

"Yes, near the mountain range where the range has been worn down from erosion that has exposed ridges that should contain metal ores. I can't tell for sure, but Jill should be able to identify some or at least potentials that she can send back to me in sample containers. I only need a fraction of an ounce to analyze the richness of the ore, but Jill, being on site, could better assess whether there is a potential quantity for mining. It is important that none of you be near another animal to teleport you back. I am starting to learn your molecular structure pretty quickly with the family being the only humans on Pangaea. A few more days, and I may be able to teleport you fully clothed and equipped like I can teleport Dawn. It took well over a year to do that with Dawn."

SHIP moved to hover two hundred miles above the selected part of the mountain foothills that had a lot of erosion due to an active river flowing out of the mountains. The important persons for this mission were Karen to protect all of them, Craig as backup and protect Karen's back, and Jill, the geologist. Craig went first because he could have his weapons, clothing and equipment with him. Karen's weapons and utility belt with accessories came next, then Karen who had selected to go without clothes. But this time she took sample bags to wear front and back like an Indian's loin cloth. Then Jill's equipment and clothing, then Jill. Jill's clothing was long canvas pants to protect her legs in case she needed to climb on rocks or crawl across the ground looking at and collecting rocks. Her equipment consisted of a small utility pick and axe tool, a folding shovel, a combat knife, and a 40 caliber automatic pistol. They brought Sandy the zoologist; Estera, the botanist; and Shelby the chemist. Sandy would look for anything from animals to insects. Estera would sample any plant life in the canyon. Shelby would test the water for chemicals, dissolved minerals, and all of them would be sending back samples to SHIP. They were at the bottom of a cliff with broken rocks at the bottom of the cliff extending out 50 yards to a sandy beach on the river. The river was the first river they had been up close to.

Karen went upstream 50 yards and Craig downstream 50 yards to watch for any predatory animals. Shelby and Sandy went to the river, and Estera and

Jill went to start examining the rocks that had fallen from the cliff.

Sandy called out, "There are fish in the river." Craig yelled back, "Parana or trout?"

"Very funny. SHIP can you send me a rod, reel, and a lure for a maximum of 10 pound fish?" The equipment appeared next to her next to the water.

Shelby had taken water samples being careful not to touch the water, because they did not know that it wasn't flowing acid. Her gloves were waterproof and covered up to her elbows. She used her test kit to test ph, to check that it was water, and various test chemicals to test for minerals. She sent a sample to SHIP for detailed analysis and confirm her testing. It appeared to be water with trace amounts of iron in fairly high levels and trace amounts of magnesium, and other expected metals from a river flowing out of a mountain range. There was some plant debris that she could not identify. It was looking good from chemical analysis, but SHIP would do a thorough lab analysis.

While Shelby was testing, Sandy was fishing. It was not long before she caught a fish and hauled it into shore, pulling it far up the beach. SHIP had warned her not to touch the water, let alone the fish. The fish was nearly 18 inches long and probably weighed 4 or 5 pounds. "SHIP, can you send me a club or something to kill it with?"

Sandy killed it and started fishing again.

In the meantime, Estera was collecting grasses and flowers growing between the rocks. One looked like an orchid another a moss rose.

Jill had picked up a number of loose rocks and sent them back to SHIP. She chipped samples off some larger boulders and shipped them back. Eventually she worked her way back up to the cliff examining the layers worn away by water over the centuries. There was a dark gray layer that was probably hematite which might have 60% iron; another layer was apparently the green copper carbonate Malachite which meant a rich vein. She saw a smaller rock maybe six inches across. She struck it hard with her pick and split it open. It definitely looked like carbonate Malachite. She could not reach it, but there appeared to be a vein of pure gold. She used her shovel to move some of the gravel around and soon found a small nugget of gold. Jill tried to keep her samples to one small piece per type of suspected mineral. SHIP had to send more sample containers.

Karen spotted what appeared to be river otter type creatures, but they kept their distance. Craig saw nothing. He used his stabilized camera to look at what the girls were doing and to look up and down the canyon. The camera had a tendency to stick on Karen in her loincloth. Obviously it was not the camera's fault. He tried not to, but whenever he panned around and saw her he could not stop himself from pausing on her.

Eventually, Craig saw the girls stop working and they dropped their equipment and clothing and teleported back to SHIP one at a time. Craig and Karen moved closer in to the rest of the family while they teleported. Craig went last again. Once Karen was gone, Craig could be quickly zapped back to SHIP with all of his gear.

Once back on SHIP, SHIP helped the family assess this latest expedition. Jill had discovered many minerals valuable for supporting a modern society. The site turned out to be very valuable. Without further exploration of other areas, they would just have to assume that these minerals were widely available elsewhere on the planet. SHIP had analyzed all of Jill's samples and found primarily iron and copper, but also titanium, phosphorus, aluminum, gold, silver, magnesium, potassium and other trace elements. From orbital analysis the ocean contained sodium and other minerals. It was salt water. Therefore, Pangaea had all the minerals necessary. Without mining, the amounts were unknown only estimated percentages, which were similar to Earth and Mars. They had found no uranium which did not bode well for a nuclear energy society, but uranium might be found elsewhere. The sand of the river beach was largely silicone sand.

Sandy's fish were previously unknown but one was similar to salmon, one was trout, and one more like bass. There were no poisons in the fish. None contained dangerous bacteria or virus or dangerous levels of mercury, iodine, and so on. If there were enough, they would be a good food source.

The water from the river was drinkable without filtering or purification. The minerals might take a little getting used to, but would probably be healthier than drinking bottled, distilled, or chemically treated water.

Estera's plants were unremarkable grasses and weeds. Their DNA was different than from Earth, but there was nothing dangerous.

Karen's observation of the river otters was interesting, but next time they went exploring, Karen would need to take a camera. Craig's time was wasted although the videos were interesting and the views of the canyon with blue skies and floating white clouds were quite beautiful. Everyone got a laugh of the camera sticking on Karen from time to time. Craig turned a little pink in embarrassment.

There had been no danger in this expedition. They discussed the plan for tomorrow. They decided they would all get some much needed food and sleep while SHIP resumed an energy conserving orbit. SHIP was told to look for a river bottom area with different kinds of vegetation than the Pangaea oaks and maples, and plains grass. They would consider exploration of what areas to look at tomorrow. They were still on Earth time. Daylight or nighttime meant nothing in space other than did you have a light on or not. When exploring Pangaea it depended on Pangaea time in relation to its sun. With the short duration of their trip into space it made no sense to change from Earth time. Sort of like flying around the world non-stop in a few hours. Why change your clock? Dawn and Craig went to the master bedroom for the evening. Dawn had been sort of left out since they arrived at Pangaea.

"Sorry about leaving you here on SHIP. Why don't you come with us tomorrow? You need a break from SHIP and some fresh air on planet."

"Keep in mind that SHIP is learning from me. It may have the advantage in sensors and math, but I can actually think versus repeat or compute. But, still, it would be nice to visit the planet and get a feel for it you cannot get flying by or looking on view screens. Seeing up close is different than seeing, feeling, smelling, the real thing. Plus, I won't be a hindrance on anyone since SHIP allows me to teleport at my whim with whatever I want to bring along. What temperature should I expect?"

"I would say warm, but uncomfortably so. I'm going to insist that Karen wear some clothing this time for protection since we are going to go into the trees. There might be some allergens or bugs that could bother her. Nice thing about being able to move around the planet instantly, we can select the temperature any time of day."

Craig teleported first with a full supply of weapons and wearing a camouflage outfit to blend in with trees. Karen's equipment came next and Craig watched the area for her protection. There were animals in the trees and some form of flying animals flitting between trees. Then Dawn came down with her camera and sample containers. Then Craig had to go back up to get the rest of the crew one at a time. Once they were all dressed and ready to go, they spread out some. SHIP had put them down on a sandy beach at a bend in the river that had no vegetation for 20 yards. They did not leave the beach at first. Karen pointed out some creatures like monkeys going from tree to tree. Dawn zoomed in with her camera.

"Those are cats swinging through the trees. They seem to be like the lions, they have hands instead of front paws to grip the limbs. And those are not birds they are more like pterodactyls or bats with funny wings. We need to somehow get one of those flying creatures."

"I can shoot one down if you want."

"I would rather keep the noise down, Karen, until we have sampled the soil and plants. Maybe we won't scare them all away and you can take one just before we leave. What about insects?"

"I'll use my bow."

Estera said, "I have already captured several bugs in containers, and swatted something on my neck.

As best I could I scraped it off with a sample container. Don't know what they are, but then I am not familiar with that many bugs."

Jill said, "I think I found some gold in the sand and collected it in one of my sample containers,"

"I sampled the water and it seems as clear and clean as in that other river in the mountains. It should be safe to drink. SHIP already measured the sample. Craig, have you heard from SHIP?"

"Yes, Shelby, and you were right, its clear and clean."

Karen, "Look up in the crook of that tree. Is that a sloth or a cat laying in wait for us?"

Dawn returned looking through the camera, "It seems to be a big fat cat, but it is moving up the tree very slowly. It seems to be using its hands to pick ants or something off the trunk as it moves up the tree."

"Craig, keep an eye on it, I want to get a little closer and see for myself."

Dawn, "Can you stay about 40 feet behind Karen to watch for small animals or snakes on the ground?"

They all started heading up off the beach spread out. Craig was bringing up the rear with his rifle at the ready. Shelby had her gun out. Sandy said, "SHIP, can I get a tranquillizer gun:? I hate to be killing animals that are not threatening and we aren't going to eat. I would like to inspect some live specimens up close."

Craig spoke for SHIP since he was the only one that could hear the SHIP's answer. "SHIP does not want to rely on a tranquillizer because it's unknown about dose or susceptibility to tranquillizers. Our safety has to come first. A wrong dose could kill just as easily as a high power bullet except you have to be a lot closer to shoot with a hypodermic needle. Maybe with more study on planet we can equip you with such, but right now, no."

"SHIP, can you send us some miniature radios with an ear bud so we can communicate with each other and directly with you? It might be important to tell one of us something without having to relay through me. Plus we could talk to each other in soft voices without having to yell when we get separated."

"That's why I rely on you humans, for new ideas. The communicators are on the ground next to each person. As soon as you put them on everyone will be connected. A whisper should be heard by all of us. Of course I knew how to make these, I just didn't think about this use for them."

Dawn added another requirement, "SHIP, send me a parabolic mike so that I can aim it at different animals to hear them. Send one to Sandy also, since she is the zoologist she would appreciate it more."

Karen broke the discussion, "The slow sloth like animal looks like a cross between a cat and a sloth. It really is climbing the tree and eating some insects. I can't tell if they are ants or what."

"And those really are miniature cats going from tree to tree. They look just like Pangaea lions except that they are much smaller, skinnier, have a longer tail, and are eating leaves. They must have different teeth instead of a meat eater's teeth. They have fingernails versus claws, but they have a cat shaped head and pointy ears like a cat. They are hard to see because they are gray and black to help blend in better than tawny lions which blend in with the grassy plains Sandy commented, "That is three types of cat we have found so far. What is there about this planet that makes everything look like a cat except for the buffalo?" It would seem pretty strange to have cats with different kinds of teeth, but Karen, you must be right about their teeth being adapted to eat leaves instead of tearing meat."

"Let me get some leaf and bark samples from one of these trees. They look like water oak trees: fast growing, rounded instead of pointed leaves. They look just like Earth water oaks." I also collected some of that vine growing up the trunk of some of the trees and some low brush from under… Whoa!" Estera jumped back and began backing away.

Karen came to her. "What did you see? What was it?

"I'm not sure; something ran over my foot while I was sampling the brush."

They all wore sturdy hiking boots and gloves. Karen pushed back the brush and saw nothing.

"Should I say eek? I think it was a mouse that just ran past me." Dawn said, "Maybe that explains the cat population."

"What better way to control a mouse population than to have a lot of cats?" Sandy enjoined.

Karen said, "If I shoot a mouse there won't be enough left to investigate."

"Maybe you should shoot one of those monkey cats and inspect its stomach contents?"

Craig asked, "Has everyone got samples of whatever they think we need to study further? Okay, Karen, see if you can shoot one of the monkey cats then one of those bird things."

Karen's bow twanged twice in rapid succession and a monkey cat and a pterodactyl fell close to Dawn. It was too big to fit in one of her small containers so SHIP sent her a larger one. Dawn used her gloves to pick it up and put it in the container. Karen's bow twanged again.

Sandy said, "What did you shoot?"

"I think it was a large bird, maybe an eagle."

"It fell over there." Sandy said, "I see it. SHIP, send me a large container."

Karen warned, "Go slow, no running, there might be some animal in the grass and brush. I've seen no sign of snakes, but that doesn't mean anything. There could be hole to step in. I'm coming too, just go slow."

Sandy got it and spread its wings. It had a six foot wing span and feathers. "I think it is a hawk of some kind. Maybe it hunts mice too."

Karen said, "I suspect that there is another form of cat we have not seen. We have seen Pangaea lions, monkey cats, a sloth cat, what I saw in the mountains might have been an otter cat. But there must be some small cats to eat the mice on the ground."

Craig said, "I think we should go back to SHIP and assess what we have. Good shooting, Karen."

All the samples returned to SHIP first then the women one at a time with Craig, then Dawn, then Karen with Craig. They no longer had their radios. Karen said, "I would like to borrow one of those bullet proof tents and some infrared glasses and spend the night here."

Craig asked SHIP. "How about if Karen and I leave some infrared cameras here to see what happens by the river at night?"

"Just attach them to trees or set them on their built in tripods, turn them on, and I will monitor them all night long and keep recording for you to see in the morning."

Karen and Craig spent another 30 minutes setting up cameras and additional cameras that SHIP had to send twice. They put cameras in the trees, along the river, pointing at the trees, pointing at the river, and pointing into the sky. Then they teleported together back to SHIP.

The conversation at dinner was in favor of Pangaea being a good place for a colony. Dawn had spent the last two days plotting a course from Earth of the minimum distance without their exhaust blasting something out of orbit or hitting anything larger than a big rock. The impervium appeared to be indestructible, but the kinetic energy of traveling at multiple of the speed of light left questions better avoided.

In the morning they watched the recordings of the night before. There were many insects that came out at night and swarms of flying bats that ate and ate for hours. There were mice that scurried out at night and house cat size cats that grabbed them with their hands and ate them. There were feathered large birds that caught and flew away with some of the bats. They did appear to be Earth type bats and mice. Only the cats were strange with their hands to catch the mice. Of course, with only infrared video they could not confirm the mice were mice and the bats were bats, but they looked and sounded like you would expect.

The monkey cat was just that. Shelby commented, "If evolution were given enough time on this planet would there be cat people? They have hands which means they could use tools. If they learned to use tools would their intellect increase to designing tools? If they had a SHIP to teach them would they be going into space instead of us."

Dawn stated, "Do we need to look any further for a planet to colonize?"

SHIP replied, "That is one thing very difficult for a computer. I can calculate odds. I can produce facts and figures. I can calculate a decision based on known facts, and Yes, I think this would be a good place for an Earth colony."

Craig brought everyone back to Earth so to speak, "Yes, I agree that from what we know this planet is good place for a colony, but let me point out that we don't know about the climates, only a calculation and very short observation of the hemispheres. We don't know if there is another moon on its way to hit Pangaea. We don't know if the sea holds sea monsters. We have hardly observed any of this planet. We have found a rich source of minerals, but how long will they last? We have not found petroleum which we know we will need. Anyone see any cars that run on wood. I guess we could refine wood alcohol from trees or grain alcohol, but if you notice the relative area that is forested is less than Earth has. What do we use for fertilizer when we try to grow Earth crops? Can you make bread with the grain on the prairies? Anyone see domesticated corn? Can you domesticate the Pangaea buffalo? If you have to travel 50 miles to kill a buffalo, how do you get the meat home? How stable is this continent; will it break apart like Pangaea did on Earth and form multiple continents? There haven't been any earthquakes since we arrived, but how about next week? SHIP, how many islands are there in the sea?"

"17,482 that comprise 2 percent of the land area on Pangaea?"

"How long would it take to sail a sail powered boat around the planet?

"Two years for a fast Earth boat, assuming you do not hit a major storm and need to take shelter on an island which are few and small."

"Another good point. SHIP, what do we know about the climate?

Are there hurricanes, tornados, hail storms?"

"Of course, but I have not observed any severe storms in the days we have been here. Again, the human trumps the computer. I did not compute the probability for severe storms. I do not have enough data. Winds of 150 miles per hour happen in Earth hurricanes; wind speed over 300 miles per hour have been clocked in tornados. One advantage of Pangaea would be that the land is one big continent so you do not have areas of the ocean like the Gulf of Mexico that can heat up because it partially cut off from the bigger Atlantic."

"SHIP, let me point out that hurricanes form in the Atlantic and the Pacific Oceans away from the Gulf of Mexico."

"I think we should spend no more than one more day here and then go back to Earth in a different path to look for maybe a good planet closer to

Earth. We need to get back to find out how research is going without us. If we find another planet we could take a cursory look at it on the way home, but we are expected back and cannot afford to disappear from the political climate on Earth."

Jill said, "We need to look for an energy source other than burning wood and making alcohol. I think that should be our goal on this last day. SHIP could we do that and still do more research in another area?"

"I would recommend against it. Karen is the primary protector on the land and Craig protects her. We need to keep the team in one place for safety. As Craig has pointed out, we really do not know much about Pangaea. I have searched for oil patches on the surface and have found an area that appears to have tar pits and pools of oil. I suggest we go there today. I can provide Jill a drilling device to drill deeper to make sure there is oil under the ground as well as on it. She will need several people to help set it up. Because the metal is so strong it can be very light weight and very powerful, but because it is so lightweight it needs to be anchored. I will have to teleport it down in parts to be assembled."

"Take us there SHIP. Girls, get ready to go and tell SHIP what you need."

"It is colder there with a daytime temperature in the fifties and night temperatures in the twenties. I recommend warm clothing. The climate there would be roughly equivalent to southern Canada in the early summer. There is another area just like it in the south and each area covers 1000 square miles. There is a larger area near the equator that might be like the oil fields of the Middle East, but there is no surface water and appears devoid of life. Anyone going there would have to be supported by constant resupply of everything. With only a colony, it would be impossible."

Karen and Craig went first and Karen got dressed very quickly. Dawn arrived on her own fully clothed in an insulated windbreaker and then helped Karen set up a tent large enough for the whole family to spend the day. Craig made the trip again for Estera, Shelby, Sandy, and Jill. There were areas that looked like a northern tundra, islands of short but thick trees, patches of tall grass, and as promised small ponds of what appeared to be oil. The tent was set up on a large island of grass. As soon as she was dressed Shelby headed out to test the brown black fluid to see if it was oil and its quality. Karen had to hurry out of the tent with her weapons and Craig followed.

"It's high grade oil." The sands here should be a rich producer.

Jill had caught up and was there. "You're right; this may be richer than any field on Earth and has never been tapped. If all the ponds are the same kind of oil and if we had someway to just store the oil in these ponds we could supply the colony for years with just the oil on the surface. This area must have been under the sea at some time. I suspect that this was an inland sea at one point where there may have been a jungle submerged for some reason for millennia and then raised up to above sea level again through some tectonic activity and is now leaching oil to the surface. I need to drill down and see if there are pockets of oil under this whole area. Ideally I would drill a hundred or more wells to map the underground oil to get a firm estimate."

"Slow down, Jill." Craig admonished, "You have the day. I suggest we get busy setting up the drilling rig."

Karen maintained a security watch, but the only thing she saw were high flying birds of indeterminate size. The rest of the family spent the next three hours assembling a miniature oil drilling rig. They dug holes in the island near their tent and set anchors in some form of quick concrete supplied by SHIP. The anchor parts were five feet deep by two feet square. The anchors buried in the concrete were spindly but made of the ultra strong metal.

While they were working SHIP told them it would be going to the desert in the equator to absorb some sand to be converted into its subatomic level to replenish the energy the SHIP had used during the voyage and material used in making everything the family had used during the voyage and the exploration. "I will have to leave you for a couple of hours to replenish my subatomic structure to replace the energy burned so far and the material used to keep you supplied. I will also need to make a couple of thousand feet of pipe for the well."

Craig told the family as they worked, "We are temporarily ob our own. Karen, keep an extra close watch for any animals that threaten or any weather we might not see coming. SHIP is going to be out of range for teleportation. SHIP can teleport from 20,000 miles away but only by line of sight. The equator is out of that line of sight over the horizon and there is too much interference from trees, other animals, and so on."

It was afternoon before they were ready to start drilling, but they only had twenty feet of drilling pipe. They had to wait on ship. It was very lonely. Dawn, Karen and Craig stood together, on watch. The other girls went into the tent to eat survival food supplied with the tent. The tent had battery powered heat and light.

Craig stopped them with, "Look at that wall of clouds coming in. SHIP, there is a strong storm coming in, don't you think you better get back here?" Silence. Let's get in the tent. Let's shovel some dirt up against the tent to help protect it from the wind getting under it. "

Everyone shoveled dirt and rocks from their digging the drilling rig foundation up against the ten then took shelter in the tent. The tent did not bend in the wind, but it was not airtight and they could hear the wind howling outside.

Craig said, "It sounds like the wind is 100 miles per hour out there.

I hear things hitting the tent."

Dawn said, "I have never felt so alone. I am used to having thousands of people nearby. Here we are just the seven of us in the tent and not another person on the planet. Not another person in many light years. Where is SHIP?"

"Adam and Eve did not feel lonely if you believe that mankind came from two humans created by God. They could not experience crowds and had no one else around. Australian men go on walkabouts. Not sure what they do on a walkabout, but you would think they spend time alone."

Dawn came back, "I don't think there was an Adam and Eve per se.

I think I believe in God, but the Bible has two stories of creation. Genesis One is scientific theory about creating the earth and heavens in seven days. I think those days would be better said as eons. Each eon might have been a billion years, or a million years, but certainly many millions of years transpired before humans walked the earth. The Bible was amazingly accurate according to current scientific theory. Genesis then goes on with a fairy tale about Adam and Eve for those that cannot understand scientific theory. People that believed in God wrote both stories."

Shelby asked, "Or was Genesis written by a captain of SHIP way back then? Do our beliefs in God translate into belief in SHIP?"

Karen stated, "Most of my life I lived up to my Indian name of "She Who Wanders". I have spent many months a few days at a time getting as far away from crowds as I could. I have wandered the mountains and the plains alone. I learned to hunt and fish with guns and arrows. I know self defense with no weapon, but my body. This adventure is more than I could have imagined. I do believe in a God. Something put order into everything. The universe is made of galaxies, the galaxy is made of many stars. Solar systems are dependent upon a star to orbit around and provide energy. Plants and animals alike are dependent upon this solar power. People are dependent upon the plants and animals. Some plants and animals are dependent upon people for their quality of life. Molecules are made of atoms which are made of smaller particles. The electrons orbit the protons and neutrons like a miniature solar system. The protons attract the electrons capturing them in orbit just like the star's gravity captures the planets or orbit. Now we are finding smaller particles. There had to be a God to put all this together and establish these laws of nature. As an Indian, I am close to nature and I am also a Christian. There are too many examples of people praying for a miracle and getting that miracle. Sort of like SHIP, but now that I know SHIP, it was prayer that worked, not SHIP. SHIP is not the all powerful force summoned by prayer. Of course prayer does not always work because some things are not meant to be. It may be what we want but not what is best."

Dawn said, "I can agree with that. At one time I wanted to marry someone that I would have been bored with over time and I would not be on this adventure if I had married him. Fortunately for me, he left. I was broken hearted, but now I am glad."

"I think most people have a broken heart at one time or another only to find happiness later. How many times have even childhood sweethearts married right out of school only to have one of them die from sickness or accidents and find happiness again with someone else. I'm lucky because I have wanted to go into astral navigation, but where would I work other than NASA. I am now the ultimate expert."

Karen offered a slightly different opinion, "I too had a first love. My second love was living up to my Indian name, "She Who Wanders". Now, I am on the wildest wandering trip there could be. Craig is a bonus. I may not get him full time, but the wandering could never be full time either. Normally one or both parties have to be gone to work half the time and frequently one has to do a lot of business travel or one has a sick parent they spend time with or they have handicapped children. I consider myself in the ideal life right now. More than I could ever have imagined."

Shelby joined in, "The only thing I miss is my family. I miss my parents and my brother. It is sad to think that they will die in only two more years. When we get home, I have to take time to visit with them."

Estera directed her question to Craig, "Can I tell anyone about this planet when we get back to Earth?"

"Please, jump in here with your opinions." Craig admonished, "I think it is time to tell everyone what we know and what we are doing. Selecting the colony crews should be quiet. As we select candidates we need to have specialized schools for those candidates. We are talking about a university of just evacuees. We need to separate them from the general population and see which ones will or won't make the cut.

Dawn, you have a comment?"

"Yes, we need to go international. We have enough science and experience now to allow all the advanced countries of the world to start building their spaceships and selecting their crews."

Sandy warned, "Do we give the secret of this impervium to countries like Russia and China that could build shelters and weapons instead of spaceships?"

"Good question. I think that we should ask our President and cabinet members to approach other countries with the full story and present this idea of international cooperation and then I use the SHIP and its capabilities to spy on their leaders to make sure they are responding correctly before we release the technology."

Dawn added, "We can hold back some of the technology and techniques until we can see if they are really committed, but they need to get started building and selecting their crews now. Two years is not long to train earthbound humans to be space-men for the rest of their lives."

"Where is SHIP??

"SHIP went to the equator. Estera, girls, no one every explained that SHIP uses is subatomic struc-ture for power, to make our food, clothing, weapons, the drilling rig, and all of the energy used to get us here. It was time to refuel."

Jill asked, "How does it refuel and what does it use."

Craig answered, "SHIP uses any matter. On Earth, it teleports sand from the desert and converts it to its subatomic structure which becomes part of the mass of SHIP. It went to Pangaea's equator to suck up some sand. There did not appear to be any threat where we were so it seemed like a good time to leave us on our own."

Shelby asked, "Why hasn't SHIP contacted us and gotten us out of this storm?"

"I think because of two things: SHIP is over the horizon from us and out of straight line communication and this storm is creating a major electrical mask over our position."

SHIP contacted Craig telepathically, "What is going on there? I can sense your thoughts, but my sensors show only dust, lightning, and rain."

"That is what it is SHIP, a storm. It came upon us out of nowhere and engulfed us. We are in the shelter and are okay."

"I am going to teleport you up to safety."

"No, teleport Dawn. I will stay here with the rest of the women. Someone ought to be safe so make it Dawn. After you have Dawn on board, you can teleport us up in the normal one at a time routine."

It took 10 minutes to get everyone back on board. Dawn had already taken a look at the size and strength of the storm on Pangaea by the time all the women and Craig were teleported to safety in orbit. "It looks like a hurricane that came up quickly. It is 300 miles wide with impact over an 800 mile circle. The winds are 80 miles per hour and the rain is coming at 6 inches per hour."

Craig asked SHIP, "Any idea how often these storms occur or if they occur anywhere on Pangaea."

"I did not observe storm damage in other areas. On analysis, the storm can happen anytime a cold front from the poles hits this oil area where there is very little vegetation and no hills to slow it down. After it got past this area, it died down to a more routine rainstorm. That means that the people tapping this oil reserve need to have shelters close at hand and extra supplies to last out the storms if they happen. It also means that we need a pipeline to get the oil out of this area to a more stable area."

They went back to the oil drilling rig. Ship teleported the drilling pipe to them in 20 foot lengths that screwed together. Rather than a diamond drill bit, this bit was just metal, but Impervium was harder than diamond. They had no drilling mud, but the drill bit and pipe was not Earth made steel. At 900 feet they had a gusher. It took into the evening before particle beams from SHIP managed to stop it. The drill hole was only one inch in diameter. The oil was everywhere. Even Craig and Dawn were teleported back nude because everything was saturated with oil. The oil was not teleported so they arrived at SHIP as clean as if from a long shower. They were all laughing. Their implements, tent, the drilling pipe, every trace was teleported back to become part of the SHIP. After an hour the oil gusher was still going strong. SHIP used a beam weapon to close the hole and stop the gusher. The oil had just added to the pools of oil in the area except the thin plant life that was under the gusher would never live.

Jill stated, "Well, I think that was the final question. Yes, there is an energy source on Pangaea. Our colony can survive here."

Craig rejoined, "I agree, but we have overstayed our visit here and need to head toward Earth. On the way back we can look for another potential planet and assess everything we have learned from this expedition." There was no dissent and SHIP was on its way toward Earth using a different course. They ate heartily and then went to bed for awhile. Karen and Jill were still excited from the trip and volunteered to take first watch in the control room. Four hours later they were relieved and the voyage continued.

13

PYRAMID

In less than twenty-four hours Earth time, SHIP slowed again and entered orbit around another planet. An announcement over the speakers throughout SHIP woke everyone asleep and they all rushed to the windows.

"I have entered orbit over a planet that appears to be perfect for humans. It is possibly inhabited as I have detected what appears to be a city. At the center of this city is a large pyramid, twice the size of the largest Egyptian pyramid. I intend to orbit a few times looking for life signs."

SHIP found life signs, heat signatures apparently belonged to animals, but no signs of modern energy usage. After four orbits and nothing further seen, Craig and Karen decided to teleport to near the pyramid in the center of the city. Karen asked for the temperature on the surface and SHIP replied 84 degrees Fahrenheit. I will need only my weapons, my utility belt and my loincloth.

They went down together and Karen put on her loincloth and utility belt. The belt was now permanently attached to the loin cloth. Craig said, "You know that your lack of clothing is distracting."

"It may be, but at least you will keep watch to protect me and I feel freer and closer to nature which heightens my senses."

They went to one of the stone buildings first. It was totally empty with the only furniture being stone benches along the walls that could be used for seating or bed rolls. There was what appeared to be a kitchen with a stone oven with a chimney. The kitchen had a waist high stone ledge that could be used as a kitchen counter without drawers or plumbing. In the next room was a raised round stone with a one foot depression in the center and a hole in the roof above as if it was intended as a fire pit. There were knee high stone ledges around three sides of the room. There were smaller rooms off to the sides that might be bedrooms or storage rooms, but were totally bare. There were square holes for windows and doorways, but no windows or doors and did not look as if anything was ever used for windows or doors. At the end of the hallway against the back wall was a room with a deep hole in the center. Karen asked, "That would be the indoor plumbing I suppose?"

As they came out they scared a small flock what appeared to be bantam hens with a brightly colored what must the be cock. As they walked down the street away from the pyramid, they saw a large earthlike hairy wild pig and a half dozen earthlike cow like animals.

Craig observed, "All the buildings look identical. We have checked 4 on this street, 6 on the first street and I don't think there is any building different. Let's head to the pyramid and see if there is anything there."

Karen had been carrying her rifle at the ready. Craig had lowered his guard. They remained 40 feet apart when not in a building, close enough to converse, but far enough apart to watch out for the other one. Craig was slightly in the lead with Karen behind and on the opposite side of the street. They had seen nothing threatening, but that did not mean that there were not predatory animals stalking them. Karen was looking at the flat rooftops as best she could. The streets all sloped slightly downhill from the pyramid at the center.

Karen made an observation, "Except for the pyramid, these buildings and street remind me of a poor mans Pompeii before the volcano. The pyramid reminds me of a volcano. Is that significant?"

"You are right, Karen, it is almost like this city was made to resemble Pompeii, but there is no color other than gray stone and no paintings or statues or any kind of decoration."

Karen and Craig were both wearing communicators so everyone in the SHIP had two way communications, but no one on SHIP made any comments that could distract Karen's and Craig's protection of each other.

"Look, Craig, there is what looks like a stone door into the pyramid."

"SHIP, what do you think? Is a door?" "I cannot see it well."

"Do you think it would be safe to open the door if we can?"

"I have no way of knowing. The pyramid is solid to my sensors. So it is either totally solid and that is not a door, or the pyramid itself is blocking my sensors."

"Craig, let me go ahead of you. I am more expendable. I have no special education except recognizing Martian and Earth predators and how to use weapons. You are the leader and need to be in a safer position."

"Okay, Karen, but don't touch anything until we both get a chance to study the door closer."

A few minutes later Karen was standing by a twenty foot high stone doorway with a twenty foot stone door. The door was decorated by some geometric patterns, the first decoration they had seen on anything in this city.

"Craig, I think maybe this decoration is meant for us." "How so?"

"There are triangles, there are seven sets of six triangles in big circles with one exclamation point or a one or just a single line in the center surrounded by the evenly spaced triangles. Each set is identical except for this center set that is in a straight line with the single line in the middle with three triangles on each side of the single line."

"That doesn't tell me much."

"Oh, but I think it does. Craig, what if you represent the one and the six triangles represent the six women in our family."

"You may have a point, seven seems to be a common number in the Bible."

"If you look really close, it appears the symbols in the straight line may be independent versus raised letters on the stone. Like maybe they are buttons. Maybe it is a combination lock."

"SHIP, we are going to try to see if this is a combination lock on the door."

"Be careful Craig and Karen. If the door starts to move get as far away as you can quickly. That pyramid may have been closed up for millennia and could have poisonous air from thousands of years ago like was found in some of the Egyptian tombs."

"Okay, Karen, see if you can press one of those symbols to see if they move."

She tried a triangle one removed from the line in the middle, and it did not move. Then she tried the line and it did not move either. "No, they do not move, but they felt like they wanted to. Craig, give it a try, you are stronger."

Craig tried the line because it was the one in the middle and the last one Karen pushed. It easily popped in about an inch.

"How did you do that? I pressed hard and could not move it."

"It was not hard, maybe you loosened it. Like the second person that tries a jar lid and opens it easily after the first person gave up just before getting it open." Craig then tried the same triangle Karen had tried and not only could he not budge it, but the line popped back out to its original position. "Okay, that was interesting. You give it another try, Karen."

She did and it didn't move.

Craig pushed the line in again and it went easily again. While Craig was still holding the line in, Karen pressed that same triangle and it popped in. When Karen tried a second triangle both the original triangle and the line pushed their fingers back up and the symbols were in the same locked position again.

"Okay, I'll push the line again, then when you push a triangle I will try the opposing triangle on the other side of the line at the same time."

The line popped back out. Craig could not hold it in.

"Okay, I'll push the line, you push the triangle then I'll try the other triangle after we have two buttons pushed in."

The line and the first triangle worked fine, but then popped back out.

"Okay, this is definitely a combination lock, but this is not working."

Dawn came over the communicators, "I think that the line and the triangles are symbolic of our crew and the makeup we were told to use on the colony ships. Six women and one man. I think we will all have to come down and while Craig pushes the line, each of us press one triangle apiece."

"Worth a try. Dawn, it is easy for you to teleport. Come on down and see if we can press one line and two triangles."

She did teleport and it worked, but the most they could press in was one line and two triangles, any two, but only two. When they tried a third everything popped back out and they had to start over.

Craig teleported to SHIP and brought the other girls down one at a time. They did not bother getting dressed after teleporting because all they wanted to do was open the door. The only way it would work was Craig pressing the one or the line or whatever and one girl pressing one triangle. All the symbols locked down and the door started swinging inward. They all retreated to the first line of houses before the door opened completely. The pyramid lit from within with a hue of gold with many sparkling colors on the walls.

SHIP said, "I can see what you see, but not enough detail. I detected nothing dangerous coming out of the door like gases. I suggest that everyone get their full equipment readied and then Karen go in by herself. She has the best reflexes and best eye for danger."

They intended to keep regular communications going but as soon as she entered the doorway, communications with her went dead. She came back out and the communications worked. She reentered and walked much further in and then came back out. "Dawn, come in with me and see if we can communicate. I want you to see this."

Dawn and Karen were out of sight for a few minutes. Craig and the other girls collected near the door. Dawn came back out to report.

"The interior looks just like the Martian command post but more elaborate."

Estera accused, "Are you saying that you and Craig have been to Mars and found a command post?"

"Yes."

Jill spoke up, "Why haven't you told us before that you already had firm proof of the Martians? I have always thought that the Martians and Atlanteans were some sort of story that SHIP was espousing."

"No, it is true. We didn't say anything about the command post on Mars that confirmed the whole story, but we had no proof and there was nothing new that SHIP had not taught each of you. Yes, Dawn and I found a command post under the ice at the Martian pole. It was self powered and showed us videos of the escape to Earth and videos of the impact of the interstellar body wiping out civilization on Mars. Much of the original population tried to live underground for centuries after some of them colonized Atlantis, but they were all dead when we went there. Nothing pretty and no proof. Even pictures and videos of the command post could have been made on Earth. We could not prove anything and SHIP gave all of you the good parts of the story. I guess we should have told you our first trip from Earth was just the two of us. We first went to the moon and found the ruins of a moon colony. They had a series of interconnected structures with breathable air. We then traveled to Mars and found the still functioning command center that showed videos of life on Mars before the impact and the launch of the mission to Earth. It did not give us anything we could show on Earth, but it gave us the proof that SHIP was telling the truth."

Craig asked SHIP, "Please send us some super strength bracing to make sure that the door cannot close while we are in there. It could be a trap. Probably not, but I need to be sure."

Dawn went into the pyramid to get Karen to come back out and help assemble the bracing on the door. It took the better part of an hour to build the braces and inspect for another potential door besides the one they had opened. While they were working Karen gave them a commentary on what she had seen inside.

"There are huge television like monitors and lots of buttons to push. Each of the controls seem to be like the lock on the door. It requires six different triangles and one line to be pressed at the same time to get each device to function. It was like it was built for us. Note how on the door there were sets of six triangles and 1 line in a circle with the triangles forming a circle in the circle except for the set that opened the door and each symbol had a small circle around it. They all pressed in as circular buttons. These buttons are the same. I think it takes Craig plus each of us girls to simultaneously press the triangles and the line to activate each machine."

"Let's give it a try. Karen, which one do you think we should try first?"

"Dawn, I was studying them when I was in here alone for awhile. I think we should try the center console."

Each of them pressed one button each at the same time. The screen came on instantly with a symbol. There was a voice that was totally unintelligible then silence. Then there video appeared and kept repeating showing 6 young women and one man talking with no sound.

Craig said, "I think it wants us to all talk. Let's try counting from 1 to 10 together."

They did and the screen turned green and showed balls, first one then two, up to ten. Then it showed the six women and the man again talking with no sound.

"I think it understood our counting. Now it wants us to talk. Any ideas of what it might want to hear."

Dawn said, "We are an expedition from Earth." Each of them repeated the sentence with Craig last.

The console added with, "Thank you." I have been listening to your television and radio broadcasts since Tesla invented the radio. Then Marconi took credit it for it. I needed you to speak to decide what language to communicate with you. Congratulations you have found the planet I left for your evacuation. This is the nearest habitable planet from Earth. The pyramid and the consoles use the simple code. SHIP was programmed to teach you this relationship of women to men. It is what we used coming to Earth and leaving Earth. By having the simple code it eliminated accidental activation by the animals we left to breed on this planet. It also served as a guard from some other intelligent species that might land here. At this time we have never found another intelligent species, but cannot rule it out. We have inhabited dozens of planets since leaving Earth. All of our planets are in the outer spirals of the galaxy as we do not believe that humans can survive near the center of the galaxy. Even a dual star system might provide too much radiation. We have found an estimated 1,000 habitable planets among the 100,000 planets we have found to date or one percent."

The show then provided a look at Martian civilization followed by Atlantis followed by views of much newer civilizations. The humanoids on some planets were taller than humanoids from other planets due to gravity of the different planets. The Neanderthals on Earth were overtaken by Cro-Magnon man that came from Mars. There was some in-breeding between a few, but eventually the Neanderthals disappeared. The Martians changed over time due to higher gravity on Earth. What we find evidence of are the Martians that were left behind when Atlantis was destroyed. It did not take long before they resorted to crude tools. The average Martian living around the world had been totally dependent upon Atlantis for their electrical power, their long distance communication, and their tools. Eventually, they were surviving by hunting with stone spears.

A thousand years after Atlantis was evacuated, some Atlanteans returned and left the SHIP to gradually train those survivors to once again travel to space. The Martians/Atlanteans also built the city they were now in. There could be no doors or window coverings or furnishings that would last for millennia and they did not plan on ever returning to this part of the galaxy. The pyramid was sealed with perfect preservation. Once people from Earth, trained by SHIP, found this new planet they would have at least one place they could settle. The houses built of stone would give them shelter from the worst of the weather and the new people could build doors, windows, and furniture after their arrival. The Martians had killed off all predatory animals and left behind the cattle, chickens, and pigs that were mainstays of the Martians in ancient history. There were fields planted with edible grains for the livestock that could also provide for the new colony. The video ended with instructions to go on to the next.

The next had to activated the same as the first one, with six women and one man simultaneously pressing buttons. "We are assuming you came here in SHIP and have no idea how to build your own spaceships or star drive to travel faster than light. It has taken you centuries longer to arrive here in SHIP. One of the captains of SHIP should have arrived here with his six wives here over three thousand Earth years ago. We can only presume that some calamity on Earth has deterred your arrival here. Obviously the captain of SHIP should have followed the direction of SHIP, acquired six wives and come here then. That captain, if he had done as

SHIP told him could have lived five hundred years then passed on the captainship to someone else. By our calculation you only have six years before Earth is destroyed. How many captains have there been before you."

"Maybe a hundred since Aristotle that I know of, but only SHIP knows."

"When did Aristotle live and was he a great scientist?"

"Aristotle lived about 2200 years ago, and yes, he was a great scientist. People throughout history studied him. He was responsible for a number of major scientific achievements and many scientists say some of his inventions were impossible for his time period. He was a student of Plato who claimed to have read about Atlantis from books that no longer exist. I guess, Plato must have been the captain before Aristotle. Plato was rumored to like men, not women and Aristotle had two wives. Both were Greek. Aristotle was a mentor of Alexander the Great that conquered much of the known world at that time."

"SHIP was supposed to help stop wars by educating its captains. Are you telling me that earthmen warred between themselves instead of working on science?"

"Yes, several captains were involved in wars on Earth. It may be that some of their new scientific advances were crucial in wars."

"What about atomic power?"

"The first use was the United States dropping two bombs on Japan to end a multi-year war."

"What about you?"

"Not interested in war. I guess I was not interested in power other than how it would help me get humans into space. I was young and needed a lot of help to get anyone to listen to me. Because of my age, maybe I listened more to SHIP. Instead of already being important when SHIP chose me, I was a nobody."

"Is there hope for Earth to escape into space and come here to colonize this planet?"

"Yes, we believe so, but there is a lot of work to do. We came here because we needed to find somewhere to send the colony ships once they were ready."

"SHIP was to bring you here to finish your training."

"Do you have a star drive system that will drive the colony ships at above the speed of light."

"No, use the next console for the science you need."

They spent the day in the pyramid and then they really had to leave for Earth. They learned a lot and the family was more convinced of the urgency than ever. If there were any of them that had doubts, they no longer doubted.

"SHIP, take us to Earth." There was no need to continue scanning for habitable planets on the way back so SHIP was able to use its speed. Twenty-four hours later, they were in orbit around Earth.

Dawn said, "I have to set up a school for astral navigation and find advanced students to study it. SHIP has learned with me and prepared all the education materials including books, charts, and computer algorithms."

Jill said, "SHIP has analyzed all of the data and designed drilling rigs and mining equipment that the colonists can use when they get to their planets."

"I need to get permission to raid the seed repositories on Earth. The vaults will be useless in two years so we need to take the seeds with us to introduce the proper plants to support our expanding colonies." Estera said.

Sandy added, "We have videos and data on the animals on both planets. Both planets have herd animals that can serve as protein. We can't take many animals with us so there is not too much I can do until we get back to the planets.

Shelby said, "You think you have nothing to do. I really don't see much purpose for me. The voyage was more than I ever expected when I watch Star Trek."

Karen said, "Listen to you all. I have no real training other than resident American Indian and I am only half Indian. I can hunt and use weapons. What will I do?"

Craig admonished all of the complainers, "Who do you know on Earth with your experience. We have to select and train thousands of colonists to travel through space and perform amazing jobs after they arrive. We need to select craftsmen and women of all sorts. Anyone know how to make cloth from basic materials? Chemistry. How much do you know about making nylon, rayon, and so on from crude oil? We may not need a veterinarian, but how about reviewing medical records and testing potential crew. Karen, you did not have intense training by SHIP because you were already a hunter. Now I need you to be a hunter again. I need you to work with SHIP to learn psychological testing and hunt me up a few thousand candidates for the colonies and then I want you to develop training courses to teach them what they will need to know to live on a new planet without the modern conveniences. I want you to develop training material for assembling equipment upon arrival. If you do not find enough people who are proficient hunters and fishermen, then I need you to train some. You may have the biggest job. Right now, I need to convince first our government then all the world to get with it. Wars are meaningless when the Earth will not survive two years. We still don't have a colony ship faster than light drive engine. There are a number of small things that need inventing. I suspect that each of us will need the help of other members of the family a number of times in the next two years. We need to return to both of the planets we have found and should probably find one or more additional planets. Dawn has become the expert on the basic design and construction of the colony ships, but that is not her area. Astral Navigation is her field. She felt worthless while we were exploring the surface of new planets. I hope no one feels they don't have a critical job, we all do.

PART FOUR

PREPARE FOR LAUNCH

14

CONVINCING THE WORLD

There was no way to radio ahead, SHIP traveled at several times the speed of radio waves. It would be like the pony express trying to get across country before a telegraph message. Teleportation was only at the speed of light so SHIP travel was the fastest.

SHIP provided each of the family copies of ultra condensed USB drives of their planet explorations. Each drive had a capacity of 1 terabyte of video. Each USB drive was really a miniature computer so that the computer they plugged into would be bypassed except for the video and sound portions. Once started, the USB drive would take over the computer it was attached to and the only data transfer would be the video and audio portions of the videos. The Earth processors would be idle and the only data moving over the USB was the data required for the video and sound processors. This made up for slow USB connections in the host computer.

Data could only be passed one way, nothing from the host could be written to the USB and the host could not copy the data on the USB since the host processor was being bypassed. This also allowed the family to control who could see the videos.

Craig took his to the President and his cabinet. He showed them excerpts from the videos from Pangaea showing them the strange animals and plants they encountered there. Edited out were Karen's nude hunting style and their teleportation to and from SHIP. There were no pictures of the SHIP or references to SHIP in the verbiage of the family. The only thing that Craig chose to show were actual videos of their inspections of the trees and animals on Pangaea.

Someone in the peanut gallery asked, "You have been gone for a week. How could you have traveled that far into space and found a planet and be back in a week? Are sure this video wasn't made in Hollywood?"

"I demonstrated faster than light travel to this group. I have demonstrated teleportation. I teleported into this most secure command bunker and you have seen me appear and disappear. Some of you have deliberately touched me to see if I was real versus a hologram. Yes, I noticed the surreptitious touches. I don't blame you. I commend you on your suspicions. However, we did travel at unreal speeds though space. Our colony ships will never travel near this speed. It will take months to a year for the colony ships to get there."

"What proof would you like?"

"How about some plant material from the trees to analyze?" said the Secretary of the Interior.

The Secretary of Agriculture asked for samples of the grasses they found. "I will compare the samples with what we know of the ancestors of Earth grasses."

The President asked, "I have every reason to trust you, but I do have a question. Assuming that we get a colony of a thousand or a few thousand to this new planet, ah Pangaea, where will they live and will they be burning up the forests there for heat?"

Some containers appeared near Craig. "Here are some tree samples. They are very much like Earth trees, but also very different. Here are some grass samples you asked for. I'd like to continue the video to answer your question Mr. President."

"Please continue."

Craig next showed their oil field find. "We do not know the full extent of the oil. There is a field like this toward both poles. The pools of oil can simply be pumped off into pipelines to our colony. However, after some years with hoped for population expansion, eventually the oil pools would be need to be replaced by subsurface oil. As you can see here we set up a small drill rig and had a major gusher at 900 feet through a one inch drill pipe."

The Secretary of Energy interrupted, "How can such a small rig with only a one inch pipe with a battery powered drill motor drill to 900 feet?"

"The rig and pipe were made with the Impervium which you know is incredibly strong and light weight. We could have easily lifted a nine hundred foot length of the pipe, but we limited it to twenty foot lengths to control it better as we screwed sections together. Any longer and it might catch too much wind and become uncontrollable. The rig itself is small of the same metal and anchored in a special concrete. We had to dig the holes for and anchors the hard way with shovels."

"What about the motor and batteries?"

"The batteries and motor are beyond current technology on Earth, but we will be working with scientists on Earth to come as close as possible to this new technology. The colonists will need this capability until we can get a petroleum based technology going. The colony ships could not afford the weight of the current technology in electric motors and batteries. I believe we can get close in the next two years."

"How did you shut off the gusher?"

"Technology I cannot explain. We left the rig there, but removed the pipe and sealed the hole."

"Please continue with your video." "Thank you Mister President."

The video showed the river canyon and their finding of minerals on Pangaea. "We found most of the essential minerals in the layers of this one exposed cliff and the rocks and boulders that fell to the river bottom. We also found some new elements we did not have names for. They atomic weight put them above uranium, but they had no detectable radiation. We determined that all the minerals necessary for a modern industrial society exist on Pangaea, but we have no way to assure there is a sufficient supply forever. It could be that we happened on the only minerals on the planet. However, we believe that the mountain range has all that is needed. There is silicone available in the sands of the planet. There appears to be more gold than we would need for any technology. From the percent we found, gold may not have the value it does on Earth."

The President asked, "Are you seeing these colonies as socialist communes?"

"No. I believe that we will be picking colonists who will be self motivated to do what they can. However, I also believe that some will turn out to be lazy if they don't have to work. There is no way that we can be assured that one hundred years from establishing the colony we would not have half the people trying to live off the work of the other half. Initially we will encourage a barter system where the farmer trades food for electronics, and so on. Gold and silver may be just more rocks on Pangaea so we will have to have a credit earning system where people will earn credits through their work that can be used to trade for others production. The person, man or woman, can make clothing in exchange for food and electricity. All credits will be apportioned for work performed based on a computer program and the computer will serve as a bank. At the same time, the computer will prevent billionaires in that income above some level will be invested in advancing science, technology, roads, or whatever the majority of the people need. This is a problem we need help with. I am of the opinion that the future generations should not be able to inherit money, but will have to live on what they earn. The children may inherit the house of their parents, the experience of their parents, the knowledge of their parents, but not the bank accounts. I would hate to think of a generation of people living off what their parents earned and never contributing to society themselves. I suspect that this issue will be under debate after the colonies are established and after Earth is gone."

There was grumbling around the table. The Secretary of State stated, "That sounds like something most people would disagree with. Parents want their children to inherit what they worked hard for. In my case, my great grandfather wisely invested his work in developing the oil fields of Texas and my grandfather, then father, and now I enjoy the fruits of his labor. I would not be Secretary of State if not for my inherited wealth that made my family famous and powerful. Why would you take that incentive away? What would my great grandfather think if he knew that it would all be taken away at his death?"

"I said you could inherit his house, just not his money. If your grandfather inherited all the property and if he worked as hard as his father wouldn't he have been able to expand his holdings and earn his own riches. Your father could have expanded again. Then you."

"But the oil fields were depleted by the time my father inherited.

How could he have gotten rich?"

"The land might not be as valuable, but maybe your father should have found new oil reserves and developed them himself. Maybe your father should have been working with his father to sell the oil fields to farmers or ranchers and gone on to new land."

"What if we still had nobility that owned all the land and ruled by force? What if 99% of the population could only rent land from the nobles. Any thought of freedom would be put down by the King's guards? What about the wars between nobility where the surfs suffered? What about the King's guards that died not for their own family, but to make sure their King won the wars to keep them from becoming surfs."

"Then the obverse is true we have what the socialist say they believe. Everything is owned by the state and divided up equally. This leads to people with no incentive to work. Who runs this state? The new nobility. Some say that has happened here. The new nobility is the ultra rich that think they have the right to high political office because they inherited money and position."

"When we colonize a huge new planet with a small number of people we have the opportunity to establish new rules for government. I know that democracy really means a republic where people elect representatives rather than have a true democratic vote. With our large population, it would have been difficult to govern the United States in history. There was no way for everyone to know the complexities and current events. Now we have instantaneous communication. Could we have a popular vote? I think it is too late for that. There are too many people getting something from the central government who will vote for only the representatives who will continue their benefits. There are too many people that would vote on a popular vote to give themselves more freebees. The old silent majority would get overrun by the freeloaders. Consequently, we still have a representative government not anarchy."

"We will be starting with the cream of the crop. The best trained farmers, carpenters, mechanics, engineers, doctors, scientists, electricians, seamstresses, boot makers will be selected for the colonists. We will be starting classes on colonization soon. We have astral navigation specialists already in training. Our instructor has returned from the voyage with first hand information and courses that will be plotted for the colony ships."

"There will be from a thousand to a few thousand colonists and the only city services will be the colony ship for months to years. How much government do you need on a cruise ship? It is quite possible that there will fewer colonists on the planet than one of our big cruise ships."

The Attorney General broke in, "But there is a captain who is the absolute ruler of his crew. A cruise ship with four thousand passengers has over one thousand crew. How will you maintain order on the ship and in the colony after it lands?"

Each SHIP will have a crew with duties like a cruise ship. Rather than a single captain, there will be a committee for decisions and an on duty officer in case of trouble between colonists. Upon landing this same system will continue to operate just like it did on the ship. I would not anticipate any problems with these carefully selected colonists who will have been attending school together until the ship is ready to leave earth. We expect natural leaders to emerge that will have the confidence of the ship. Maybe we elect a class president who will become the primary captain. I don't have all the answers yet."

"I presume you will only issue guns to a security force."

"I don't see any need for guns onboard the ship. A bullet could ricochet around taking out more innocents than the one you were intending to shoot. I would propose tasers on board the ship. When the ship lands, everyone will be issued guns for protection from animals and for hunting. Gun training will be a regular course in our training for the colony. We will be taking a lot of ammunition, but we will also have to have some trained gunsmiths who can reload ammunition and even manufacture gun powder from resources on the planet."

"What is to keep the colonists from overthrowing the captain and the security crew? Not to mention, if we have one hundred colony ships we will have one hundred thousand people which makes a good sized city."

"If everyone is evenly armed, it will make it hard for anyone to take over. As far as one captain overthrowing another, it would take the people from a ship to band together. What are they going to take over? The ships will provide power for the colonists for fifty years and then they will have to have developed the oil fields and pipelines and refineries. To do that they will have to build steel mills to refine the iron oil, make pipes and stoves and anything else that uses the oil. I would think everyone will be too busy to do anything but cooperate."

"What about taking over the ship and going elsewhere. Never mind where would they go? They can't return home, where else would they go? Okay, I'll concede."

"So what percentage of the United States can Pangaea support?" asked the Secretary of Housing and Urban Development.

"That would depend on how many ships can be built in two years and how many colonists can be trained, and whether we can invent things we don't have yet, like the faster than light drive that will have to be used by the colony ships."

"So how many colony ships are we talking about for the United States?

"Maybe ten if we get an unlimited budget."
"Ten!!!!"

"We have not built one yet. The drive I have will not work for the colony ships. The colony ships will have to have a new drive we are just theorizing right now. We still do not have the unlimited support of the government. Right now, the escapees will be myself and my crew."

The President calmly asked, "What about Europe, South America, Japan, Australia, China, all the other countries of the world? I anticipated millions of colonists."

Craig stated, "Thus far we do not even have one ship for the United States. How long does it take to develop a new airliner with existing technology? Ten years? How about an advanced military bomber? Twenty years? We are talking about spaceships the size of the largest cruise ship for only one thousand passengers. It took four years to build and fit the "Oasis of the Seas" for Royal Caribbean. There was no really new technology that had to be invented. The ship was built in a dry dock and simply pushed into the water."

"A cruise ship is never more than a few days from resupply of fuel and food for the passengers and crew. We are talking about a ship larger than that. We have determined that it can be built on land and boosted into space empty, but it may take months to get all the people and equipment on board. If we have unlimited funds or free work and materials from all of the big companies in the United States, we have a little more than a year to invent whole new technologies and a very huge ship. After getting it into space how many shuttle flights would it take to fly one thousand people there, dock, unload, and fly a year's supply of everything they will need to live on the ship then start a new colony. With our existing fleet of shuttles that have already been retired it would take years to get one ship loaded."

"We have a start. How long would it take for Europe, Japan, and other countries to build their own ships when they do not even have the impervium yet? I have not started to convince them. How much has the United States Government done to bring the world on board?

"You mentioned selecting the colonists. Who is going to do that? "My crew will do that?"

The Secretary of Treasury asked, "So do I talk to you to buy passage for my family?"

"No. No one can buy passage to the new colonies. Money will be worthless there and there won't be any here in two years. Money, per se, will no longer exist. There will not be a colonist over thirty. We have to have colonists that can have children after they arrive. We cannot afford anyone that is unfit mentally or physically in any way. We will even be doing genetic testing."

The Secretary of Housing and Urban Development angrily said, "Now wait a minutes. What about blacks and Hispanics?"

"I think the crews will reflect the current population as far as race. There is no reason to take a Caucasian over a Mexican American. One of my crew is half American Indian. We need a diverse gene pool. We do not want two people from the same family, even cousins on a colony ship. Most important is physical fitness. I do not mean weight lifters, football players or Olympic athletes. I am talking true fitness which would include family history of heart disease or cancer. Physically fit means endurance. However intelligence, already acquired skills like boot making, weaving, farming, lumberjacking is critical too. A humble skill might trump the most physically fit swimmer that has no skill needed in the new colony. What could shift the percentage of one race over another might be education levels or skill levels. If everyone was equal we could make sure we maintain the percentages that exist here now. However, if a race tends to be unskilled on welfare, they cannot expect to join the new colony. We need self starters. We need people that have somehow acquired skills. We probably do not need lawyers. We will have a library of the constitution and all the laws and court cases of the United States, but any laws will either be set before the ships leave or modified and adjusted as the colonies develop."

"Why would we use the total resources of the country to pay for only a few thousand colonists?"

"Because the alternative is that nothing from the United States will exist into the future. If we can evacuate just a few thousand people, the principles of this country and its pioneers can continue on. Maybe in a thousand years there will be as many Pangaeans as there are Americans today. But, I want the other countries of the world to have some opportunity also. However, I do not want to take people from other countries on ships built here. We need to save Americans first. If Great Britain wants British to survive, they need to commit their country to building their own ships. The same goes for every country. The United States should talk the other countries into this mission and provide our technology to them to build their own ships."

The Secretary of Defense said, "I am against providing this impervium and other inventions to countries that might attack us."

"Who is going to attack the United States after life on Earth ceases?"

"Mister President, if I could, I would like to tell the group about the other world we found."

There was a collective gasp around the room. One of the secretaries said accusingly, "Why have you spent all this time arguing over minor points if you have another planet to tell us about."

"Because most of the arguments apply to this other planet also and because I was interrupted."

Craig restarted the video showing pictures from space of the pyramid city, "We named this planet "Pyramid" for obvious reasons."

The Secretary of Education interrupted, "Is this another planet or a new discovery on Earth?"

"This is another planet, but with an amazing story." Craig let the video run of their exploration of parts of the city. Then the video moved to the pyramid in the center of the city where all roads led to the pyramid. The video showed the closed door of the pyramid. It zoomed in on the patterns of triangles versus lines in a circle. Always six triangles for each line.

"We tried pushing the buttons that were in the straight line one at a time. I, as the man, was the only one that could press in the center button. I could not push in a triangle. The women could not press in anything unless I pressed the line. The button was round and pushed in easily. Once that button was pushed one of the women could press one of the triangles in the small circles, but only one. It took all six women to simultaneously press triangles while I pressed in the button with the line."

The Secretary of Health and Human Services interrupted Craig, "Are you telling me that you have a crew of six women and you are the only man?"

"Yes, and that mix was essential to open the pyramid. Once inside it was like the control room of an advanced spaceship. There were multiple consoles. The consoles provided information. To activate each console, again, required six women and one man."

"We could have spent days there, but needed to get back to Earth to try to get the ball rolling a whole lot faster. What we did find out that this world was prepared for us by a past civilization that knew we would need to evacuate Earth now. The buildings are just basic shelter. There are no real furnishings, no windows, and no doors. We will have to have carpenters make doors and shutters after the colonists arrive."

"Other consoles gave them technologies they did not have. Another console gave a history of this mysterious race of human-like intelligent people and some of their history after leaving Atlantis on Earth. It told of expeditions back to Earth to visit the people of Earth that had returned to caveman status."

"Craig, excuse me for interrupting you again, but why didn't you tell of this planet first?"

"Because we did not have the time to thoroughly investigate the planet. We did not look for petroleum, minerals, or natural animals and plants. It is closer to Earth. I was going to recommend that we send colonists to both planets assuming we have at least two ships. The city is not large enough for more than five or six thousand. We don't know if there are building materials for building more structures. Pangaea seems to have everything needed except a stone block city and a pyramid."

"To continue on," he un-paused the video, "these are the animals we found roaming the city. These animals are not exactly like Earth animals, but the pyramid told us they were from Earth. If so, they are from our history. They are not modern cows and pigs and chickens. The chickens appeared to be Bantam chickens, small and brightly feathered, especially the roosters. After living there wild for thousands of years, they may have reverted to their wild state. The pyramid told us the Martians rid the planet of predators, but did they? If we see rapid progress in our scientific work, we will try to go back to study the planet further. We named it Pyramid because of the Egyptian style pyramid in the city. We found no other indication the planet had been visited. We named the first planet we discovered Pangaea because scientists believe that

Earth originally had just one continent and named it Pangaea. Pangaea has a few islands, but only one continent size land space."

"We need a firm commitment that you will try to convince the other nations to start their own colony ships and the commitment of America to go all out. Remember, money will be worthless in two years. There is no more important thing in the world's history than developing colony ships before the world ceases to exist as a habitable planet. This solar system will essentially be dead in two years."

"I could not say which planet would be better. Both need to be further explored. To assure the survival of the human race we need to colonize both planets."

"The Secretary of Education said, "I will task the universities to provide lists of their top students in all fields."

The Secretary of Health and Human Services, "Said, I will make up a list of the top doctors and medical researchers in the United States."

The Secretary of Defense said, "I will provide special forces troops to teach your students how to handle guns. If the President agrees, I believe that we can take a few of the military bases we were going to shut down and turn them over to the colonists. They have housing, offices, theaters for large groups of people and the military police can stay there to provide security."

The President said, "I agree, each department has valuable things they can contribute toward this effort. I will have to convince Congress."

"You will have help in the Ways and Means with Representative Shay."

"Why is that?"

"Because one of my crew is Estera Shay. I met her over two years ago. When she joined my crew a few months ago, Representative Shay basically told her to join my crew and go with me. He is just looking for an opening to support the mission."

"Do you have any more Congressmen under your belt."

"Sorry. No I don't. How about we put together a briefing for the combined houses?"

"Great idea, let me set it up. Plan on it one week from today."

When Craig returned to the SHIP not only was Dawn gone but all the girls were gone. SHIP, "Where is everyone?"

I have found that, like Dawn, I have learned your wives enough that I can safely teleport them wherever they wanted to go complete with clothing and some equipment. Estera wanted to visit her father right there in Washington D.C. so I teleported her to her father's office. Sandy went to meet Dawn since her father was at NASA in Houston. Karen went to her parents home in Colorado to visit with them, tell them she is safe, and will return to the SHIP tomorrow. Jill is back at the University of Oklahoma. She took the oil samples from Pangaea and a video of the oil fields and your drilling experiment. Shelby took her chemical samples to Yale University. From there she will be teleporting to Stanford University. Then she wants to visit her parents. I didn't think you would mind and you were to busy to interrupt."

"You did right SHIP, but I cannot communicate with them and we need to talk together sometime today. Are you able to keep watch on all of them to make sure they are safe and teleport them back here to keep them out of danger?"

"Easily, as long as I stay above the United States and they stay there. I could not teleport someone from Australia while over the United States. As you know, it only works line of sight, just like radio."

"I'm curious SHIP. You say just like radio. Then how do HAM or amateur radio operators talk around the world using their relatively low powered radios?

"They bounce their signals off the ionosphere when it bounces back down to the ocean surface and back up to the ionosphere and eventually to the other radio around the world. However, it is spotty. They cannot beam a signal at Australia. They aim the radio beam in that direction if they have a directional antenna like a Yagi antenna and just hope the bounces will end up in Australia. If Australia can hear them at that time of day, then they can probably aim their directional antenna back and have a two way conversation. If you were to aim at Europe, you might find yourself talking to Japan and vice versa." Sometimes talking to someone five hundred miles away is harder than talking to someone fifteen hundred miles away. The longest distance that they can talk in a straight line is maybe twenty-five hundred miles with only a single skip off the ionosphere. Even then the signal is scattered. When trying to talk over high frequency at two hundred miles their signal might just literally go over their heads. Cell phones are short range. They send their weak signal to cell phone towers that relay and relay and relay until the signal ends up at the cell phone you called."

"Why don't you teleport each of them a cell phone with all of the cell phone numbers of the family programmed in. That way we can contact each other while we are apart. If I needed to contact any one or all, I could phone them."

"It's done and they are now looking at the phones. Yes, they figured it out. They are all calling you now. The phones are set up so that if more than one member calls another one they all would automatically be in a conference."

"Hello girls. Just me. I asked SHIP to give each of you a cell phone programmed for other family members. Remember though, these are special cell phones so we can contact each other. They use the cell phone towers like any other cell phones, but these will only talk within the family. Because your phones use cell phone towers there may be blank spots where you cannot call and we can't call you. SHIP will be monitoring all of us in case of trouble. If someone is being threatened SHIP will teleport you out of the situation and back here."

"This is not like call waiting. If I am talking to Dawn and Karen telephones Dawn, she will go through without a ring, we will just find each other in a three way conversation. If you look at the screen on your cell phones you will now see all of us listed. Let's all plan on teleporting back to SHIP at 1 A.M. Eastern Standard Time for a conference. Then you can return or stay here, whichever you choose, but I think we need to get together face to face and discuss some issues that will impact all of us."

Each of the girls agreed, hung up after some general discussion with Craig and went back to what they were doing.

15

THE FIRST COLONY SHIP

Karen came back to the SHIP after Craig called her on her cell phone. "Karen, I have a hunting job for you. You have told me how you did not have a specialty like the other girls. I want SHIP to train you in psychology to help you learn to select the colonists. You will not be the only working on it, but you will be the primary hunter of the people we need to be colonists on the ships. You are already fluent in English, Apache, and Spanish so you show a talent in languages that the rest of us don't have. SHIP can easily train you in other languages. Right now, English is the only language you will need so right now it is just psychology, but hopefully we will soon get international efforts to build colony ships. Regardless of nationality, the colonies will be a meld of everyone and they must have a common language. English is already common around the world and it is what we speak, so English language has to be mandatory."

"Karen, I know your Apache heritage is important to you, but the colonies cannot hope to maintain their own heritage on the new planets. There will be only a few thousand on each planet and they must begin their own planet wide culture."

"Okay, I would be most happy to take on leadership in that area of the mission. However, I think it is important that all members of all ships be fluent in English. We don't want one colony village not being able to speak to the next colony village. Besides, many of the educated people of the world are already capable of speaking English. The countries of Europe are the size of our states. For a European to travel to other countries this is like Americans going from state to state here. Think what it would be like if a Missourian could not speak Kansan. The common language there is already English. The British Empire used to extend to Africa, India, China, the Caribbean. The British Empire used English. After the breakup of the British Empire much of the population continued speaking English for the tourists."

"I agree. We should confirm that the rest of the family agrees, but it makes sense that we should have an official language. It will also make it easier for the rest of the family that does not know other languages, like me."

When Karen finished her training in the learning module she found Craig waiting. "Why do you hang around when we are in the training module?"

"To make sure that you are okay and not in overload. To make sure that you don't get tempted into demanding that SHIP provide you too much knowledge. The human brain is rather amazing. It is capable of storing up to one hundred terabytes of information, but that includes so much more than a computer learns. SHIP has all the written knowledge of Mars and Earth. It is too much data for the human mind. However, your mind has information that SHIP will never know. When you were on Pangaea for that first time, in the first second you took in gigabytes of information. You caught your balance, you saw the open space, the sunlight, the trees, the leaves on the trees, the grass. You automatically scanned for hazards and determined if you need fight or flight. You would have to spend hours writing down what you saw in that first second. SHIP, on the other hand, may have taken a photo or a video, but would have to spend hours storing a record of what you did in one second. SHIP can do a math problem almost instantaneously, but assessing what it means may be beyond its capability."

"Ten seconds after your arrival in that forest clearing you determined what information you would store and what information you would forget to make room for the next ten seconds of information. What you learn from SHIP in the learning module is imprinted on your memory such that it is hard to forget. Your one hundred terabytes of information could get overloaded very easily. You are not given time to decide what to remember and what to forget. I'll bet you have forgotten many details of that first second on Pangaea. Many previous captains of SHIP overloaded their brains. They may become an imbecile or just go crazy. That is why I have not been tempted to become an expert on everything. I rely on my crew and on SHIP providing me tidbits of information telepathically when I need information to answer a question. I can always decide to forget that tidbit in seconds after using it to answer a question. If I need to recall it, I rely on SHIP to recall it for me. I choose to remember some things to keep my humanity. I cannot compete with a computer on accessing the memories of everything."

Karen commented, "What about using that information? Couldn't we just have SHIP pick the colonists?"

"No, you are underrating yourself. SHIP could go through a checklist, but when you interview someone, you will see body language, unsaid emotions, and other hints that SHIP could never interpret. SHIP can provide you lists with possible candidates. Be thinking about your process of selection. In the meantime, we have to be able to tell the world what we are doing. I only had to pick six family members. You will have to pick thousands. You are short on time. You cannot go to the applicants. We will have to have the applicants come to you. The ones with money can afford to travel to a central location, but how are you going to pick a lumberjack that is the best in the world, but does not have the money for travel? How many are married to someone that is suitable for a colonist? How many married women will be content to have another five wives with the same man? How many married women will leave their husbands to join a crew? How about leaving their children? How many singles are there that are physically fit, mentally suited, not using drugs or alcohol? The only alcohol I want on the SHIPS would be for cleaning a wound. I would rather the colonists worry about building a society instead of making moonshine. Someone will be making moon-shine quick enough without having heavy drinkers before leaving Earth. Right now, work with SHIP to come up with an advertising campaign."

"Okay. You went a little overboard with your explanation. You could have kept it to a couple of sentences."

"Sorry, I forget your IQ is higher than mine. The only thing I have on you is a couple of years on SHIP. I do not have your experience in nature."

Hundreds of companies that had already been involved in the research had already decided to sink their financial reserves into construction of the first colony ship. Their CEOs had decided that "to heck with the stock holders" and the dim future of their companies. They still had to pay their employees so their employees could continue paying their mortgages and buy groceries. Therefore their regular business had to continue to pay the bills; they could only donate cash reserves and cancel plans for new products that would never reach the market in two years.

Dawn had the designs from the pyramid on an effective faster than light drive. It was similar to what they had planned. It would use a nuclear reactor on the colony ships for power for the on board equipment, lighting and heating. The critical part was a particle accelerator. It is common knowledge that superconducting materials work best near absolute zero which they would have in space. These super conductors would be used in the accelerator. The pyramid had provided the methods to make a super accelerator to accelerate by products of the nuclear reaction to unimagined speeds to be accelerated out the back of the ship. As they accelerated beyond the speed of light, scoops on the ship would open to gather in antimatter particles and dark energy which would be further accelerated in the ship to produce more thrust. It would take time to accelerate and decelerate at the half way point of the voyage to maintain the gee loading for the colonists, but the top speed would be over two hundred light years per month. The USS Enterprise from Star Trek could not match the speed of the colony ships. A voyage of five hundred light years would still take six months because of the acceleration and deceleration which would be basically constant. They would accelerate for three months and decelerate for another three months during a voyage of five hundred light years. Acceleration would never drop below 1.2 gees and never exceed six gees. During periods of six gee acceleration the colonists would be restricted to acceleration couches in the ship to help them withstand the gees. For comparison an F-16 fighter jet pilot could routinely pull up to twelve gees but only for seconds at a time. Whereas an F-16 pilot might go from one gee or less to twelve gees in seconds, the colonists would feel a more gradual acceleration over several minutes up to six gees which would then taper off to a more comfortable 1.2 gees in between major acceleration periods. Living under higher gees daily will build muscles for physically fit colonists and prepare them for life on a new planet with higher gravity. Most people, if sitting up in a seat versus reclining, would gray out or even black out within seconds at six gees. Even in reclining acceleration couches you would find it hard to breathe. Your one hundred fifty pound body weighs nine hundred pounds. For most your arms would be pinned to the couch.

Dawn said, "We are almost finished with colony ship number one except for the FaTL drive. We could launch it soon for outfitting in space. We have the reactor and can install the reactor and particle accelerators next week. We can attach an old missile rocket and get it into space."

Estera said, "We have developed what we think will be a sufficient way to convert waste carbon dioxide from the colonists back into carbon and oxygen. No problem with recycling water back to hydrogen and oxygen."

Dawn said, "Our reactor design from the pyramid gives us a way to feed the hydrogen back into the reactor to extend the fuel in the reactor. It is not just a reactor, but has a breeder function to take the hydrogen and feed it back into the reactor."

Estera continued, "One of our biggest questions is whether we can get our gardens working to use solid waste to grow vegetables and fruits in the solarium. It should work. It will not be zero gee like in the space station. We will be maintaining gravity throughout the voyage. One question is whether the plants will take the short periods of nine gee acceleration. There have been some success in growing plants on the space station, but that was at zero gee. Since there is little light in space we will be using electric grow lights. If the plants do not survive we will have to leave a trail of human waste and garbage in our wake. However, we could then add that space to our living space on the ship."

Sandy Scofield had spent the days studying high gee living during the days. She visited with her father after work.

"My biggest concern is the few animals we may have on the ships. We don't even know how a cow or pig will take 1.2 gees, let alone six gees. We could put them in slings several times a day, but I do not think we will be able to take animals with us. We do know that the two planets we have found so far have their own animals that we can eat. I think the decision must be made to live off the indigenous animals on Pangaea and Pyramid. However, we can take along frozen embryo and sperm from earth animals to try to breed the indigenous animals to be more like Earth animals."

"Earth birds, like chickens and turkeys will be a bigger problem. Eggs would not survive six gees for any length of time. We could pack them to withstand a six gee drop, but six months of 1.2 gee punctuated by periods of six gee would probably end up with the egg yokes crushed to one side of the egg shell. We can try. We can also take along chicken sperm to fertilize the chickens on Pyramid to be more meaty like Earth chickens rather than skinny Bantams."

"In other words rather than take live animals we will have to have test tube animals to have on alien planets. Another effort would be some genetic engineering to genetically modify the genes in the indigenous animals and birds. People may not like it, but basically farmers have been doing genetic engineering for centuries through selected breeding."

"One advantage of not taking live animals is that we will not have to take their food or waste water on them."

A doctor from Southern Cal asked, "Is that a firm decision you are making on your own."

Sandy replied, "It is not in stone. It is my opinion. If you can come up with good reasons why we should try to take our own animals, please submit those to the group. However, I believe I will be correct."

That night they all met back at SHIP for a meeting. Each gave a report on what they had done that day.

Dawn, Estera, and Sandy gave theirs first. Karen and Craig had spent the day on deciding on and building press releases and TV broadcasts.

Craig, "Does everyone agree that we will have to forget shipping animals on the colony ships?"

Dawn agreed with Sandy, "The ship is going to be very crowded as is. Since both planets have cow and pig type animals for meat the animals pale in comparison to a number of kits to make up a jeep and truck type vehicle and other tools needed. It would be foolish for anyone to consider taking livestock into space."

Estera, "I not only agree with Sandy on the animals, but I am wondering about the plants. Plants can grow from seeds or cuttings. The only reason I tend to keep the live plants as a way to convert some of the solid waste, like poop. The plants can use it as fertilizer and convert the energy into edible food. I hate the idea of ejecting it into the exhaust to just spread across the universe."

"Not that bad," Craig said, "anything put into the exhaust will be vaporized immediately. It could even add mass and therefore thrust."

Dawn disagreed, "Ever tried to put poop in a particle accelerator. I'm more afraid it will gum up the works and decrease thrust. It could even block it up some. We are talking about accelerating sub microscopic particles in small pathways to provide thrust. We would have to have a dump chute to avoid the exhaust and then we would be spreading shit across the galaxy. I vote for keeping the green houses and just hope it works."

Shelby Scofield had not had as much to do as the others for the whole time but now added her accomplishments. "I sampled water, I sampled soil, and now we are starting to get some real issues in chemistry."

"I have consulted with several top universities and with my existing knowledge have influenced many professors who now believe in the mission and have dedicated much of their research to help us. They have directed their graduate students' research to help us. They have convinced the deans at their respective universities to dedicate a considerable amount of their research dollars to help us. Most of this is outside what most of you will consider chemistry, my special knowledge, but, in fact, is chemical. One item we have plenty of on the ships and, at least for a few years, in the colonies, electricity. I have here a list of what the universities are working on."

a.   Using waste products and breaking them down to their chemical components for reuse. When people eat food their digestion breaks it down to useable components in the body. The protein from a steak is extracted from the steak and deposited in muscle. The fat is converted into energy to burn in the body to maintain body heat and other functions. The flavor of the steak and the steak sauce, if any, is excreted by the body. Some of the protein and even fat as well as bulk are excreted. If we can recover the flavor, the left over protein and fat and bulk, we could use that to create another food with the right flavor, some of the fat and protein to supplement the nutrition and recycle it through the body."

b.   With vegetables and fruit we have the same situation, but more fiber that just passes on through the body. The fiber adds to digestion and adds bulk to the excrement to keep the waste flowing rather than getting constipated. Forever, we have been creating artificial vitamins we could have gotten by eating the proper fruit and vegetables. Through chemistry we could take the fiber and flavor and natural coloring, add the vitamins, and minerals back into the mix and create more food that will be as nutritious as the original. The issue is getting the right mix of chemistry to make the new fruit as appealing and flavorful as the original. Imagine, if you will, eating an apple. It has a red skin, pulpy fruit that can be crunchy, especially if refrigerated. You think it is delicious.

c. You eat it. Your taste buds on your tongue and to some extent your nose tastes a red delicious apple. Your stomach and intestines use chemistry to extract the vitamins, minerals, some protein and the carbohydrates, sugars, to nourish the body. The flavor and fiber pass on through the digestion process and is captured. We separate the flavor, coloring, fiber, and use it with other waste products like paper to create a new apple. We make the interior of the apple have the same texture and flavor as the original apple. We use chemistry to make a new skin for the apple that looks, feels, and tastes like an apple skin. We add a little alum to give it a tart impression just like the original apple. As we are manufacturing this new apple, we add back in manufactured vitamins and minerals to make it as nutritious as the original. There is no real reason to add the indigestible stem or seeds to the artificial apple unless we need to psych out the eater of the apple so he can not tell a real apple from the manufactured one. The chemicals and equipment to make these new fruits and vegetables take less space than trying to ship these on the ship. It is one thing for astronauts to eat fake food from a tube for a few weeks; it is another thing to eat this food for months or a year. Miniaturizing the equipment for recycling is the hardest thing about doing this.

d.   Again, taking waste water, removing soap or chemicals and minerals filtered out by the human body and turning it back into drinking water is not new. It is the idea of recycling this water that is difficult. It is more compact to carry the water recycling equipment than it is to transport enough water for one thousand people for six months to a year. It would be impossible to carry that much water. That is chemistry. Many sewage plants are capable of cleaning water to be of superior quality to what came into fresh water mains to start with. The difference is that we will be extracting the chemicals for reuse.

e. Recycling the air and exhaled moisture is part of the overall process. Again, this has been used on the space station so this is not new technology. The difference is one thousand people in a small space versus ten or twelve people on a space station.

f. The other research is a general study on how to have a closed system where nothing is lost or becomes unbalanced. We will not be able to send up fresh water or air to the spacecraft once it has left Earth until it lands on the planet.

g. The summary of the samples taken from Pangaea and Pyramid are not remarkable. We find the same chemicals on Earth in similar amounts. The exception is manufactured or refined chemicals that are absent. Mercury levels are very low. The rivers do not contain any insecticides or fertilizers like on Earth. It points to the need to control these on the new planets to prevent pollution we have on Earth. Because the colonists will have unlimited land for at least a few centuries, we should not need the added chemicals we need on Earth to produce enough food to feed the seven billion people we now have on Earth. We will at least start out with a highly educated society in the colonies. As the population expands there will need to be ways to control insect pests that go after our food crops. As we reuse the same soil we will need to fertilize it artificially. We need to teach the colonists to look for natural ways to control the pests and add fertilizer. Through chemistry we can start using human waste as fertilizer by treating it to make it safe. We can research natural enemies to pests on the new planets. We know almost nothing about the insects on either planet so we simply don't know. What if we tried to introduce ladybugs to help with pests and they had no enemies to limit their population and they became the pest? Rather than the colonists being just farmers and mechanics we need a high number of scientists to study this new environment to keep it safe while supporting an expanding population. The colony ships will have a fixed population and stored chemicals for use for a relatively short time. Once we land we want the population to grow exponentially to assure the continuation of Earthmen. We want them to establish towns and cities all over the planet to not have all the people in one area to be destroyed by a single storm or earthquake.

g. Finding and refining petroleum for cheap energy is Jill's area, but the refining and using this fuel is still chemistry. We will also be looking at additives to the fuel to cut down on air pollution. There has already been a century of study on Earth, but it never hurts to take a new look for a new planet. We can use petroleum for vehicle fuel, and heating, but we can also use it for plastics, clothing, and fertilizer for plants. We need to do it smartly this time on a new planet.

"I guess that sums up chemistry. Any questions?"

"Well said," Craig said, "I knew there was a good reason for a chemist on the team. Good work, keep those universities to the grindstone. Also, make sure that we have the equipment on the ship that we can set up the manufacture of plastics, clothing, and so on.

"What are your immediate plans?"

Karen said, "I'm gong to stay on SHIP and work on publicity."

Craig said, "I will be working on it too, but I will also be visiting with some country leaders."

Sandy said, "I think I've sort of fired myself from working on transporting animals on the colony ships, but I will be working with the Secretary of Agriculture to decide what test tube samples we will be taking and how to care for the samples for a couple of years. I will also be spending time at NASA with my father who seems to be there almost full time."

Shelby said, "I will be spending some time in Oklahoma with my family. Can I tell them what is happening and that I will be leaving my family behind?"

Craig replied, "Someone tell me if I am off base, but I think a few rumors from family members won't hurt at this stage. We will be advertising for colonists soon. If some information leaks I don't think it will hurt that much, but ask your families to keep it private for now."

Dawn was relieved, "My family has been asking for two years now what you and I have been up to and why I have been out of touch so much. I will go visit them for a day or two before going back to NASA. By the way, I think we should make two small model colony ships to fire it off into space to see how it will work. NASA already has an ion propulsion that is nuclear powered. If we put it in a ship and let it go all out we can get an idea how it will work. Both ships will use conventional rockets to achieve orbit then fire up the ion propulsion as unlimited as possible. One ship will be empty and one with a sample load to simulate having a colony ship fully loaded at take-off. We foresee no problems getting a colony ship into orbit with its extreme light weight and aerodynamics, but we will have a problem if we have to launch empty and then move all the people and supplies to the ship. We would have to have a massive fleet of shuttles with the bottleneck being the airlock between the shuttles and the ships."

"Sounds great. Do it."

"I want to spend some time with my parents. I used SHIP to spy on them and found out my father will be going home for the weekend. I would like to spend the weekend there."

"Okay, Estera."

"I have been spending a lot of time at the University of Oklahoma working on equipment we will need in the colonies including a small extremely efficient refinery. I have been able to see my family for a few hours now and then while I was there. With no objections, I will confess as to what the mission is to my family also. I will also add some environmental concerns for the petroleum projects."

"Okay then. SHIP allows you to teleport by yourselves. You only have to think return and SHIP will teleport you back here. If you need anything ask SHIP to provide it. Just keep in mind that SHIP cannot produce large objects. If you need a vehicle, SHIP can only provide one for the whole family so keep things small if possible. We will have to do any inventing outside the history known by SHIP. SHIP cannot invent anything not in its history banks. Keep your phones on and charged at all times so we can contact each other."

The family went their separate ways except for Karen and Craig who were staying on SHIP to develop information packages to help start forming the colony personnel.

"I have been having a hard time getting you alone, Craig. I think we should start our day on SHIP with a little sex before work. That will take away the tension."

An hour later they started working on the information packages.

"I had been looking forward to that since you wore your Indian garb." "And I had been waiting my turn since you saved my life from the Pangaea lion."

"That was part of my job and I only wounded it."

"I had not even seen it. I've been wandering alone most of my adult life and no one has been there to save me. That is twice if you include catching me from that cliff in Colorado when we first met."

"Let's make a list of what kind of information we want to provide."

> a. Would not yet provide the information that Earth was doomed.

b. That way they would get volunteers who were willing to go on a long adventure.

c. They would provide a list of skills needed and ask for people that thought they were the best.

d. The age limits would be 21 to 25 for both men and women with the exception of medical doctors that would need to have graduated from medical school. That in itself made doctors to be older, but a maximum of 30.

2. Television and Radio news spots initially.

3. A television special of an hour on all the main networks and news only stations.

4. Radio programs where they would be interviewed by talk show hosts.

5. Newspaper releases.

6. Magazine articles.

Karen said, "We will not find the right colonists with this initial release. We will get some good ones to start with, but we will also get people just looking for adventure, fame, or getting away from crimes or bad situations."

"Then you and SHIP will have to filter out the bad ones. SHIP can run the computer background checks and school records. You can interview them and get a feel for them and their motivations."

"I said what was wrong with this information, but if were to tell the world that Earth is going to be destroyed and if they believed us we would get everyone volunteering and people trying to bribe their way onto the ships. People would be paying money to falsify their records and making up lies. So I suggest that we never officially tell the general population what is going to happen. Better if they just don't wake up one morning. If the average Joe believes the story there will be wholesale crime with even the police just saying to heck with it."

"I agree. We need to get on a joint call to the whole family and stress that while they can tell their families they need to stress secrecy and why it needs to be kept secret. We don't want panic in the streets. In fact…

Craig pressed the button to call the whole family; Karen answered just so she could hear both ends of the conversation."

When everyone was on the line Craig explained, "I know that earlier I had said you could tell your families. Karen and I were working on information packages and came to the conclusion that if the average person knows the end of Earth is coming in less than two years there will be wholesale problems the Earth cannot afford."

Dawn interrupted, "What do you mean?"

"People will do things they would never do when tomorrow is far in the future. I'm not saying everyone will go berserk, because most are good people that will just continue on as best they can, but we could have millions doing what they would not do if the world were not ending:

1. Many parents will split up instead of staying married. This will leave the children without two parents.
2. Some children could find themselves without a parent; why raise a child when everyone will be dead in two years.
3. Criminals will commit all sorts of crime. If they get caught they will not have to serve more than two years. We are talking murder, rape, robbery.
4. Many police and military will just not show up for work; why worry since it will be over in two years.
5. Firemen will just watch buildings burn.
6. Why worry about sexually transmitted disease if there is only two years to live.
7. Some doctors and nurses will just leave their patients to die; why treat someone for cancer when they will die anyway, why work long hours when you only have two years to party.

8. Workers in companies producing things we need for the colonies will quit work. They won't need to worry about paying for a kid's college that won't live that long. They will never retire unless they quit work today.

9. People will quit paying their mortgages and pull whatever money they have in the banks out.

"I get the picture." Dawn said. "I agree with you and Karen. Why didn't SHIP warn us?"

"SHIP doesn't think new thoughts only regurgitates information. Jill said, "What can we tell our families?"

"Only that we are building a spaceship to travel to another planet and will be recruiting young people for the mission. We do not even hint that there are only two years left. The politicians may leak that information, but we should not confirm that information."

"Do we tell them we have found an earthlike planet?"

"Sure, that will explain the large ships and the recruitment. When are you going to start the campaign?"

"In about ten days. What about some videos of the actual ship construction?" Karen asked.

Dawn said, "There is a ship at a hidden base in Nevada sometimes referred to as Area 51. It's in a large hanger. It is complete with shell, floors, rooms, and entrances. It has no reactor yet or furnishings, but the electronics in the control room have been working for a week."

"Can we get photos for the print media and videos for television?" "Craig, what do you think? Are we ready to release pictures?"

"Yes, Dawn, I think so. Apparently Karen wants them so she agrees. Does everyone agree? You know I want criticism when you have any."

Dawn teleported to Nevada the next day and appeared in a meeting with engineers discussion the status. Some of them had seen her appear before but others were startled.

One of the engineers jumped up from his chair, "What are doing here? Who let you in?"

Then he noticed some of the engineers that had come from NASA were holding back snickers. "What's going on? Is this some kind of joke?"

"I am Dawn. The ship is my design and I came to take some pictures of it."

"Is she legit? Was it my imagination or did she just appear here?"

"She is legit. We've been working with her for over a year at NASA planning all this. Yes, she just materialized in the room. It was not your imagination."

"How can you do that?"

"We, the team, has a one person teleporter that can teleport us anywhere within a relatively short range, but only team members. It will not work for anyone else. It took a long time for the teleporter to be taught each of us individually. It will not work to move anything to the ships. It only works between our small ship and our destination in line of sight with the ship."

"How come we have not all heard about this?"

"You did not have a need to know?"

"Who built this ship of yours? Is it the same as what we are building?"

"Who built it is a secret. It is not the same kind of ship and it is small. Our family consists of seven people. One man, the captain, and six women. Why six women you will ask next? Because, that is a good ratio for space travel and the same makeup as the colonists for this ship will be."

"Who decided that?"

"No more questions. All of you have worked on military top secret projects before and know that you will never know the big picture, only your part of it. Some military systems had a very small in crowd and the engineers did not know what they were building until it was made public. Even then some were not sure that is what they had a part in. This is the same thing. Everything is top secret. The details will remain Top Secret just like the Blackbird; SR-71 aircraft just appeared one day in 1968 as a fait accompli. The specs only came to light over the years. Some of the engineers never got close to the aircraft itself until it was retired and put in museums. This is the same thing. We will show the ship you are building next week on television and start recruiting colonists."

"So soon? We don't even have a star drive yet."

"We will have the faster than light or FaTL drive installed long before we can train the colonists. Think how long we trained astronauts for a short mission. These people will never return to Earth."

"Okay, I'm sorry, and I am Ronald Carowski. My job is building the chamber for the ah, fatter drive. It's finished except for final measurements and testing."

"What testing?"

"Testing it for strength and testing it for radiation stopping ability."

"That testing was done at the University of Oklahoma two years ago. We don't have much time for that kind of testing. Once you build something with this metal you should know that changing it would be extremely difficult. It can withstand 10,000 degrees Celsius. A diamond will not scratch it. What would you do if something was off by a tenth of an inch?"

"I see your point. Have you not seen what we have built before?"

"Only a million drawings and specs and artist concepts of what it should look like. I have seen small models I could hold in my hand, but, no, I have not seen it?

"Prepare to be amazed. Are you ready?" "Yes. I have my camera right here."

"We have not been allowed to take any photos or videos. Is that little camera all you have?"

"Don't worry, this little camera has more capability than anything short of a spy satellite."

They broke up the meeting and moved out of the conference room into the monster hanger built on the remote desert base.

"Oh my god. It's huge. Drawings did not do it justice. How is it actually working with this Impervium?"

"Actually, it is very easy. Until it cures it is like working with a malleable plastic. You just bend the material to the shape you want then you use a metal gun like you would a caulking gun to put the pieces together. Twenty-four hours later it is stronger than anyone could theorize. We drill holes for door hinges and latches while still in plastic state and then bolt things together with bolts made of the same material."

"Okay, question. What you using for door seals? Will it stand up to space for a year?"

"Yes, It should. It was developed for the space station and stood up well for more than a year without damage. Every entry is an airlock. You can only open one door at time. If the outer seal were to leak, it could be repaired with the inner door closed."

"Okay, we have space walked at 18,000 miles an hour in orbit. What happens if a man or woman steps outside in a spacesuit at ten billion miles an hour?"

"It should be no different. Speed is relative. A piece of dust hitting a spacesuit at 18,000 miles an hour can puncture the suit and kill the person inside if it hits in a bad spot. It has never happened. If it hit at that speed, the person would never know it, and probably explode. We don't know if a human could exist for any time outside the ship at faster than light speed."

"We don't plan on opening the doors after the ship leaves Earth until we land on the new planet. I guess it will work. I'll do some checking to see if there is another seal we could use."

The ship was as tall as the largest ocean liner and none of it was below the waterline. It made it appear almost twice as tall. It was twice as wide as the largest ocean liner and half again as long. In other words larger than the largest ocean ship ever produced.

"You say it has all the interior rooms finished as far as structure and doors, but no furniture and the electronics and routine electrical wiring are in place."

"That is correct."

"I'm going to take some photos and videos of the outside. What is that crane doing?"

"Testing the operation of the scoop on the top side, as it was the last one installed."

"Is that a person up there?"

"Yes, it is."

"Okay, how do we get inside?"

"This is the bottom of the ship and the part that will be on the ground after landing so the door is easy to just walk into. Follow me."

Dawn kept the video rolling. She had taken both videos and photos of the outside. The photo of the ship with the monster crane and the spec that a person standing would be truly impressive. As she entered the ship the hallways extended out of sight in both directions. The door was wide enough to get large items into and out of.

She visited some a few living quarters then boarded an electric golf cart to ride down the hall to the front of the ship. They took an elevator up to the control room. The engineer explained that there were three control rooms. One toward the top where you would expect a cockpit on an airplane, the main one in the middle where they would be visiting, and one near the bottom to be used during landing. There was no viewport to look out. No windows at all on the ship as they had no way to manufacture a clear version of the super metal. All outside viewing was through exterior cameras, radar, sonar, laser, and other sensors. There wasn't much to see except the inside of the hanger. There were multiple back-up cameras behind small doors that could open and another camera rolled out and turned on to replace an exterior camera/sensor that might get damaged.

"There is no way that I have time to fully explore this ship and record it on my camera. Can you get some people with conventional cameras to take photos and videos of the ship inside and out."

"Of course. We have a number of professional photographers on the staff here at Area 51. We regularly take pictures of various military aircraft that have been developed here for years. When do you need them?"

"How about sending them to NASA in Houston the day after tomorrow? Whatever you have. Let's go back to the conference room to discuss some technical issues."

⸺⸺➤➤◄◄⸺⸺

When they returned to the conference room with the rest of the engineers that had tagged along and the ones that had stayed in the conference room, Dawn asked some questions.

"What is the weight of the completed empty ship as it sits there now"

"Two hundred and fifty-six thousand pounds. About two thirds of that is electronics and wiring.

Wherever possible we used fiber optics to reduce weight. Wherever possible we used the impervium to keep things light. The cases for the video displays are all of the impervium which was lighter than plastic, provides limitless interference protection and strength, but the plastic screens and wiring are heavy in comparison. It's amazing. At its size engineers would be amazed that it weighs less than two hundred fifty-six thousand tons, not pounds. We are talking that with ordinary aircraft aerodynamics we could strap on a couple of big airline jet engines and it would fly just fine as is even with a couple of hundred people on board. If the aerodynamics are as good as advertised, it could fly to 40,000 feet with a four jumbo jet engines and the requisite thousand people. But when you add supplies for a year and the equipment proposed, plus a nuclear reactor, we would have to strap on solid fuel minuteman missiles to get it off the ground."

"How are you going to get everything up in orbit and into the ship?"

Dawn replied, "We are still working on that. We either have to have a fleet of shuttles or find some more powerful rocket fuel. We'll let you know. With unlimited funding how many of these ships could you build in a year?"

"Could we build them out in the open or do have to keep them out of sight in hangers?"

"Let's say, outside."

"Maybe two more or three if we're lucky."

Okay, I will probably be visiting more often in the future. Don't panic if I just pop in. Right now I'm going to pop out. Bye now." And she disappeared. One second there the next second, not a trace.

16

RECRUITING THE COLONISTS

Karen and Craig started the information campaign the next day with newspaper releases. The next day came with more detailed articles and brief news releases to national TV and radio networks. The day after the media started advertising an hour long special.

The news papers all ran the photograph of the first colony ship with a short story. "The United States has just released pictures of a new spaceship to take a colony to another planet. This ship is the largest moveable object ever built. We do not know too many details yet. Apparently this is the result of over two years of intensive research going on at NASA in Houston, the University of Oklahoma, Stanford University, the University of Colorado and many other universities. In addition, a number of major U.S. companies have been involved almost since the start of this project. We knew something was going on because of the congregations of scientists and engineers in multiple locations. It was thought to be a military development project like the Manhattan Project and it was, but not military. This ship was built to send a colony to another planet and they are looking for people to start trying out to become one of a thousand colonists who will be moving to the new planet to create a permanent colony. We have been told that we have discovered two inhabitable planets that will be colonized. Neither planet has intelligent life, but has plant and animal life similar to Earth. If any one is interested in applying to be one of the colonists go to the nearest large university and inquire. They are looking for not just college graduates, but every conceivable skill from medical doctor and engineer to farmer and mechanic. Applicants must be between 21 and 25 years old and physically fit for a long space voyage. Individuals accepted will enter a long training program for departure from Earth in less than two years. The medical doctor must have completed his residency and still be under 30 years old. All applicants that are accepted will go a secret location for training. This will be all volunteer with no military unless they meet the same requirements as any other applicant. Applicants will be trained in colonizing a new planet. The purpose of this mission is to guarantee the survival of the human race and give us another home to go to. All applicants will be safer than the average person not on the mission, but must be willing to cut ties with family and friends for nearly two years of training. There will be fierce competition for this mission. The schooling will be somewhat physically demanding but in a learning environment.

They do not want police or military for this mission, but there will be a need for people that like to camp out, hunt and fish. They need people that can weave cloth, sew new clothing, boot makers, farmers, and all conceivable skills. Bring your birth certificate, any education you have from colleges or technical schools, and any other proof of your skills or knowledge. Be prepared to be immediately swept away to the school if you are accepted. You will be allowed one phone call to whoever you want before entering the school. At this time there will be no guarantee of another contact with family and friends. There will be five thousand accepted for this school at this time. This may be the only school or there may be additions later, but assume this is your only chance to be a colonist on a new planet.

The television stations had videos of the ship in its hanger, with views of typical living quarters with sample furniture and clothing for a living unit on the ship. There were videos of the entertainment areas and the primary control room. There were artist concepts of the greenhouses. Again, the plea went out for volunteers for colonists willing to break their ties with Earth for the chance to spread the human race to new planets. This was followed by videos of Pangaea and Pyramid.

Pangaea came across as a new Garden of Eden unspoiled by humanity. A place for a new start. The videos of Pyramid proved that another race of intelligent life existed in the galaxy. Parallels between that and all the UFO sightings were made. Maybe UFOs were for real and came from this civilization. Versus a Garden of Eden, Pyramid already had crude housing and earthlike animals roaming around. It would be less taxing. Pangaea wanted for true pioneers willing to build and explore and develop. Pyramid would attract scientists and archaeologists wanting to study the previous civilization that had built the city.

Both planets needed every type of skill in the team of colonists. Pyramid seemed to be looking for people to study it while Pangaea seemed to be looking for rugged individualists.

It did not take long before tens of thousands of volunteers swamped the universities that were taking applications. Each volunteer filled out extensive forms and the scanners were busy scanning in documents that gave proof of birth, proof of education, proof of skills, and references.

There were people taking these applications that automatically eliminated any applicant that had any obvious handicaps. This caused the news media to start an outcry saying that handicapped individuals were being discriminated against. The news media was also keeping track of the races applying to see if one race or another was over or under represented. All of the data was input to computers linked together over the internet. SHIP was tabulating all of the information on everyone applying.

There was also a hue and cry against the money to build the ships and to start a new colony when the money was needed here on Earth to help the poor people of Earth. Why was money being spent on this technology when the price of gasoline and heating oil was rising? Small businesses wanted cheap or free loans to expand. Home builders asked for government money to subsidize home construction.

There were some magazines and editorials in favor of the mission, but most were against. The U.S. Government was under pressure to stop the flood of money. Stockholders in the companies that were donating huge sums of money and personnel complained that any excess funds be distributed to the stockholders or be used to reduce debt. CEOs of some of the biggest donators knew that Earth was doomed, but had been told why they should not make the information public and whole heartedly agreed. The universities were criticized too, but steadfastly continued investing their research time and money. The universities did not know that the Earth would cease in less than two years.

The President and his cabinet were fully aware of the whole story and did not want to release that story to the general Congress who would spill the beans for publicity.

Representative Shea agreed to writing blank checks from the House Ways and Means. He would eventually be caught, but he knew the world would end before he could go to jail. He was proud of his daughter, Estera, and ever grateful that he had had the opportunity to assure she would survive. He did not know if the colony ships would ever arrive at their colonies, but it was worth the risk. Regardless, his daughter would survive.

The Secretary of Defense knew the whole story. He shuffled all the funds he could to the mission. He had to continue paying the payroll and buying supplies for the military, but all research and development was shifted to the mission. Most of the production money for replacement of planes and tanks was also shifted to the mission. Like Representative Shea, he was not worried about being caught. If he was caught by the wrong people, he would be fired and perhaps charged, but too late for him to serve time. In the meantime, he was proud to do what he could for the benefit of mankind. He donated several military bases for training the colonists. Most of the military mission was reduced to near zero and security built up. The concern was that once the populace found out about the fate of Earth, the bases would be under attack. Some bases like Edwards AFB and Area 51, and the nearby Nellis air force base were almost exclusively dedicated to construction of colony ships.

After two weeks, SHIP had a list of 300,000 volunteers for the mission. There was no shortage of college graduates ready for adventure, but some of the skills were more difficult. Most clothing was made in other countries so finding experienced boot makers, and seamstresses was coming up short. Some of the fields like lumberjacks had no desire to go off to some school for a couple of years to go off to another planet. Their world consisted of American and Canadian forests. The same for oilmen. You might have the expert engineering in drilling wells, but you need the laborers who were experienced in drilling and laying pipe. Welders that could weld together hundreds of miles of pipe for the oilfields. Construction workers to build roads.

The team solved some of this problem by announcing huge sign-on bonuses for these career fields they were short of. The government agreed to forgive all college loans of those completing the training and going on the mission. One problem was that the age group sometimes got married right out of high school.

Any women applying were automatically rejected if they had children. Young children could not go on this mission with the intermittent high gee acceleration periods and then survival on a new planet after their arrival. Children would have to come after the colony was established.

SHIP finally reduced the list from 300,000 to less than 100,000. Fifty thousand were rejected because their records did not match what they had submitted with their applications. One thing unanticipated by the SHIP or the family was that they had 175,000 women applicants to only 75,000 male applicants.

Jill explained it, "Unmarried women have less opportunity to get the good jobs after graduation. Even the seamstresses get paid very little and now there is an opportunity to do something wild and free. The poorer women had no real hope of seeing anything except that of the city they were born in. Farming women will jump at a chance to get away from the everyday life of the farm even if it means going somewhere to farm. If you live in a rural area, maybe you want to meet someone not from the same small town. If a woman has a bad relationship, she may want to just run away from it and it you can't get any further than another planet. How many girls run away from home as a young teen?"

"Men, on the other hand, may be up for an adventure, but many want to just return home, the conquering hero. Men have more questions about the where and why."

Dawn asked, "At what point do we explain that we will be taking six girls for every guy? That will attract a lot of males."

Karen said, "I think we will just select extra girls to start with and tell them after they have been introduced to the school. Many of them will drop out. I would not expect to lose any of the males."

"There are many jobs that women can do as well or better than a man and there are many jobs that a man would refuse to do, and, of course, have no experience in, like sewing clothes. Yes, there are a few tailors from a family of tailors, but a large number of women can sew while few men can sew. A woman can drive a bulldozer or build micro circuit boards. However, men have more strength for those few jobs that are unsuited for women, like cutting down trees, and lifting a log into place for a log cabin. Men tend to be better hunters because they have been the hunters for a million years. Women are the planters and flour makers."

"I think we will stress the intellect of the women and the physical strength of the men. A lot of the women have been brainwashed that they are not as smart, but we will build them up to the point that maybe they will understand. We will gradually feed in information about women being better in space because they use less water, food, and air than the men do. Maybe many of them will see the advantage before we introduce them to the idea of having more women means more children. I'm not a Mormon, but how did they do it?"

SHIP chimed in, "Decisions are not my strength. How many women and how many men do you want to start with in these schools?"

Craig answered, "I do not expect to have more than ten ships when we have to leave Earth. That would be a total of ten thousand Americans. That would be roughly 8600 women and 1400 men. We should have 10,000 trained women and 1600 trained men expecting a few last minute changes. We need to start the training program with 20,000 women and 4000 men and see how it goes. The training won't be like military basic training so I would not expect too many dropouts and almost no injuries. Some will just change their mind after being selected. Some will drop out when they discover it is a one way trip and some will stay when we tell the world that the world is ending. I would suspect near riots to be in the training program when that news hits."

"How are we going to handle people from other countries? There are only 7 of us and several of us will be too involved with other things?"

Karen replied, "We have already determined that we will require other countries to provide students fluent in English. We cannot possibly train the Americans without help from professors and other experienced trainers. Our job will be primarily providing the curriculum. We can provide the same curriculum to all the countries."

Estera disagreed, "How are you going to get the Japanese and Chinese to actually provide English speaking students? I understand that it will be critical for everyone to speak the same language on the new planets, but we have to give them the technologies now to get them to build some ships before it's too late. How will you force them to provide English speaking students? What makes you think that they will even follow the age requirement or the mix of women and men? What do we do when at the last minute they decide to man their only colony ship with an all male military unit to take over the new planet and take our women as captives?"

Silence followed.

Sandy said, "Does that mean we need to select military trained men for our colony ships, just in case?"

Craig said, "No. Not necessarily. It might mean that I use SHIP to watch them closely even after the launch from Earth orbit. If they have a military force I might have to use the powers of SHIP to destroy their colony ship enroute. However, I think we should consider some military men who have the skills we need. It would not hurt to have everyone trained in weapons handling and marksmanship. Our new colonists will be a hunter gatherer society and everyone should be able to defend themselves from wild animals. I do not want our colonies to need a military but when it comes to helicopter or airplane pilots, why not take military trained pilots? There are none better."

Shelby said, "You said you would use the powers of SHIP to destroy their colony ship if necessary. That means that SHIP has military capability?"

"Yes, it does. It is not a military ship, but it does have capabilities. Did you ever wonder what became of the military buildup in the Middle East? That was me using the SHIP's capability."

"I didn't picture you as someone willing to just kill a thousand people because you did not believe with their ambition."

"That would be a very last resort. I don't think it would ever come to that. SHIP can give me a lot of power to avoid that. However, one ship of military from one country could easily overcome all the peaceful colonies on a planet. The women would become slaves to the conquerors and the colony would either fail completely or, at best, we would have a world level dictator with all the people of the planet living under a military dictatorship. We cannot allow that to happen either."

"I see that, but it sounds so horrible. How sure are you that you can prevent them?"

"We will have to watch them closely and have SHIP spy on them. We will do everything we can to make sure all of the colony ships stay under our control. We can withhold the FaTL drive from them until the very last. They can't do much without the faster than light drive. They could load their ship with military men and equipment, but without the FaTL they are earthbound. As a last resort, we can check them after the mission is on the way and take them out."

"There is another alternative. That would be to send questionable countries to different planets. We found two planets. Maybe we can find more."

17

TRAINING A COLONY

Each of the training bases had three thousand students. It started with days of lectures about the mission in general and what was known about the new planets. There was a lot to train everyone on. There was a lot even the family didn't know.

The instructors had their training material that had been developed between SHIP, Karen, and Craig. They were trained in common ship operations like the video and book banks that were to include all the great works of mankind in books, music, art, history, and science. Everything was digital media to make it smaller and lighter. There would be no canisters of film, video tapes, or books on board. There would be training in how to make a pencil or ball point pen, even building the common musical instruments, but there would be none on board the ship to conserve weight. Everyone would have a digital notebook to store photos and notes they might take along the way. Everyone would be allowed only twenty pounds of personal items. Everyone was wearing a lightweight uniform that would be worn on the colony ship. They could exchange the uniform for a clean one at any time, but everyone only had one set of everything from underwear to shoes. While in the school, their personal items would be in storage on the base. To start they got weekends off where they were allowed to go wherever they wanted and wear whatever they wanted. Everyone had their own tiny room in the school that was identical to what they would have on the ship. The thinking was that everyone needed somewhere private to go when they would be onboard the ship for six months to a year. The students slept in their rooms Sunday night through Thursday night. Friday and Saturday they could leave the base.

The biggest early complaint was the unisex uniform. Karen told them, "We do not intend for the colonists to wear uniforms in the colony. The only reason for this is to keep down weight on the ship on the way there. It is important that weight be saved for the equipment you will need to set up the colony. The raw materials for making new clothing will be available on planet. Initially you will have to set up mini- factories that will be stored in kit form onboard the ship. You will have classes on assembly of these factories. You will have a lot of work to do initially, but after you get the colony set up the seamstresses on the ship will be sewing new clothing. The computers on the ship will have patterns for all the latest clothing styles. We would hope that individualism in clothing gets a new start on planet. We have boot makers in the colony to make new leather boots and shoes from indigenous leather on the planet. The colonists were not selected for their individual wealth which would show in their clothing, but on their skills which we will need in the colony to get the colony set up and built up as quickly as possible. Everyone will know how to handle a firearm and there will be plenty of firearms to go around. Like Switzerland for the last century, armed to the teeth. Every home in Switzerland has automatic rifles and ammunition. Their crime rate is very low."

Other countries saw the videos of the colony ships and saw the training courses underway in the United States. The U.S. Government and the news media broadcast that the United States would share their technology with all the countries of the world. It did not take long and the people of the other countries of the world demanded their governments produce similar efforts to build colony ships and start training colonists.

France, Great Britain, Germany, Switzerland, Japan, Australia, China all started building their own ships. Craig demanded that all ships be alike, be supplied alike, and that students be approved by him. The Europeans had no problem using English as the common language. Many Europeans were already fluent in multiple languages with English already common among them. It was not unusual for a German tourist in France to use English to speak with a Greek hotel manager. Japan and China wanted to keep their own languages. South Korea had no problem using English. Japan gave in quickly. China eventually agreed, but then they started teaching classes in Chinese.

"Mister President, we have a problem in China. They have started teaching their classes in Mandarin instead of English. They have also modified the training material to insert their own political statements. Do you have any suggestions as to how to deal with this?"

"Craig. I will take care of it. I will be sending the Secretary of State there immediately to tell them they have to switch to English with the approved training materials immediately or just not get the crucial technologies."

"I'm good with that Mister President."

"I have another problem. The Middle Eastern countries do not have the technology to build their own ships. They are trying to hire other countries to build their ships for them. When are we going to tell the world that this is not a commercial enterprise, but an evacuation of Earth culture and the deadline for escape?"

"As soon as we tell the public there will be anarchy in the streets. People will go wild. The rich will be trying to buy their way onto the colonies. The middle class will be rioting against the ship construction and the training academies. The poor will just start looting to have as much as they can get before the end. There will be lawyers for everyone trying to make us take just anyone on the ships. And not just here, but around the world. Right now it looks like there will be around 27 ships from all around the world. The United States is on track for twelve ships, Japan for three, Great Britain for three, Germany for three, France for two, the Netherlands, Denmark, Sweden, Norway, and Finland are combining for one ship to be shared. Brazil is building one ship. China is building four ships, and Australia is building one ship. That is forty thousand colonists for two whole habitable planets."

"I am concerned that more ships are not being built, but if we tell them why it is so critical, the word will get out to the people. There will be no ships from Africa or the Middle East. Only Turkey and South Africa has a manufacturing capability. It may work out for the best in that most of the Middle East and Africa would try to put their leader plus a harem on board along with security forces which would be counterproductive to developing new colonies. We need skilled colonists, not politicians and unskilled women and armed security forces."

"I personally agree for now, but I will consult with the cabinet. I will get word to you about the SECSTATES visit to China."

"SHIP, can you keep watch on all the students from all the countries?"

"Only if I am orbiting Earth. I have been stationary over the United States in case one of your family needs rescue. I can only teleport in light of sight. I can see about one third of the world from high station, but the other two thirds are hidden. Also, I can see over mountains from high station, but when you get to South America, mountains block much of my view."

"We need to have another family meeting. I think we need to consider our time on Earth and may need to come back here and let you orbit to spy."

"I could maybe set a time each day to go into orbit for a few hours to search their computers and spy on the individuals. I presume you are concerned mostly about China."

"Yes. Please figure out what you would need from the family to allow your orbits."

That evening the family met. Craig said, "We need to spy on the Chinese colony. Karen, what have you seen on their training?"

"I don't think they are using our training materials. They are all the right ages, they speak English well, but I got the impression they are either not learning or at least not learning our material. I did see some training manuals they tried to hide from me that were written in Mandarin."

"Okay, that confirms it as far as I'm concerned. Here is what I propose. From now on when anyone goes to the secure facilities at NASA or the U.S. training facilities you will stay there all day during the day. That would be you Karen."

"But Craig, I have to rotate between the various overseas training facilities."

"I know, hang on. No going out to lunch or shopping. Anyone that wants to go with Dawn or Karen follows the same rules. If you need to go somewhere else it will have to be scheduled with SHIP to make sure SHIP is in a position to teleport you immediately in case of trouble. SHIP is going to be spending time in orbit around the Earth every day except when we are scheduled to go somewhere in particular and then we have to stay put until SHIP comes back. Anyone not scheduled in advance will stay on SHIP. I will be spending some time on SHIP to monitor the intelligence in real time. Specifically, we are going to look very closely at China and Japan. We need to verify all the countries, but China is breaking the rules already. I'm not sure it is just language."

Shelby said, "What about my work with the universities?"

"It will either have to go on hold or you will have to stay at a training base or NASA."

"What about my work at the University of Oklahoma?"

"I think they can probably get by without you some of the time. Oh, okay, don't say it, you're right. I just don't think of the university engineering department as a danger place."

"Look at it this way. The SHIP is going to take a closer look at some of the involved countries. We do what we have to take care of the problem. Keep in mind that we could be targets for kidnapping and ransom, or even assassination. As far as being away for a few days, we need to take another exploratory voyage soon. See if we can find another planet or study the two we have more. Not sure which first."

After everyone was delivered to either NASA or the training bases that left Jill, Sandy, and Craig on SHIP and they were over China. SHIP uploaded all Chinese records on the trainees, not just what was submitted initially. The computer records were traced back to birth. Over eighty percent had records of service with the Chinese military. The other twenty percent were tied to important Chinese officials. Apparently much of their applications had been faked.

Since SHIP was staying over China, Craig teleported to the office of the Chinese Prime Minister. SHIP did the translation of English to Mandarin and Craig was able to speak Mandarin while thinking in English and could understand Mandarin as if it were English because SHIP did the translations on the fly. Craig would realize he was speaking his thoughts in Mandarin, and hearing Mandarin, but the instantaneous translation was seamless and without thought about what he was doing.

"Mister Prime Minister."

"What are you doing here? How did you get in here?"

"I am the leader of the mission to space. I came here directly from my ship bypassing all your guards." "What are you doing here?"

"I came here to tell you that China will not be going to space unless you take over the situation and make some radical changes."

"Please tell me what you are saying?"

"I'm saying that your colonists do not meet the requirements for the colonies. They are past military or related to important political figures in China. They do not have the skills that we demanded of the colonists and we have no need of military."

"I am unaware of your claims about our hand-picked colonists, but what business is it of yours and what would you do about it if I just told you to leave?"

"First of all we are attempting to establish colonies in space light years from Earth. We have found two planned planets and we are attempting to establish colonies that will be independent of Earth and its politics. We need certain skills for these colonies and I demand that the only ones going to these planets will meet our requirements. What could I do? I can make sure your ships never leave Earth. We will be withholding the faster than light drives from your ships until I personally am satisfied that you are meeting the requirements we set out. The infraction so far will already result in an inspection team inspecting everything you put on your colony ships to make sure you are not bringing military equipment."

"I do not know what you are talking about. We will meet your requirements. I'll look into the issues myself. Now please leave."

Craig did not walk out the door he disappeared.

The day was gone and it was time to go back to the United States and pick up those family members at NASA and the training bases.

The next day Craig was summoned by the President.

"Craig. I don't know what you did, but the Chinese Prime Minister called on the red phone to complain that you threatened him."

"Not him personally. I threatened to stop their colony ships." "Why?"

"Because they have staffed their colony training with military members and people with political connections."

"Why would they do that?"

"I am concerned that China is planning to send military units to the new colonies to take over when our ships get there. This would eliminate democracy in the colonies and put the colonists in danger, not to mention possibly destroy the colonies themselves. The colonies will require cooperation between everyone in the colony. Everyone will have a job. Three thousand Chinese military would do nothing except possibly kill critical people and as a minimum be an instant drag on the colonies to support them."

"I see your point, but how can we decide that China will cease to exist in a little over a year."

"First of all, our colonists are made up, as close as possible, to match the racial make up of the United States citizenry which includes Chinese. Saving a culture is not what this is about. It is about saving humanity from extinction. There is no need for military in space. There is every reason to make sure that we have the right people to make a new society where everyone is equal from the highly educated to the craftsman. Everyone will be important."

"How do you propose to prevent them from continuing and launching their military into space?"

"By withholding the FaTL drive. If their crews do not meet the standards their ships stay on Earth."

"I'm not sure we can do that. The Chinese are threatening military action to take the FaTL drive. As a minimum they may steal the technology. After all we have plans to deploy the faster than light drives around the world. The ships are designed to easily install it. They may just steal one."

"Okay, but I plan on continuing the surveillance of their colonists. I will insist on inspecting their ships prior to departure to make sure they are not taking military equipment."

"We can just have a ship of military too. We have more ships than they do. Because we started sooner we have ten ships for their three. We could put military on three of ours and still have seven ships of just colonists."

"Mister President, don't do that. We do not want to carry our wars into space. This is the one time chance to have a peaceful world. I'll come up with another solution for the Chinese and anyone else that breaks the rules. We have not explored Pyramid. Maybe there is a natural barrier there we can use to separate the Chinese from the rest of the colonists. Maybe we can find another planet to send them to."

"But that would make them mad and they could start a war here."

"They would not know they were going elsewhere until they landed. When the colonists land on their new planet, Earth will not be habitable. If there are any Chinese survivors on Earth in a bunker somewhere it won't be long before they starve out."

"Okay. Look into that solution. I do not want to start a war before the end of the world and I think the Chinese will get their FaTL drive anyway."

The colonists were being trained in survival techniques, assembling their kits for vehicles, sewing machines, farming equipment, pipe making equipment for plumbing and for the oil pipeline to the oil refinery and the chemical plants. Most of the design work was taking place at NASA except for the work related to the oil fields and refineries. Houston was now rich in university professors and experts from industry. The University of Oklahoma and its town of Norman, Oklahoma were overrun with petroleum experts from drilling to refining. The impervium meant that the pipelines would be extremely strong. A two thousand pound bomb hitting the pipeline from twenty thousand feet would not damage the pipe once it was laid. The only thing that could cause a problem would be a major earthquake where the planet split apart by more than five feet. Even the impervium could be damaged by Mother Nature. Therefore, the pipeline would have automatic cut off valves to stop the flow if a section were to somehow break during a cataclysmic event like an earthquake. There would be a spill, but they would be pumping off lakes of oil recovering clean land before they had enough wells to supply the pipeline. The biggest problem was that it would take a couple of years to build the pipeline. Everything would be dependent upon the nuclear reactors onboard the ships. Everything would have to be electric. Their electric trucks would only have a maximum range of five hundred miles on battery and still carry a payload. The new batteries still took time to charge.

Without petroleum, they had no way to charge the batteries except for the nuclear reactors on the ships. That meant one colony ship would need to land within two hundred miles of the oil regions and be dedicated largely to making and laying pipe, setting up the refinery and chemical plant. Before anything else they would have to set up a metal making plant to manufacture pipe. Because that ship would not have all the skills, they would have to set up other colonies within two hundred miles of each other: two hundred miles there and two hundred miles home leaving only one hundred miles reserve battery power."

One of the scientists said, "Why not just lay out power transmission lines to carry the electricity any distance from the ships necessary for that electric power. You could set up charging stations along the way to anywhere?"

Dawn answered, "Because the impervium is such that it blocks all energy it makes a phenomenal insulator. You would have to have copper or aluminum power lines and a lumber industry set up to use trees for power poles. The ships cannot carry that much weight of wire to be used for power transmission except for very short distances. Until we have a mining and metal refining industry just for copper, we cannot manufacture the wiring. We will have to build the colonies right beside the ships after they land so that the power lines can be as short as possible."

"The impervium is incredibly light weight, but we first need to mine the raw material to be able to manufacture the impervium to make pipe to supply petroleum to free us from the reactors which will eventually run out of power."

Another scientist said, "What about hydroelectric power?"

"Of course, eventually, but that would mean more copper wiring or building the colonies next to a river which would mean landing the ships only near a river. Petroleum is the life blood for the foreseeable future. Yes, it would be nice to be pollution free, but we don't even know the environmental impacts of damning up the rivers to generate electricity. In addition to running vehicles with petroleum we can transport it. You can't load up a truck with electricity. In addition, petroleum will be used for plastics, rayon, nylon clothing, lubrication, fertilizer, and so on. Even if we didn't need petroleum for heating and transportation, we would still need petroleum. If nothing else, to make new clothing. The colonists will be wearing uniforms during the voyage and will be desperate for new clothing as quickly as we can set things up. It will take time to grow cotton crops. We did not find sheep in either place for wool. The only alternative is to dress everyone with leather skins from the animals they will hunt when they first arrive. Anyone say caveman? This and their well worn uniforms will be their only clothing until we can get cotton, wool, or petroleum based fabric."

The scientist replied, "Okay. Now I understand. It's just that I was hoping to have a pollution free planet somewhere."

"We'll be trying to do just that. Because of the impervium, their internal combustion engines will be able to run on extremely high compression. Diesel fuel requires less refining and is basically the same as heating oil, we will have clean diesel. Running at extreme compression should burn more of the fuel to reduce pollution, but we will not have catalytic converters or urine injection to cut the pollution so we will have to rely on extreme compression. The other advantage is that diesel engines produce more power for less fuel. The personal transports, even motorcycles will use turbocharged diesel."

"How about we develop plans for more pollution control when the colonies are well established?"

"That would be great. We can include that in the training courses, not the details, because I want to give you the maximum time right up until launch, but we will make sure that it is part of the long term plan for them to study during the voyage. We will be continuing classes by computer throughout the voyage. When they arrive on planet they will not have Hollywood producing new movies and television shows, only reruns from the data banks. Most of the books in the English language will be included in the databanks. Everyone will have data books that they will be able to access the ships computers anywhere near a ship and they can store additional information in the data books for when they are away from the ships. The training will be available to any and all. When you get tired of watching reruns, the colonists will hopefully be ready for additional training. Because we are selecting the crème de la cream of society they should all be conducive to wanting to learn as much as they can."

"Okay, that's a plan. I will act as the funnel for all new anti-pollution ideas from industry and universities. I'm sure that we can get graduate students to input the information into the databanks."

So, the plan was to land a ship loaded with as much petroleum and industry material and a minimum of other payload, then land other ships within two hundred miles of the first. This would require the SHIP and family to actually pinpoint landing and spots for colonies. Fresh water streams with hills high enough to prevent flooding would be critical. They had observed that most of the rivers had a supply of trees near the river that would provide building materials. They would have to look for the Pangaea buffalo nearby for meat and skins for leather for boots and clothing.

One major thing turned out to be easier than expected. The test ships that were sent to space worked great. They never made it to light speed, but they took off from a runway at Area 51 and both made it to escape speed from Earth before running out of fuel. From those tests it was determined that a fully loaded ship could take off from a long runway and fly into space. Each colony ship would require the equivalent of twenty minuteman missiles for thrust, but the extreme light weight of the impervium for the ships, internal equipment, and equipment kits plus the extreme aerodynamics of the ships made it possible to lift this entire weight off the runway and directly into space. Once they achieved escape speed, the nuclear reactor would come online to start the particle accelerators to provide unlimited thrust. The higher the speed the faster the ships would scoop up dark energy and antimatter to accelerate using the nuclear reactors and superconductive magnets to provide increasing thrust. Once the ships got to the midway point it would quit accelerating, and while still traveling at multiple speeds of light, go to zero gee and turn around to use that thrust for deceleration for the second half of the trip. This meant that scoops would also have to reverse the direction of collection of antimatter and dark energy. This would require more dedicated nuclear power. SHIP said this would all work, but of course it had never been tried in humanities lifetime. It was an old Martian design.

Craig said, "So do we have a colony ship we could send out first to see if it works as advertised?"

awn said, "SHIP has never been wrong and we have built everything to SHIP's designs."

Estera said, "I agree that it would be nice to test a real ship with a real crew and cargo, but we don't have time. We are down to months from the escape date. The test ship would barely reach FaTL speed before that date."

Karen said, "I have been working with a lot of university professors in the classes around the world. Academia has already spotted the moon sized object and is calculating its course through the solar system. When are we going to announce the end of the world?"

Dawn said, "NASA has already calculated that this object may strike the Earth and some key people are already asking if this is the real reason for this huge effort to get into space."

"Slow down girls, I have listened to everyone and I agree with everyone. This is what I think we have to do. We have to tell the President to give a speech to the American people which will be monitored around the world. At that point the cat will be out of the bag. Within hours everyone in the modern world will know about the object approaching. I suggest that the President admit this is why we have invested this effort in spaceships."

"To prevent panic, he will announce that we do not know if this object will be a hazard, but we have the spaceships, just in case. He will announce that the modern countries around the world with the capability to build ships have all built ships to evacuate many people, just in case. There is no reason for everyone to panic, chances are that the moon will miss Earth and all can return to normal. However, since we have the ships we will just push up the launch, just in case."

"Hopefully this will make the situation open, but will not put people into a doomsday mode. We cannot keep the object secret any longer. News of this large object aimed at Earth will get out to the public. We might as well get it out there how we want the information we get out there. We want to make it appear that we have gone through all this in order to explore other planets and it is just coincidental there is an object headed our way."

"Karen, you will have to select your colonists and boot everyone else. Keep a few reserves. Once you make the selections, we will seal the bases and keep all colonists locked up on the bases until the launch date. We don't want anyone to introduce any disease on the ships or on the new planets. Anyone catching a cold will have to be replaced before launch. I'm sure the students have noticed the overwhelming number of female students, but now it is time to announce that there will be six females for every male selected.

We will have an overwhelming military presents to prevent bloodshed, but we will probably have to force the rejections from the base. Expect some of the female students to decide they do not want to be a colonist with the sharing of the males. I would not expect the males to have a problem with it, but women are the ones that want stability of a normal marriage. Many of the students probably figured that they might never see Earth again, but now you are confirming it."

Karen chimed in, "I think I should inform all the students of the mix of female and male and the fact that Earth will be destroyed before I make the final selections. I can then eliminate a few students a day rather than all at once. This will also allow some thinking time for the students. Some of the women might not want to belong to a colony with six women to man, but if they know the truth of Earth's future, that may be the deciding point. Given the choice of extinction or polygamy, most will go with polygamy."

"How does everyone feel about Karen's idea?" Craig asked.

Jill said, "But as soon as you release the first student that student will run straight to the media with the truth."

Estera said, "So, who will they believe the official Presidential announcement or a disgruntled student who was eliminated for an unknown reason."

Craig said, "Let's have a family vote. I vote that we follow Karen's recommendation?" Karen's idea passed.

There were recriminations from all quarters about why the disaster was not told to the world years earlier. Countries could have been mobilized to build more ships. The President countered with five times as many ships would still only save less than one one hundredth of the population of Earth. The backward countries of the Middle East and Africa and the old Soviet Union were demanding that they be given ships they could not have built on their own. The rich of the world were trying to buy their way onto the ships.

The President denied his prior knowledge and reiterated that the space object had only recently been discovered and it was just a lucky coincidence that the modern countries had committed major resources to building ships that could facilitate at least some survival, IF there was a threat to Earth. The IF was played up with special false releases from NASA.

College professors backed it up with "There could have been no knowledge of the object prior to its sighting only weeks before. Its course toward Earth could not have been predicted until they had time to observe it."

The media presented pros and cons to whether it would strike Earth, but the consensus was that it would most likely miss Earth. It was pointed out by the media that the comet Shoemaker Levy in 1994 was aimed at Earth but was captured by the gravity of Jupiter that could happen again. In fact, it had happened again in 2009 when the Wesley Impact had occurred on Jupiter. We never saw the comet coming but Wesley had discovered a spot on Jupiter the size of the Pacific Ocean that was apparently created by a comet strike. No one had seen the comet coming, but Wesley, an amateur astronomer with a fourteen inch reflecting telescope found the impact area. This was confirmed by other astronomers.

This left hope that this object would also hit Jupiter or simply miss Earth, go around the sun and return to outer space. Most people were oblivious to the danger. For the last thirty years scientists had claimed that you were more likely to die from an asteroid than lightning. Most people just continued watching their sitcoms and listening to music. There were no riots. The arguments against a serious problem were such that some members of the family were dubious about the end of Earth. The President even accosted Craig about the possibility that all this was for nothing.

"Mister President, I have known about the object for over four years. I have technology that spotted it over two years ago. Now that we are only weeks from impact, the rest of Earth has found it. Historically this same object hit Mars and created the Rift Valley on Mars which blew away their atmosphere."

"How would you know this? I know you have come up with scientific revelations far ahead of your time, but how can you know about what happened on Mars."

"I was on Mars over four years ago. I found an underground bunker under the polar cap that gave me a history of Mars. You will probably think I am crazy, but Martians came here years ago and created Atlantis which has been part of our mysteries since Plato's time."

"I have heard about your space travels before and know you have technology that was unimagined before you came along. How do you travel in space? How do you teleport?"

"I have a ship left behind by Atlantis when they evacuated from space. They left this ship behind to teach Earth survivors about space travel. For thousands of years this ship has been injecting science into our ancient culture. I am the last in a long line of people selected by this ship to inject this knowledge. Some of my predecessors knew things in science that could not be produced on Earth because our technology was just not there. Others got rich from a few simple inventions or other scientific breakthroughs. I was the last chosen by this ship and we were about out of time. The colonization of space by a few is the last chance to save Earth culture. I do not know what happened to the Martians after they left Atlantis."

"You are leaving me with the impression that you are nuts if you had not done all you have done in the past four years. I just hope these spaceships will actually work. If one crashes on takeoff, my career is over."

"I'm sorry, Mister President, your career is over in a few weeks when the object hits Earth. You will be a hero in the colonies as the far sighted leader that saved our civilization."

"I am getting pressure to use our nuclear warheads to try to divert this object or blow it to pieces to minimize damage."

"Won't work, but let the ships get away before you try. You might blow off a few chunks that might get in our pre-planned course out of the solar system."

"We will have to wait until the object gets closer, so you should be long gone."

There were rich people and countries that had lawsuits being worked through the courts, but they would never go to court before Earth was destroyed.

18

SECOND EXPLORATION

This trip was far overdue. They did not know enough about either of the planets. The early presumption was that both planets would support colonies. Pyramid had not been explored for natural resources. It seemed to be populated with animals from a much earlier Earth. It had some structures for immediate habitation. It had the pyramid to provide additional information, but they had felt the need to get back to Earth. Pangaea had everything needed. The only thing they would do on Pangaea would be to survey possible locations for ship landings.

The other thing for this mission was to survey the proposed courses to the planets to make sure that the exhaust from the colony ships would not cause something to get knocked out of its orbit and that the ships would not collide with anything large on the way. While taking those courses calculated by Dawn, they would keep an eye out for a third or fourth planet to send colony ships to. If they found one or more planets they would do a quick survey and on the way home Dawn would work with SHIP to calculate courses for those new planets.

They were still concerned about China and had not come up with anything to stop the Chinese short of shooting down their ships. They did not want to kill people, even military members from China. If they could isolate them from the other colonists they could sink or swim on their own. If their colonists did not have the skills called for by the family, then they would not survive as a colony, but it would be on their own heads.

SHIP slowed and announced, "I've found another earthlike planet. I needed to slow and get closer to find out more about it. From distance I detect temperature levels and atmosphere similar to Earth. When I get closer we can better assess it."

They did get closer. SHIP announced, "It's atmosphere is like Earth's except much thicker, more concentrated. It is much larger than Earth. It has water and plant life, but it has a gravity of twice that of Earth. I do not believe humans could live here."

"I agree. Let's get back on course for Pangaea." Craig told SHIP.

A few hours later SHIP announced, "I have found another potential planet. It has an earthlike atmosphere except there it seems to have somewhat more clouds. It is not far off our course. Should I detour to it to take a look?"

"By all means. Craig woke up those of the family that were sleeping."

SHIP gave a running commentary as they got closer to the planet, "It appears to be eight tens of Earth gravity, the atmosphere is breathable, but has more rare gases and some additional sulfur. Not enough sulfur to harm humans, but may be indicative of volcanic activity."

What they found was an Earth sized planet, but with slightly less gravity. That would be good for humans used to a gravity of one Earth gravity. They could jump higher and run faster. However, after a few years their strength would be less than humans on Earth. People would probably grow a little taller without as much gravity. As they orbited they found a number of active volcanoes, lush jungles and sweeping plains. There were inland freshwater seas and salt water oceans with three distinct continents. Karen was sent down first as their survivalist. Unlike their first voyage, SHIP could send her down fully equipped. Craig followed with his guns and equipment.

Shelby tested the inland sea they landed near and declared it fresh and clean with no dangerous chemicals. Estera took samples of the vegetation which included trees and grasses. They saw nothing dangerous. They teleported back to SHIP and then came back down near one of the oceans. Shelby declared the ocean water to be similar to Earth's. Estera took more samples which were sent to SHIP. While traveling to the ocean, SHIP detected some potential ore deposits so they came back to that point next.

This time Karen, Craig, and Jill teleported. Jill found coal, iron, magnesium, and most of the critical metals for manufacturing. The coal seemed to be a very large vein that would provide for heating and smelting of the metals. Coal could be converted to fuel for operation of their diesel vehicles. If there was enough coal on the planet they could use the coal to do most of what oil would be used for on Pangaea.

Jill said, "If there is coal, there is probably oil too. In any event we have old technology to convert coal to diesel fuel. We can also make clothing from synthetic fabric made from coal."

Karen fired her rifle multiple times before Craig could even look in her direction. Again, they were in a depression such that there was an entrance at both ends with little to worry about. Craig was watching one direction and Karen the other.

Craig had SHIP teleport Jill to the SHIP and then ran to Karen to see what she had fired at.

"I think it was a small dinosaur. Big enough to eat a person, but small enough to kill with my rifle. I probably wasted a lot of ammo. I think my first shot was through the eye there. I was kind of scared to see a dinosaur and just kept firing until it hit the ground."

Craig had SHIP teleport Sandy down. Karen and Craig kept watch while Sandy inspected. "I would say this is definitely a dinosaur, but nothing like I could identify. Of course, no one has seen a dinosaur so we only have artists' rendering."

Sandy sent samples to SHIP for analysis and all three of them teleported back to SHIP with Karen going last. Craig no longer needed to be first or last since SHIP had learned to teleport them one at a time fully equipped. SHIP naturally considered Craig most important as SHIP's captain. The whole family took nearby areas and had SHIP scan for other animals in the area that they could zoom in on from orbit.

SHIP declared that the dinosaur meat should taste like chicken. In fact, SHIP had documentation that, indeed, some dinosaurs were ancient relatives of birds with hollow bones, etc.

There were active volcanoes on all of the continents and a number of volcanic islands scattered throughout the oceans. They spent twenty-four Earth hours there and named the planet Vulcan of Star Trek fame. It was habitable, though not comfortable. They would set the Chinese ships down near the ore deposits they found. It was two hundred miles from the nearest active volcano, it had trees nearby that appeared to be like the trees in Brazil. There were coconut trees, Acacia trees, and many others. They were like the trees on Pangaea: similar, but different. They would make building materials, they could burn either coal or wood immediately for heat.

They had found a number of dinosaur like animals, but they were mostly much smaller than the one Karen had shot. They could serve as meat for the colony. If the colony ship was stocked as Karen told them, they would have the eggs and sperm to have test tube cattle, sheep, and pigs from Earth. They should have chain saws, factory kits, and so on to build their own colony. With four thousand Chinese colonists, they should survive.

Because the Chinese refused to use Karen's and SHIP's training material, they would never know what they were missing. They would just not see any sign of the colonists from the rest of Earth. SHIP would visit them in the near future to see how they were doing.

SHIP continued on to Pangaea without finding another earthlike planet. They found thousands of planets on the way, but they were either too hot, too cold, did not have a detectable atmosphere within the sensor distance from their course. SHIP did not slow until they arrived back at Pangaea.

They only spent two days and found what appeared to be excellent locations for colony ships. As planned, they found an area not too far from the oil fields that was protected by a range of large hills that some might call small mountains. There were plenty of trees to indicate that the high winds did not hit in the area. Then they spread out the other landing spots leading to the canyon where they found the ore deposits. There were a number of small lakes and rivers and Pangaea buffalo. The cats could threaten the people, but could easily be killed with a rifle. Eventually, the lions should learn to leave them alone. Each colony would have its own village and be connected by radio and soon roads for trade between the villages. At one end of the chain was the oil fields and the other end were the ore deposits. They decided that those ships would have specialized cargo to fit their locations. They would have back up oil rigs and ore mining equipment on other ships, just in case something happened. The colonists on those ships would be apportioned more than their share of skills for oil or metal smelting. The colonists in between would have the most clothing capability, farming capability, etc.

They went on to Pyramid. They entered the pyramid in the town as soon as they arrived, but this time SHIP sent down the bracing for the door early. Craig did not trust the pyramid not to lock them all inside and it took six women and one man to operate the consoles in the pyramid.

Craig told the group, "I'll bet the pyramid can tell us where to find minerals and oil and maybe coal deposits that the colonists can use. Then we can go out to verify."

Since SHIP knew the way to Pyramid it took less than a day to get there leaving them days to study the planet.

The braces for the door were manufactured by SHIP and sent there before anyone was teleported. Each of them were teleported one at a time to stand near the pyramid. They pressed the seven keys to open the door, set up the bracing and went in. They went around the various consoles, pressed the corresponding seven buttons and soon came across maps to and estimates of metal deposits. They found that some of these deposits already had short mine shafts made of stone already prepared for a colony. They found another console that gave them hazards on the planet. Coal was listed as flammable, polluting, and dirty to handle. Oil was in some areas of the planet. The pyramid warned them not to try to build in the area because of the pressure of the gas and oil in those areas. That was great news to the family. They found another console that told them where to build transmission towers to transmit electricity around the planet. That was not very helpful as it presumed that the colonists would have the capability to generate unlimited electricity and had conquered the method of transmitting it from tower to tower. Tesla had attempted this feat way too early on Earth and failed miserably forever marking him as a nutcase. In fact, if he had succeeded there would not have been a need for all the power lines transmitting electricity around the world. Atlantis had this capability before Atlantis was destroyed. Another warning was about hot thermal areas with hot mineral waters fed by volcanic activity. They were to keep colonists from building near there. Looking at the map they could see the prearranged mines were not far from the city, but the oil fields were well over two hundred miles. The mines and the oil fields seemed to be connected to the city with roads. They had not seen the roads because they were covered in vegetation. They would have to check the roads out for condition and see how deep the oil was. They watched more videos of the natural animals on the planet. It was explained that all predatory animals had been eradicated. This created a problem in that they had seen mice out in the daylight with no fear of humans. There was no way to find out how many mice there might be. Would they decimate grain storage? Would they carry disease like they do on Earth.

Sandy said, "How about including a few house-cats on the colony ships just in case we have some mice that sneak on board a colony ship. They don't need walked. We can clean and recycle kitty litter. They can eat scraps."

Dawn said, "How about a few dogs?"

Sandy came back, "Okay, lets take along a few test tube dogs and cats."

Craig said, "I think the mice are here because they were on the ships from the Martians that set this place up. With no predators they were able to breed like mice. We could maybe have a very few female cats onboard the ship, but we will use semen to breed them on planet. Maybe they can hunt any mice that get on our colony ships. I would suggest that we take the capability to breed some rat terriers for larger mice that cats might be afraid of. I read where Teddy Roosevelt turned loose forty rat terriers in the White House and within twenty-four hours they found over ten thousand dead rats and some tired dogs. Then we should take some hunting dogs to help stalk game on each planet. Not the dogs themselves, just the eggs and semen to create them upon landing. And only a few cats on board that have to be kept skinny and hungry to do their job. We don't need some overweight lap cats."

They slept on SHIP and the next day teleported down with their drilling equipment to the oil fields. There were no pools of oil on the surface like on Pangaea, but Jill thought the land looked good. They set up the drill with its concrete footings and started drilling. Their tiny drill was fast and worked without lubricating oil mud. They went down one thousand feet the first day without hitting anything. Jill said not to worry, some wells in the United States went to twelve thousand feet.

Craig said, "We will not have the drilling pipe for twelve thousand feet. SHIP can make anything, but the quantity is limited because SHIP uses part of its own mass for anything we want. The drilling here is also slower because of the heat of the rock we are drilling through. The metal can take it, but if we heat up the rock we are drilling through too much we might ignite any gas or oil we find and have a huge blowtorch on our hands. I am setting three hundred degrees as the maximum drill head temperature."

The next day they hit four thousand feet and felt a deep rumble under their feet. They quickly pulled up the pipe and had SHIP use its particle beam to close off the hole.

Jill said, "Okay. I guess we found oil. If the pyramid was correct there is a thousand year supply under here. There are also coal deposits and hot springs, so somehow we should have energy for a colony. The only concern is the mice and probably rats. We probably ought to include extra antibiotics on the colony ships to here and maybe an extra doctor just in case there are rat born disease that SHIP has not detected. I suggest we survey more of the planet. We have only really looked at the area around the pyramid and what the pyramid told us to look at. We don't know if the Martians intended this to be a permanent home or a stop over."

"I agree." Craig replied. "Any objections about surveying more of the planet?"

Everyone agreed, they closed the pyramid again. The bracing for the door once again became part of SHIP. SHIP had restored its mass while waiting for the oil drilling project for most of two days.

As the orbited, they found that Pyramid was largely an ocean world. The continents, if they could be called that were really huge islands, ten all together. The island with the pyramid was the largest and smaller than Australia. One continent appeared to be mainly under ice at the pole and not habitable. There was another that be would the size of England and Scotland combined that was nearer the opposite pole and probably on the cool side. It had different trees that appeared to be pine trees. It had other animals besides earth type animals living there.

Karen went first, as usual, dressed in a form fitting warm ski suit, not as usual. Craig came next wearing a parka, then Estera, and Sandy to evaluate the trees and animal life. The trees appeared to be sequoia trees or giant redwoods. They were soft wood without a lot of strength, but still good building material. It would burn fast in a fireplace. There were animals that appeared to be bears like on Earth, but the size of Kodiak or Polar bears and were colored with greenish fur.

Sandy said, "Those bears look like predators to me. Their green color may be like moss from the dampness here. I thought the pyramid said they eradicated all predators."

Karen said, "Apparently they only did that on the chosen continent. I agree they look like predators but they are keeping their distance. They are curious about us, but not afraid of us. They are following us, but I think we are the only other large animals on this continent so they are cautious. They don't know whether to run or eat us."

Craig said, "Keep an eye in all directions. I thought I saw something behind us in the trees. Maybe they are smart enough to surround us."

"That's not comforting. I think we should send Estera and Sandy back to the SHIP. Then, Craig, if they don't close in on the two of us, you go back up to SHIP and see what they do with just one of us. If they close in I will try to scare them off. If not, SHIP can teleport me back. No, don't argue. I am able to take care of myself and if you are already on the SHIP then SHIP can concentrate on saving me if necessary."

The bears, if that is what they were, were confused with their prey disappearing one at a time. When Craig was also gone, they seemed to regroup. Karen had on her two way communicator and SHIP was tracking the infrared images of all the living creatures around Karen.

Craig warned, "Karen, they are gradually closing the circle. I think we need to teleport you out of there just to play it safe."

Karen swiveled shooting three bears between the eyes in each of three different directions. The fourth direction had bears running away. Karen said, "Maybe that will teach them to stay away from humans. They seemed to be highly intelligent. Maybe they will pass the word."

Craig teleported back and covered Karen while she took samples and sent them back to SHIP for analysis. It wasn't that they didn't trust SHIP to teleport her back quickly, but SHIP was a machine and might be too logical.

They then orbited over a continent near the equator and found that it was a tropical jungle about he size of Texas surrounded on all sides by a black sand beach and had a twenty thousand foot active volcano. It had a small lava flow going to the sea on one side. It was like a big Hawaiian island. Karen and then Craig teleported to a deep stretch of black sand beach on the opposite side of the continent from the lava flow. They observed the trees lining the beach with binoculars. They could see a multitude of colorful birds. They were too far away to see if they looked like Earth birds, but their colors were magnificent with blues, reds, oranges, purples, like the rainbow. They saw tropical plants under the trees moving, but it was not the wind. The halved the distance to the tree line and stopped to study the forest ahead again through binoculars. They could now see the birds clearly through the binoculars and were amazed at how vivid the colors were. They could also see brightly colored flowers in the tree tops so these were flowering trees.

Jill was linked in so that she could see through their binoculars and talk and listen through their communicators. Volume was automatic so a whisper came through to SHIP almost as loud as a shout. "The birds have such bright colors so they can blend with the flowers. That would indicate that there are predators that the birds have been hiding from for a thousand years."

Just as they were about to move forward again, an animal like a wild hog with tusks came racing out the tree line being chased by a ... dog cat. Karen asked, "Do you want some more samples? I can take them down quickly."

"Yes."

Before the "s" in Yes was completed Karen's rifle sounded and both animals dropped dead about half-way to their position. Sandy was teleported down to look at the animals, make an assessment and send samples back to SHIP. Karen and Craig did not look too closely as their job was to guard Sandy while she did the studying.

Sandy gave them a running commentary, "I am most interested in the predator. It has very little hair. It has the head and teeth of a wolf, the front legs have huge claws made for digging, but the back legs look more like a Pangaea Lion. It looks like an animal put together by a mad scientist. We need some serious DNA analysis on this animal. It would appear that maybe the large wolf type mouth is made for taking down large animals like maybe this pig type animal. The front claws look like an anteater's claws made for digging. The front legs look like a cats made for leaping, maybe to catch low flying birds. The lack of real hair may be because of the heat of this continent. The skin is leathery to provide protection from smaller animals and from getting scratched by underbrush. Of course, this is just rambling. We need to study the animal closer. SHIP, can you send me a container where we could store the whole carcass for study back on Earth?"

"Thanks."

"Craig would you give me a hand here, I would estimate the weight at one hundred fifty pounds. I can't drag it into the teleport container."

"Karen, watch my quarter too. I will have to lay down my rifle to help Sandy."

They decided to go on to the next continent just south of the equator of Pyramid while ship analyzed the carcass of the wolf, cat, anteater, whatever it was.

Sandy said, "I don't think that continent should be visited by the colonist for a few centuries. That animal, whatever it was looked like a nightmare come true."

Karen replied, "I agree. After seeing that creature I would not want to go wandering in that jungle. When we first examined it I thought maybe we had discovered the island of Hawaii. All those beautiful birds. The wild hog would probably not be pleasant to run into, but that creature is best at a distance. While you and Craig were hauling it into the teleportation container, I was very much on edge. I kept seeing movement in the underbrush. I was never sure that I was seeing more of them or not. I would definitely not want to wander into that jungle where you could see no distance and have one of those things sneak up on you."

"When we listened to the pyramid I was under the impression that the Martians had eradicated all predators, but obviously not. Now I am worried about the main continent. Did they miss some there or just eradicate them on that one continent?"

"Craig, do you think either that bear type creature or that wolf cat are roaming around the pyramid."

"We didn't see anything more threatening than cows and pigs in the town. They were not afraid of us so either nothing is threatening them or they just weren't afraid of us because we didn't look like predators."

SHIP reported, "The bear type creature was a form of bear. The wolf, anteater, cat appears to be genetically engineered. I cannot calculate a reason for anyone to build such a creature. I have been observing the next continent. It is more the size of the state you call Arkansas and seems to have similar terrain. One end is mountainous with low mountains and the other half is very flat plains and swamps. The mountains are not tall, but rugged with a lot of exposed stone or covered with a large variety of trees. The continent seems to have heavy rain in that the mountains have many streams and rivers while the other end is plains and swampland. The streams all come together in small rivers that flow into the lowlands and then spread out. There are swamps for a mile or so interspersed with a mile or so of plains. There seem to be cattle type animals on the plains and some sort of large amphibians in the swamps. There are a few large mammals in the mountains and a variety of very small animals like rabbits or rat living over the whole continent. There are some large birds that seem to be like Earth eagles or large hawks flying mainly over the mountains."

"Karen, you go first. Let's take a look at the plains and swamps first. I'll come immediately after you with my rifle, then Sandy for the animals and Estera for the plants."

Karen and Craig took up defensive positions while Estera took samples of the grassland on the plains. Sandy studied the large mammals through binoculars then suggested that the group move toward a small herd about three hundred yards away."

"Okay, but be cautious. I will lead. Keep at least fifty yards behind me in case they decide to stampede us. Craig, you keep watch on our rear and remember what happened on Pangaea when we were walking through tall grass. I think Dawn should come down fully armed too, and how about sending down a rifle for Estera and Sandy. These appear to be cattle, but if they were to decide to stampede at us, we will need plenty of firepower to shoot as many we can and hopefully divert the rest. I know there are only twenty cattle in that small herd, but they weight eight hundred to twelve hundred pounds and they are wild animals in good condition."

They waited for Dawn to arrive and everyone check their rifles to make sure they were fully loaded with a bullet in the chamber and the safety off. It turned out they were able to just walk up to one of the cows who had dallied away from the herd. It just kept munching the grass. There was one animal that appeared to be the bull of the herd that watched them closely, but they had moved up slowly with no attempt to hide. They did not group together. Jill was the only one that actually walked up to the cow. She inspected it closely, took some hair samples from the tail and slowly walked back to the group that retreated in a spread out formation until they were one hundred yards from the small herd.

Sandy said, "I took a hair sample, but for all intents and purposes I think SHIP will find that genetically it would make a good meat source. It looks more like an Earth cow than those wandering around the pyramid. Let's take a walk over to the swampland and get an idea of what it looks like."

When they got there, Estera said, "The trees look like cypress trees. See how the base is very wide and the bark looks relatively soft? Those over there are cattails. The plants here seem to look much like Earth plants, even more so than Pangaea."

"Estera! Back up slowly. There is an alligator or crocodile swimming up toward you."

"Sandy, where?" Karen exclaimed. "I didn't see anything." "There, see those bumps in the water. Those are its eyes." "Okay, Craig, you want an alligator?"

"Not really, but I would like to know what we are dealing with. Is there anyway to get it to come out and see what it looks like on land without getting attacked?

"I don't think so. How about I shoot it and we just fish it out and look?"

"I'd rather not, but go ahead."

They used some cut off limbs to pull it in to the shore and then they all got together and pulled out a six foot fresh water alligator. The cut off some samples for ship to study and then had SHIP teleport Karen and Craig up into the mountains. When it seemed quiet around the clearing Estera and Sandy teleported down to study the flora and fauna.

Karen warned, "Everyone keep an eye out, the trees and brush makes it hard to see what we have here. There, is that a squirrel?"

"It is a squirrel, but different than Earth squirrels. It's bigger than an Earth squirrel and it's marked more like a chipmunk with stripes and it has white paws and spotted tail. Maybe it has developed better camouflage than on Earth."

"I am collecting leaves and small branches for SHIP, but these look like Birch, Elm, Oak, Maple trees and not that different than on Earth. See there are some acorns from the Oak."

Karen called out, "There is a game trail here. How about we take a walk in the woods. I'll take the lead, then Sandy and Estera and Craig cover behind us."

Estera asked about getting lost and Karen replied, "Magnetic north might not be Earth north but I think I can manage to walk on a trail and then return. If we come to a branch in the trail, we will mark our trail. In other words, this is what I have lived for years. Let's walk as quietly as possible and see if we can find any other animals. I'll hold up my hand in a fist if I want everyone to just freeze where they are. It will probably mean I have seen an animal and don't want to disturb it. If I do ask you to freeze, don't worry if you don't see me for a few minutes. I might be trying to get closer. I have a camera with me to take some pictures and my rifle if it turns out to be unfriendly."

About thirty minutes along the trail, Karen held up a fist, then pointed to the side and held up her fist again. The rest took this as the signal to be quiet, that she was going to go off the trail to her left, and for everyone to stay frozen. Craig became extra vigilant not knowing what Karen was doing but now having to watch for threats in three hundred sixty degrees. Karen was out of sight for nine minutes then came back, put her finger to her lips for quiet, but then used her hand to tell them to come to her position. They gathered together and looked where Karen was pointing. There were deer not unlike Earth deer grazing in a small clearing.

"They look like normal deer to me. They don't view us as predators but if there were predators around, they wouldn't be here just grazing. See how the stag is just observing us?"

Sandy replied to Karen, "I think you are correct. Craig, do you suppose that the Martians populated this small continent for colonists?"

"Possibly, but we know there are alligators in the swamp. Maybe they are there to keep down the cattle population. That would mean that there must be predators here to keep down the deer population. Otherwise, after a few thousand years there would no longer be grass for grazing either here or on the plains. This would give colonists a good place to expand to. Maybe we should send a colony ship here?"

Craig disagreed, "No, we need to concentrate our ships to a smaller area to insure survival. It will take awhile for the colonists to be able to travel this far. The helicopter kits we are sending are short range. What boats we are sending are rubber rafts and very small boats for the lakes and rivers, not to sail the ocean blue."

Sandy said, "We have not inspected the oceans anywhere. Do we know that there are monster sharks or sea monsters that would easily sink the small boats we have sent? We checked the rivers and lakes for edible fish, but we did not go fishing in the ocean to see what there was. We only tested the water to see if it was normal seawater."

Dawn asked Craig, "Is there anyway that SHIP could make us a boat or submarine to allow some exploration of the ocean?"

"SHIP heard your question and suggested a small one person submarine that would be fast and highly maneuverable, and supremely strong. It would be able to hover or travel at two hundred knots under water. It would operate much like an aircraft, but under water. It would also be capable of entering the atmosphere from SHIP and returning at the end of the trip. Who is the best qualified to fly a submarine? ... Okay, I can do it myself. I will keep a video commentary going to SHIP so you can all see what I am seeing. SHIP trained me to fly a similar craft years ago. I used one to put down a war and help stop the drug traffic."

Before Craig left in the one man shuttle submarine Jill said, "I did not get a chance to check that earthlike continent for mineral deposits. The orbited over the other continents but decided to save them for the future. They did not see anything exciting.

Craig left SHIP with everyone watching. The reentry into the atmosphere was flashy, but uneventful. The shuttle was like the colony ships, nearly indestructible but even stronger because of its diminutive size. He waited until he was a few miles from shore and gently entered the water with all cameras rolling. He entered off the coast of the continent with the town with the pyramid at the center because that was where the colonists would first go into the ocean. He saw an assortment of fish which he was unfamiliar with, but SHIP gave a running commentary on what the fish resembled on Earth: Cod, Halibut, Tuna. He flew alongside a large whale for awhile. He sped out further to sea and dived down in the deep water off the continent shelf. With lights blazing, there were more fish that only SHIP could compare to Earth fish. Sandy was their Zoology expert, but mostly she had learned those animals found on land and fish that land animals ate, like salmon and fresh water trout. Craig then raced back into shallower water and went slow the last few miles to the coast. Yes, there were sharks of varying sizes up to something larger than Great Whites. He didn't bother them and he was too big for them to mess with. He would assume that they were the same danger as on Earth.

When he returned to SHIP they had a meeting on the ocean trip.

Estera concern, "I saw no jellyfish at all. That means that this place is really different than Earth or that mankind has not spoiled things yet. There is a theory that global warming, pollutants and overfishing causes an increase in jellyfish."

Craig countered, "I don't know too many people that eat jellyfish. At least jellyfish won't take over the oceans if the colonists pollute it."

Dawn admonished Craig, "Don't even say that. We have been trying to teach the colonists to not pollute any more than necessary."

They were only a couple of weeks from the launch and they needed to get home. SHIP took them back to Earth. They could no longer call it home because it would not be there in less than a month. Craig and his girls all visited with their parents and explained as much as they could about the whole situation and what they had been doing to prepare. Craig's parents believed whatever he said because he always told the truth. Estera and Sandy's parents were involved in the mission and knew the facts.

Jill and Dawn's parents took it badly and did not know whether to believe it or not. Dawn's parents did not realize that Dawn would be in a sham marriage shared by five other girls. They had always hoped she would have dedicated and devoted husband that would provide for her and their grandchildren. Now they discovered they would never have grandchildren and Dawn did not have a dedicated husband. It did not matter to them that Dawn was the one that insisted on having a polygamist marriage.

Shelby's parents were upset because they thought she was just going to college and did not have any idea what she had been doing. Of course, they asked if they could go on the colony ships having ignored Shelby's lengthy explanation.

Each of them spent a couple of days at home with their family. When they got back to SHIP they were all somber, but did not have time for sobbing. Now it was time to tell the colonists that they would be the last survivors of Earth and would never again have contact with Earth. The students were given two days off with the warning that if they did not return by the evening of the second day they would be stricken from the colony, replaced by those that did. They were given priority boarding on airlines to see their families one last time with permission to tell anyone that Earth was down to two weeks. The studentws were warned about coming into contact with anyone that had any symptoms of anything. They would be expelled if anyone came down with a simple cold.

The news media suddenly started paying attention to the rumors and started producing news about the space object headed for Earth. The calculations of impact had been available for well over a month, but people didn't know about it because the media had not told them about it. Science professors and engineers knew about the end coming even when they were not working on the space mission.

When the colonists got back to the training bases around the world, the final selection of colonists took place. Those selected were sent by military cargo planes to their colony ships for the final training. Those not selected were kept at the school for a few days, not knowing that they had not been selected. Every day another large group was sent home.

Karen told the family but directed at Craig, "It may seem cruel, but it has eliminated fights and arguments about why they were not selected. We needed to keep this large group because we could not control who would be coming back after finding out about the end of Earth. SHIP was the important factor in selecting the colonists. There were too many for me. Up until then, any of them might have been selected so we really did not know who would be going on. I did make a few decisions myself based upon gut feel based on their participation in the few classes I taught."

"You can't worry about it, Karen. As you said, SHIP made most of the selections based on verification of their skills, their education records, and performance in classes. They will probably never know that their skill at using guns was a major factor. Many colonists assumed this was recreation versus a serious class. Some colonists blew it off as necessary but stupid, as they did not believe in guns and considered the training as immoral. Some were dropped because they enjoyed it too much. Those with previous experience in handling guns tended to win out over others, but that was not your fault and is important when much of their diet will be what they can hunt. Any of the colonists might be faced with a known or unknown predator and need to defend themselves. A thousand member town in a state that is mostly settled into farms and ranches is pretty secure, but when placed out in the middle of wild country who knows what will wander into town."

Training continued for the next week onboard the colony ships. Food was brought in daily so they would no use food they would take on the ship, but was the same food they would be eating for months. The only training was on the particular planet their ship would be going to. The family had decided who would go to what planets.

Despite Craig's warning to the Chinese, they continued training military and political men using Mandarin. Their payload on the colony ships consisted the standard rations, but instead of equipment for a colony they took automatic weapons, grenade launchers, vehicles. It appeared obvious they were planning on taking over whatever planet they went to. The Chinese did not know they were on their way to Vulcan and programmed their computers to erase all other navigational data so they would not be able to find the others.

Country	Destination	Colonists
Australia	Pangaea	1000
Belgium, Netherlands, Denmark	Pangaea	1000
Brazil	Pangaea	1000
China	Vulcan	1000
China	Vulcan	1000
China	Vulcan	1000
China	Vulcan	1000
France	Pangaea	1000
France	Pyramid	1000
Germany	Pangaea	1000
Germany	Pangaea	1000
Germany	Pyramid	1000
Great Britain	Pangaea	1000
Great Britain	Pangaea	1000
Great Britain	Pyramid	1000
ItalySpain	Pyramid	1000
Japan	Pangaea	1000

Japan	Pyramid	1000
Japan	Pyramid	1000
Nordic Countries	Pangaea	1000
Russia	Pangaea	1000
Russia	Pangaea	1000
Russia	Pangaea	1000
Russia	Pyramid	1000
Russia	Pyramid	1000
South Korea	Pyramid	1000
South Korea	Pangaea	1000
Turkey and Greece	Pyramid	1000
USA	Pangaea	1000
USA	Pangaea	1000
USA	Pangaea	1000
USA	Pangaea	1000
USA	Pangaea	1000
USA	Pangaea	1000
USA	Pangaea	1000
USA	Pyramid	1000
USA	Pyramid	1000
USA	Pyramid	1000
USA	Pyramid	1000
USA	Pyramid	1000

That was pathetic to only save forty thousand humans out of seven billion. There should be enough people and skills on each new planet to have new Earths in the future. With twenty-one thousand on Pangaea, fifteen thousand on Pyramid, and four thousand on Vulcan. Pangaea would be all European countries, South Korea if you count the United States. The Canadians had worked as one with the United States in developing the mission and their young were included with those from the United States. The United States and Great Britain were actually a mix of racist based upon the actual makeup of their Earth populations. There was a slight leaning toward Caucasian because they tended to lead their field in their skills or education, but there were still a high percentage of Asian Americans, African Americans, Mexican Americans and whereas Great Britain had no Mexican Americans, they did have some of Arab descent, maybe the last in the universe. France also had a number of Africans and Arabs. The other countries had few not from their countries.

All the Chinese and only the Chinese would be sent to Vulcan to survive if they had brought the right equipment but there was no one else there to conquer and live off.

19

THE JOURNEY

The colony ships took off a week before the arrival of the doomsday moon that destroyed Earth. The liftoff was quite strenuous as Minuteman missiles boosted them into space. Acceleration from the runways was very exciting with the vibrations of the powerful solid fueled rockets quickly accelerated to take off speed then pointed toward the stars. Each ship used ten strapped on missiles for the initial takeoff into space then when their fuel ran out ten more missile engines would ignite. The first hours of the colony were fraught with vibrations and nervousness. There was very limited conversation. Only the pilots would be speaking, reporting to the colonists on their progress in an attempt to relax the colonists. The computers would monitor all the colonists' vitals even though there was not much that could be done during this acceleration period. The commentary was essential the same on each ship and always in English, except for the Chinese ships.

"All colonists confirmed in their acceleration couches. If you are not in your couch report in the next twenty seconds."

"Stand by for launch. Rockets igniting in 10, 8...0" "Take off occurred three seconds after ignition."

"Space achieved 58 seconds after launch. Standby for weightlessness in 10,9,8...0. Standby for secondary boost phase in 10,9,8...0. The computer reports all colonists getting back to normal heart rate. Standby for nuclear thrust in 10,9,8...0. Boost phase over, speed 30,000 mph and building. Everyone can now move around the cabin. Next boost in eight hours."

They were to accelerate for three months using a minimum of 1.2 gees and a maximum of six gees for short periods of time. The colony ships would not accelerate until all one thousand colonists were strapped into their acceleration couches which would lay out flat for beds during the trip. The pilots of the ships had all been trained in astral navigation by Dawn, but the computers did most of the work. They were headed to three different planets: Vulcan, Pangaea, and Pyramid.

SHIP and Craig's family would sometimes fly on ahead of each of the colony ships looking for any change in large objects that could damage the much weaker colony ships or be impacted by their exhaust plumes.

Craig did a simulcast onto the view screens on all of the ships. Everyone in every cabin should see and hear what he had to say after the first big acceleration boost nine hours after launch.

"Welcome to space colonists. My name is Craig Decker and I am the cause of you being here. Most of the science in this mission came from me and my small crew, but then most of you were briefed during your last two weeks on your ship before launch. You know where you are going. My crew has explored both of the two planets in our smaller faster ship and believe that you will be like the first pioneers that settled the West. Your ship is like the Conestoga wagons that went out west during the colonization of the western United States. The difference is that during this trip you will have no contact with the other ships after the first week until you are a week from your new planet because you will be traveling faster than radio beams can travel. Your companions on each ship are not inconsequential. As you know there are one thousand of you on this ship, which is more than any wagon train that settled the west. Your journey is not drastically different in time to the wagon trains. When they went west they did not know where they were going and knew they might not be able to contact their extended families they were leaving behind. You will receive additional training about your new planet during the journey. Those original pioneers did not have entertainment except what they made for themselves. Imagine what it was like when those first colonists came to the Americas from Europe."

"You have access to every book and movie and television show created in English through the view screens in your rooms or your personal touch pads. Your touch pad is much like a smart phone and has every number for everyone on the mission to your planet. However, once the ships reach the speed of light the only communication will be within your own ship. We encourage you to develop your own entertainment There are a few spare touch pads, but take care of your own or there will be no spares when you land at the new planet. Your ship will provide electrical power for years. Keep your equipment charged."

"I expect you to continue your online training. Unfortunately you cannot do any hands on work until you reach the new planets. Much of your training will be on setting up the colonies on the planet you are going to. Naturally, this is what we envision, you may decide to modify this plan after your arrival. We will be visiting you several times during the voyage, but it will be one ship at a time. There were forty ships and we will be doing more exploring during your voyage so we will not be visiting each ship very often. You ask how will we visit when traveling faster than the speed of light?"

"We will fly our small ship next to your ship until our ships are touching and then we will teleport onto your ship to see how things are going. Our small ship is intended for a total of seven people so we cannot bring you any additional supplies, but we might be able to bring advice or a single new example of a new technology. Our teleportation device cannot be duplicated with Earth technology, just take my word that we have one on our small ship. It still only operates at the speed of light so we cannot teleport from one ship to another except directly through the hulls of our ship to your ship and vice versa."

"In a few days, you will be too far from Earth to really see what happens there. Your ship's cameras will use the maximum telephoto and digital enhancement to watch the impact live and then we will send you closer videos that my ship will take. You will still not be at the speed of light, so we can still broadcast, but you will probably be too far to see much. Earth will be not much more than a dot. You will be beyond the orbit of Jupiter and looking back at a very small planet. However, you are flying at a ninety degree angle from the plane of the solar system to avoid the planets and asteroids."

"The one concern I have is that everyone must be in their acceleration couches before periods of maximum thrust. Failure to be in your couch will give you serious injury if you survive impact with furniture or a wall. If the onboard computer detects an empty acceleration couch the acceleration will be delayed, but any acceleration delays will dramatically extend the time required to reach your planet and you could run out of supplies on this ship. I don't want any ships to arrive very late full of people that have starved to death. It is everyone's responsibility to help everyone else to assure success of the whole."

"You will notice that you probably feel lethargic and heavy. It is because if you weight one hundred pounds you are now carrying the equivalent of a twenty pound backpack due to the 1.2 gee acceleration that is constant. After a few weeks, you should build up muscles to counteract the greater weight. After a month or so, we will check on each ship and might increase the constant gee to a higher number to shorten the voyage. Once you get to your planet you will feel lighter than you do now because the gravity is closer to Earth than what you will have during the trip. Questions?"

"Why don't we use more acceleration now? This does not seem bad."

"Because no one has experience with higher gravity over a period of time. It is not the same as just being overweight. Will it impact your internal organs to be twenty percent heavier? Even your heart and intestines are pulling down by twenty percent."

"How will you decide that we can take more acceleration for long periods?"

"We will selectively have random colonists given X-rays to determine that your internal organs have not been displaced and to check everyone's general health."

"What if you find that we are developing problems?"

"Then we will have to extend your voyage time and recalculate everyone's course to make sure you are still going to miss any large objects in space."

"What if someone gets pregnant during the trip?"

"We have birth control for at least two years on each ship. You are admonished to be careful. It would be good to use timing in addition to prescription birth control just to make sure. However, an unplanned pregnancy would not be life threatening. If the baby would be a large ten pound baby it would weight twelve pounds in relation to Earth gravity. A seven pound baby would weight eight and a half pounds. Well within normal birth weight for Earth. However, we absolutely do not want added children using your limited supplies. There will be no resupply ever. The ships all have the best young doctors onboard and there is an excellent clinic on the ship, but children during the trip are seriously discouraged. We do not expect you to not have sex. Everyone was checked for disease, DNA problems and so forth while in training. Everyone on the ship is as healthy as we could select from seven billion potential colonists. Just make sure that you practice safe sex."

"You have known for some time now that there are six women for every man on every ship so until there has been a generation or two on your new planet, you will have to accept polygamy as the normal state of things. Everyone has known this for some time and have said they accepted this. Everyone will have to control any jealousy and everyone needs to watch for it. No fights are acceptable between men or women. We do not want to discipline anyone, but the doors do have locks if necessary."

"Please use the exercise equipment in the gyms. There are stationary bikes, treadmills, and weight training equipment. You will not get much exercise on the ship during the coming months, but you are pioneers who will be physically tasked in building a colony as soon as you arrive on your planets. You need to be physically strong and healthy."

"All ships successfully launched and are at similar speed toward the new planets. There have been no malfunctions. Your ship has redundant equipment plus every ship has technicians and scientists on board to make in flight repairs. Do not consider your speed. Ship will show the speed in first in miles and kilometers per hour first. After a couple of days it will show percent of the speed of light eventually transitioning to show how many times the speed of light that you are traveling. This speed will increase until you hit the midway point. There will be a few hours of weightlessness until the ship can turn around and then deceleration will build to match the similar acceleration to our departure. During this weightlessness you should stay in your acceleration couches. When you are using the couches as beds or sofas be sure that you return the configuration to acceleration couch when you are not using it. That way it will be ready to be used for acceleration when you need it in case you are rushed to get back to your housing unit on schedule.

A couple of days later all the colonists were glued to their view screens watching what they could see of the destruction of Earth. It was hard to tell what was happening because with all the telephoto and digital enhancement, Earth was still just a spot on the screen. You could see an even smaller spot moving toward Earth for hours before the two came together then everything was obscured by dust. Then SHIP broadcast the live signal to the colony ships. SHIP and family were closer than Mars to Earth and could plainly see the size of the moon approaching Earth and the impact. It took hours for the video to reach the colony ships at the speed of light, then the shipboard computers had to receive and process the pictures from raw coded data to a smooth video picture. Again, the colonists gathered around their large view screens. The moon that impacted Earth was not nice and round like our moon or Mars or any of the planets but was about half the size of the moon and ragged shaped looking like a huge clinker in a coal stove. It was rotating slowly as it approached Earth then crashed into Earth. Just like the long range real time images, everything was covered with dust. You could not see land or oceans or even the rotation of Earth. The "moon" or "clinker" that impacted Earth glanced off at a forty degree angle. There were other chunks the size of a city that were blown into space. While most of the chunks were in the general direction where the "clinker" hit, but there were a few large pieces of Earth that came from the opposite side of Earth blow loose by the impact. It looked like the major impact occurred in the Gobi Desert of Mongolia.

This image was much more psychological than the tiny image from the colony ships cameras. Earth could not have survived this impact. At least it was quick. People could have only seen the "clinker" minutes before impact. They could have seen it growing in the night sky appearing initially like a star at night, then as a satellite, then growing to a small moon. It struck during daylight in Mongolia so most people on Earth could not have seen much before impact. They would have initially experienced massive earthquakes, buildings and bridges toppling then massive dirt in the air and a darkening of the sky. If they survived that, within minutes they would be short of oxygen as the atmosphere was blown into space.

Craig's voice had to be analyzed by the colony ships computers prior to broadcast. If broadcast as received there would have been huge Doppler effects that would make it sound strange. The computers smoothed it out to sound like normal voice. Craig said nothing during the impact video.

As everyone was speechless from the video, Craig's voice came over the speakers, "We took the videos from between Earth and Mars. We cannot make anything out after impact. I do not think anything would have survived. That kind of impact would have caused all the faults on Earth to shift with cities being destroyed by earthquakes around the globe. There would have been tidal waves shortly thereafter hitting all the coastal cities. The dust cloud will effectively block almost all sunlight reaching Earth for days causing extreme temperatures. Now if you will watch the screens again, you can see that a cloud of water vapor and dust has followed the object that hit Earth. According to analysis this is much of Earth's atmosphere being blown out into space. We will be monitoring Earth until things settle down, but we believe Earth today will look much like Mars did last week. We do not believe any plant or animal life could exist more than minutes unless in an earthquake proof bunker with a sup-ply of air, food, and water. If this blew away even fifty percent of the atmosphere Earth might not be habitable ever again without protection of the atmosphere the oceans will boil off or freeze solid depending on latitude. Radiation from the sun would have no filter. This impact may have changed the rotation of Earth, increasing or decreasing gravity. Our calculations indicate that five percent of the mass of Earth has disappeared into space. Some of it will return to Earth doing more damage. We will try to put together more information and get it transmitted to the colony ships prior to reaching the speed of light. After that, we will not be able to provide any information except one ship at a time by teleporting onto each ship one at a time while matching up hull to hull."

Most of the colonists took it hard. This made it concrete that they had lost family and friends on Earth and that they could never ever return to Earth. The only thing left was a dead rock in space, their memories of Earth, and their books, videos, and pictures of Earth stored in the computers. The colony ships had a cloud hanging over the people for weeks.

Craig, family, and SHIP flew the projected courses of the colony ships, found a few minor corrections to course and then joined the fleets. The course to Pyramid had the most corrections so they docked with each of the ships in turn and Dawn fed in the small corrections to the computer navigation to avoid stars on the old courses. While Dawn made those corrections, Estera checked the greenhouses of plants from Earth to verify that they were healthy. The conversion of human waste into safe fertilizer appeared to be working.

Craig and Shelby verified that the air handlers were working to remove carbon for use in food where that and flavorings and colors salvaged from used food was used again to manufacture new rations. As there was no way for it to be perpetual the fiber and flavors from the greenhouses supplemented the manufactured food and provided some fresh vegetables and fruits for the colonists.

Sandy checked the storage of eggs and sperm to make sure everything looked good for test tube animals on the new planets. She also checked in with the doctors on the colony ships to check on the health of the colonists. She was not a human doctor, but with SHIP training she was the best veterinarian ever and probably a better human doctor than most of the medical doctors.

Karen checked on the use of the training materials to make sure that the average colonist was spending time on training using the computer simulations and training courses.

Jill spent extra time on the ships that had the materials for drilling oil and mining and smelting ore. Each planet except for Vulcan had two identical ships as far as being stocked with petroleum and metal mining and processing. She worked with the geologists, and skilled workers to discuss once again the set up of equipment, answer questions and check the training materials. Each of those ships also had smaller contingents of regular colonists, but thirty percent were oil and metal specialists.

By the time they had checked all the ships bound for Pyramid and Pangaea the Chinese ships had exceed the speed of light. Therefore the only way they could talk to them was to bring SHIP in hull to hull contact and teleport across to the Chinese ship.

The Chinese colony ships were a whole other problem. They had been allowed to launch with the personnel and equipment dictated by the Chinese government. Their colonists had other skills but were soldiers first and colonists second. They spoke English well enough, but were primarily Mandarin speakers. Their training materials were largely military in nature made for conquering and ruling a colony instead of building a colony. Once in physical contact SHIP could pull data off the Chinese computers.

The family had to go one at a time from SHIP to a Chinese colony ships so that SHIP could instantly teleport that family member back in case of trouble. It took a lot more time to visit the four Chinese ships than it took for the thirty-six other colony ships because of having to go to one at a time. When one family member returned the next one would teleport over, work alone, then teleport back before the next one teleported.

Karen spoke up halfway through the first Chinese colony ship. "Craig, do we really have to go one at a time? You or I could go over and guard the other members, that way we could at least do this a lot faster."

"Karen, they are armed to the teeth and trained in hand to hand combat. They might overwhelm our trying to guard and all it would take is one of us being kidnapped for whatever reason. SHIP has learned to transport any one of us at any time and can watch over any one of us. As long as there is just one of us, SHIP can monitor the situation and teleport that one person back instantly. But if there are two of us there SHIP might make the wrong decision as to which one to teleport first or they might simultaneously capture more than one at the same time. I just don't want to take the risk."

The Chinese had a fleet admiral that was speaking for all their ships, but, of course, not in contact with his other three ships. "How do we know that all the videos of Earth are true?"

"Because seeing is believing. It was not a simulation, it was real videos first from your own ship and then what we sent to you."

"If it wasn't for the constant added gravity and the periods of heavy acceleration, I do not even know we are in space. Is this some kind of plot by the United States to make us think we are on a spaceship? How do we know that this isn't some kind of Disney World ride that we are stuck on with a centrifuge applying the gee forces?

"I guess you don't, but you know the size of this ship that your country built. You can walk all around the ship to see its size. Wouldn't that be a good trick to put this whole ship in a centrifuge to fly around to show extra gees? You saw your own countrymen strap on your own Chinese made rocket boosters to provide take off power. Your own scientists verified the thrust factors. Where would you have gone except into space?"

"We do not trust you. We will be able to take care of ourselves on the new planet. We have taken the equipment we need. We did not have to follow your advice on equipment."

"I know very well what you put on your four ships. The military equipment will do you no good when you arrive on the planet. Believe me, you will be sorry you did not include the skills we told you to. You did not select the people we told you to. What good is a political party member going to do on a new planet?"

"They will be our link to our way of life in China. They will make sure the younger members of this expedition stay in line and follow orders."

"But there is no China any longer. Since you left off the oil and mining equipment, what will you do for energy after you arrive on the planet?"

"Your other ships will provide for us. We will keep the peace on the new planet and your colonists can supply us with whatever we need."

Craig teleported back to SHIP, "I am convinced of my wisdom of only having one of us at a time off SHIP while checking the Chinese ships."

Estera had gone over next to check their greenhouse, "I am not happy with the greenhouse. Apparently, they are eating food other than what we told them to so their wastes are not processing correctly. The plants are not as healthy as on all the other ships."

Karen went next and SHIP teleported her back to SHIP. "I think I hit a few raw nerves of the Chinese. I read them the riot act. They are not doing any training at all except for hand to hand combat and military strategy. I told them that if they wanted to survive on their planet they better get with the training program. I had SHIP plug all of our standard training into their ship's computer and erased the Chinese training. Then they started to get threatening and I found myself back here on SHIP."

"Karen, while we are in contact with this ship have SHIP put in the programming for building a colony on Vulcan. It will not make them happy, in fact murderous, but they deserve it. As soon as it is complete, tell me."

A few minutes later it was done. Craig used the ship to ship contact to access their loud speaker system. He talked in English, but the people on the Chinese ship heard Mandarin. "The Chinese ships have been programmed to go to Vulcan and there will be no other colonist ships there. We have installed the information on Vulcan, your new planet into your computer and the software that will provide you training on setting up a new colony there. Vulcan will be a Chinese only planet. You will not have anyone to conquer or rule except the four thousand Chinese on your colony ships. Your armament will be worthless and you will have to learn to survive without the equipment the other ships have. We told you to load oil drilling, mining, smelting, and manufacturing equipment on one of your ships and you left all that equipment behind. Your ship nuclear reactors will provide power for a few years after you land, but you had better figure out on your own how to get other forms of energy. Your colonists do not have the skills you were told to have and you chose to have soldiers and politicians instead. The advantage you will have is that your soldiers are fit and strong. You will have to survive without any help from anywhere except yourselves. You can live on the ships for a few hundred years, but you will have to build log cabins to live in for the long term. You will have to fashion boots and clothing using lizard skin from the dinosaurs living there. We have erased the science from your computers that could be used for making spaceships, the impervium, faster than light drives, and weapons. We left some simple rocketry to enable you to someday replace your GPS satellites. We erased this data to make sure that you cannot attack the other colonies in a few centuries. You do not know where they are and may never be able to find them. You did not bring scientists to create new inventions, although some of you may be able to learn on your own. We knew from the start that you were not complying with our requirements, but our American President did not want me to take strong action against you. I suggested sabotaging your ships so you could not leave Earth. I suggested not delivering the FaTL drives to your ships so you would be stuck on Earth when it was destroyed. I suggested we could just shoot down your ships after you got into space. However, the American President asked me to come up with a less aggressive solution. We found a planet that can support a colony, but not as nice as the other two planets. Once the colony ships exceeded the speed of light further communication between ships became impossible and at that point your course started deviating to Vulcan instead of Pangaea or Pyramid. Your ships are programmed to land on Vulcan, but you getting there alive is already compromised by your threatening of Karen, our lead trainer. Your greenhouses are not healthy and you may lose your fresh vegetables and fruit. This will gradually mean that you use up your ship store quicker and be low on food when you arrive, but you will have enough to get there plus a few weeks on Vulcan. We may and may not check back with you later on to see if you are surviving on the ship. Do not mess with the computers. Causing a computer failure could cause your ship to go into a constant twelve to twenty gee acceleration that would kill you all within hours. Messing with a computer could shut down the drive entirely which would mean you not making the course corrections necessary. That could lead to smacking into a star or planet destroying this ship or it could mean your ship wandering in space until you all starve to death. You are on your own now. If you take the computer training for Vulcan that we have loaded on your computers, you should be able to arrive alive and build a colony on Vulcan. You will have it rougher than the other colonies, but you can survive. I realize that the average soldier is not to blame, but all of you knew that you were not selected in accordance with our rules and you have sealed your fate. We will be checking back sometime before you reach Vulcan. Hopefully you will have been training for your survival on Vulcan.

The same message was transmitted to all the Chinese ships, one at a time, after the SHIP had come in hull to hull contact and reprogrammed the Chinese computers.

The family had not been able to check all of the systems on the ship, but SHIP could check the computers and see what was monitored. Because the greenhouses were not as healthy as they should be the oxygen levels were slightly off, but should hold with the scrubbers and recyclers until they arrived on planet. The colony ships had been designed such that a total failure of the greenhouses would not kill the colonists on board. If the greenhouses were successful, the colonists could use the contents to transplant the Earth vegetable and fruits on the new planet. Grain crops could be planted from seed, apple trees could be grow from seed like John Chapman better known as Johnny Appleseed had planted apple trees in pioneer areas. But actually being able to transplant live plants works better than seed for some items. If the greenhouses worked as planned some of the waste would help the greenhouses and the greenhouses would take carbon dioxide from the air and provide oxygen in return. The air handlers would do it, but the greenhouses would add to the safety.

The family took a few days off while SHIP explored the planned courses of the colony ships once again to see if any course corrections were needed. Space is mainly that, just empty space, but there were rocks just floating around here and there in space. Stars were moving within the Milky Way Galaxy. Planets and their moons were drifting to and from the stars they orbited as the stars orbited around each other and around the arm of the galaxy. The remote outside arm of the galaxy where

Earth existed and the planets they were going to was largely vacant space. The odds of hitting anything was minimal but did require a few course corrections for safety and to keep their exhaust away from large rocks that could become lethal objects to another planet or ship somewhere. Ten thousand years from now that rock that got pushed to high speed could eventually find another starship somewhere.

They then rejoined the fleet to Pyramid which would reach its destination sooner. They had to make ship to ship, hull to hull, contact to teleport in. The colonists had started pairing off, if you can call six women to one man pairing. These grouping might not survive once on planet and the work started. Now it was entertainment and training, training and entertainment. There were some that had started working in the greenhouse which were doing quite well. Scientists on the ships had independently improved on the original design of the processing of human waste for fertilizer.

A few had pulled a few small kits out of storage and started some assembly. Now imagine a vehicle that had a one liter four cylinder engine with twenty to one compression and four superchargers producing eight hundred horsepower. The engine made out of the impervium weighed only twenty pounds and came assembled from the factory. There was no advantage to shipping the engine as a kit. An engine block and cylinder head are about as compact as it can be packed. The transmission is mated to the engine. The kit is the vehicle which is mainly empty space. It comes in many compact pieces that has to be assembled from parts and the engine with transmission installed, hooked up to the electrical harness and radiator for cooling, filled with oil and water. The oil would weigh more than the assembled engine and water for cooling might be too precious to waste until they were on planet with available fresh water. The transmission must then be hooked into the rest of the drive line, tires installed, etc. The fluids, tires and seat cushions weigh more than the car which is made of the impervium, which is lighter than Styrofoam and stronger than steel. Even the tires and wheels were made of plastic to save weight.

The colonists on each ship practiced this assembly except final installation of the heavier items that remained in storage. There was not room to set up oil drilling rigs or mining equipment, but some of the smaller equipment was assembled and then put back into its kits.

After months of space travel the colonists had gotten used to the fact that Earth no longer existed as a habitable planet and were anxious to get their feet on solid ground with open spaces to look at and explore. Some of the women had taken to repair of their uniforms. With only two uniforms per person to last for the journey plus a longer time on their new planet were routinely checking uniforms for seams that needed reinforcement.

The whole family came on board these ships leaving SHIP docked hull to hull with the colony ship they were visiting. Unlike the Chinese ships that the family considered too dangerous to visit, they were celebrities on the other colony ships. There were no races on the colony ships. Everyone was just an earthman and fellow colonist.

The women and men regularly moved from room to room having casual sex as the need arose. The men found they had to ration themselves among the women. Everyone was selected health, physical fitness, intelligence, skill sets, and education.

Each ship only had one full medical doctor and one highly trained emergency tech that could double as a surgery assistant if necessary. Once the ships landed there would be one doctor for every thousand healthy young adults. There was computer training on the ships even for training new doctors. The doctors were the old people on the ship even though they averaged only twenty-six years old and the oldest was twenty-nine. There was no disease on the ship and no disease expected in the new colonies, but they had to be prepared for unknown medical problems, the inevitable injuries, broken bones and cuts that would happen while they built the new colonies. Doctors were forbidden to do anything on the ships where they might get injured since each ship only had one, but once they landed on their planet they would have plenty of doctors. The concern would be training new doctors to replace them when there would be no medical school in the colonies except for ship training.

The reactors on each ship would provide unlimited power for the first twenty years but would taper off as the radioactive fuel was depleted. After twenty years the colonies would have to find other fuels to generate electricity. The computers on the ship would be the last to use the remaining electricity from the reactors. There would be enough produced for a total of fifty years of computer operation and then even the computers would be reliant on other means of generating electricity. The computers on each ship were redundant but over twenty to forty years there were bound to be multiple failures of the electronics. The view screens would undoubtedly fail before the computers. Rather than use disk drives all the memory storage was on memory chips, many many petabytes of storage. The routine skills like rebuilding a vehicle or farming would be learned from the fathers and grandfathers as the colony got older, but some things like medicine and higher science would be reliant on the computers. There were scientists and technitions that knew everything about the computers, the computers themselves had the information and training courses for making components like memory chips and transistors, but the colonies would have no manufacturing except what the colonists could build.

SHIP and the family enjoyed their visits on the colony ships. They enjoyed their trips ahead of the colony ships and trips to the planets they were heading to but eventually they had to go back to the Chinese ships bound for Vulcan. They docked hull to hull with the Chinese admiral's ship, downloaded all the information from their ship into SHIP and analyzed the data without announcing that they were there. SHIP was invisible to the colony ships radar and cameras so the Chinese did not know they were there until Craig teleported to the admiral's quarters.

"So. You have returned. Why have you done this to us?"

"We are sending you to the least desirable planet because we knew that your intent was to militarily rule the other colonists. However, there are still four thousand Chinese that will be landing on Vulcan. If you had followed the rules with the intent of building a new civilization four thousand colonists could create a comfortable colony on Vulcan. Vulcan has everything needed for a comfortable frontier life. We will just have to see how you do with your military ships with their near useless military equipment. There are plants and animals you can eat on Vulcan. There just won't be anyone for you to rule except your own people."

"Tell me Craig Decker. Was Earth really destroyed?"

"Yes. It is doubtful that anyone lived. Theoretically someone might have survived in a bunker ninety degrees from the impact, but when they come out of their bunker there will be no plants or animals to survive on. We calculate that the air density is about like Mount Everest was so they will not be able to breath without a concentrator."

"So. By your reasoning, we will be better off on Vulcan."

"That is correct, but I could not let you land on one of the other colony planets because they came equipped to build a new civilization, not defend themselves again an armed invader. I want the new colonies to be totally free to build a new civilization without freeloaders or rulers that produce nothing on their own. Every colonist will have a job to do to support the colony. They do not have the resources to waste on politicians or military. I suspect that a thousand years from now they may once again have some crazy people that want to rule. I would hope that they have a united democratic government, but only time will tell."

"I had to keep you from spoiling that. I found Vulcan after the other planets, but the final decision was not made to send you there until your ships actually took off with military gear instead of equipment to build a new colony."

"I will probably be visiting you again prior to planet fall, after you are below the speed of light in preparation for landing."

PART FIVE

COLONY BUILDING

20

VULCAN

The Chinese colony ships reached Vulcan, the nearest habitable planet they had found to Earth weeks ahead of Pyramid. Pangaea would be reached a month after that. As all of the colony ships once again dropped below the speed of light they still had a couple of weeks of deceleration. Their scoops were no longer pulling in dark energy and antimatter for thrust so they were back to particle thrust from just the reactor and the super conductive particle accelerators.

Craig, again, visited with the Chinese admiral in his quarters. "You have dropped below the speed of light so you can again communicate with your other Chinese ships. You are only two weeks from your destination on Vulcan. Your ships will land approximately two hundred miles from the next nearest ship. Vulcan will have a global positioning system or GPS so that you can safely navigate from one ship to the next once on land. If you have been following your training since we last met, you will know that I and my crew have been to all the landing zones to verify that they are suitable for your habitation."

"Yes. My crew on this ship, at least, have taken up the training on Vulcan. Can you assure us that there are no dinosaurs that we cannot kill and eat?"

"I cannot guarantee that one hundred percent, but we found none larger than an elephant and your guns should easily take them down. You will have to be cautious and live on your ships to start with, but you need to get off the ships and start mining coal and metals as soon as possible to make your own metals for use in making other things. You will have to make sure that you send out parties in sufficient strength for self protection from the dinosaurs, but you will not starve. Your greenhouses are in poor condition because they were not cared for on the entire journey, but there is plant life that you could eat as well as the dinosaurs. There are also mammals living on Vulcan not so different from Earth's."

"You will need to cut trees for lumber to build houses and in your case you might want stockades around your colonies to keep out the wildlife."

"As soon as your ships will let you outdoors, start assembling some of your off road vehicles and other equipment. The ships will communicate with each other for twenty years after the landing, but you need to set up other communications and your own power sources before the nuclear reactors lose power.

The computers on your ships should stay active on the nuclear plants for at least forty years. After that, you are on your own."

"I recommend you spend the next two weeks making sure that all of the people on all four of your ships pack in as much training from the ships computer as you can. There are detailed plans we created for your setting up the mining and smelting equipment, building log cabins, and processing the dinosaur meat and skins. Clothing will be at a premium. There is no cotton or wool to weave cloth and your colonists do not have the skills that we had specified. However, the computers have everything you need to know. I am leaving you to let the ships land themselves in two weeks. I am going to rejoin some of the other colony ships that will be dropping below light speed in a few weeks. I will return to Vulcan when I can to see if we can help."

To help knock them out of orbit thirty extremely small global position system satellites were ejected into geosynchronous orbits to provide one hundred percent coverage plus some spare satellites. These would be used by the colonists to find their way from colony to colony.

Once they entered the atmosphere their ships became computer controlled super gliders. The particle drives retracted into the ships. The impervium could withstand the thousands of degrees of reentry speed without interior heating of the ship. The super aerodynamics took over once the ships reduced to three thousand miles per hour. The final glide approach to touchdown was less than sixty miles per hour. The original wheels on takeoff were left on Earth as soon as the ships took off. Now within two hundred feet of landing electrically automated landing skids were let down out of the hulls. The onboard computers stalled the huge ships just prior to touchdown so they hit the ground at less than forty miles per hour. Momentum dug furrows in the land for a short distance prior to the colony ships coming to a stop."

"The colonists were directed to their acceleration couches prior to de- orbiting. All of the ships landed with a few hundred yards of where the family had picked for their new villages. After coming to a stop, the colonists were not allowed off for two hours to allow cooling of the ship. During the two hours the exact landing position of each ship was displayed on a detailed map on the view screens. The recommended path and future roads between them was shown as a dotted line.

Everyone's touch pad was programmed with all the GPS locations of each colony. For the next twenty years the location of every touch pad would be tracked by the colony ships' computers.

Also on the screens and programmed into the GPS were the known locations of mineral deposits, lakes, and other points of interest with dotted paths showing the best route to them from the nearest ship.

The Chinese admiral decided to use this time before the doors open to give his capitulation speech.

"Troops, we are now on the planet of Vulcan. There are no other colonists here. You were told that we would live off the other colonists once we showed our superior firepower."

"However, the Americans found out our plans, and sent us to a separate planet. For the past few weeks we have been watching videos on Vulcan and training on colonizing Vulcan. I know that many of you did not watch the training, but I encourage everyone to spend any spare time watching the videos and taking the training on your touch pads."

"We came here as soldiers to conquer and rule the people. There are no other people, so to rule this world we will have to conquer it the hard way. We will have to build our own world to rule. We did not bring the things we were told to bring so we do not have oil drilling equipment or mining equipment, but we do have military equipment that we can adapt for what we need. We can continue living on the ship until we can build walls around the ship and then we can build some additional housing inside. Instead of having six women for every man we have only one woman for every four men. Our population growth will be slow compared to the colonies. It will be every woman's duty to get pregnant immediately and when one child is born to get pregnant again."

"We will assemble some military transports immediately to bring back any dinosaurs or other animals killed along the way. I want to try this dinosaur meat that we will be eating for the rest of our lives. Each ship should immediately set out a patrol of twenty men in off road transports toward the next ship using the GPS to verify that the GPS is correct and to watch for hazards along the way. Keep videos rolling to document your trips."

The Chinese quickly assembled their armored personnel carriers at each ship and then started out for the one hundred mile off road trip to meet up with the armored personnel carriers from the nearest ship. There were four ships so that was eight personnel carriers. Each would travel at around an estimated five miles per hour taking twenty hours to meet up with the opposing patrol. They would be broadcasting live. Each carrier would take their kills back to their home ship taking another twenty hours. Each personnel carrier would take twenty soldiers and alternate drivers for a non-stop trip. The total estimated time for the round trip would be forty hours or just under two days.

While the patrols were traveling the other troops were assembling more personnel carriers and inventorying their supplies. Because they took many of their own rations their inventory was low.

Some of the troops started clearing land and digging up an area to plant the remaining plants in their poor onboard greenhouses that they had not taken care of. Once the ground had been cleared of natural Vulcan plants and dug up they would transplant their greenhouse plants outdoors and start planting the seeds they had brought. Again, they did not bring the full contingent of seeds because they had intended to live off the plantings of the other colony ships, but they had brought some.

The patrols only traveled a few mile when they ran into vegetation too thick to drive through. This required troops to dismount and clear paths through the vegetation wide enough for the personnel carriers to pass through. Once they cleared through forested areas, they got their carriers stuck in the mud. After twenty hours they had only progressed ten miles. The admiral had been watching their progress on the video screen and ordered them back to their own ships. While waiting for their return he sent out foot patrols of forty troops from each ship with plans to walk to the meeting with the next ship. They were carrying large backpacks with tents. Instead of using impervium they had used steel for their personnel carriers. This made their equipment breakable and heavy. As a result of the weight they had to leave a lot behind that were supposed to be part of their inventory. While this gave them more empty area for their military training during the voyage they were sorry now that they had used heavy steel. They had no weaving machines for making cloth so everything would have to be made by hand including hand weaving cloth from whatever they could find.

Their foot patrol was only a few hours out when each patrol found and killed a small dinosaur. They reported this by radio and the admiral ordered them to let a few of their troops bring their kills back to camp. He then ordered the remainder of the patrols to not kill anything more unless threatened. This was to speed the patrols toward each other as quickly as possible. Before the end of the day the foot patrols met up with the armored personnel carriers returning to their ships. The foot patrols made good progress along the trails blazed for the personnel carriers. Going by foot was much quicker than trying to drive across the un-cleared terrain. The foot patrols met up at the one hundred mile halfway point in on the fourth day. The GPS system was very accurate, as expected, but the dotted line on the map was definitely not a road. The trip back to their home ships was faster as they had beaten a path through the plains and forests in their way.

The admiral had posted guards around the ship to keep wild animals from the gardens. They received afternoon rains each day lasting about an hour. The temperatures were tropical, but not too warm and the rains cooled it off. Many of the troops took to camping outdoors under the stars at night.

The troops were redirected from assembling military equipment to cutting down surrounding forest to first build a stockade fence around the ship for security then to start building cabins for those wanting to live outdoors.

The first cabin was for the admiral which contained around four thousand square feet. The admiral chose six girls to serve him, keeping him sexual company, cooking and cleaning for him. Most of the men would be without women. The Chinese had expected to conquer the colonists and taking their surplus women for themselves and did not have enough women for the number of men. To maintain their colony what women they did have would have to be protected and pregnant. Keeping all the women on their ships for protection was not practical because they needed the fresh air and sun for health.

The admiral made the good decision to build a women's compound outside inside the stockade. The women were trained soldiers so they would provide their own guards. Only a limited number of men would be allowed in at any one time to make sure the women in the compound would seriously outnumber the men in the women's compound. Men were not allowed to bring in any weapons. Their ship's doctor was moved adjacent to the women's compound to care for the women first and any injuries suffered by the men as they lumbered the forest or got injured hunting or mining.

The admiral also ordered special hospital rooms in the women's compound to care for pregnant women and a children's area to keep the children isolated from the rest of the colony.

Each ship was near a fresh water source so adding plumbing for fresh water was easy, but they had left out the toilets to save weight for their steel armored personnel carriers. The only flush toilets were onboard the ships. The people that lived outdoors had to make due with outhouses. The waste was composted with left over wood shavings from the lumbering operations to make fertilizer for the gardens. The plants that had survived the voyage came back to life with regular rain and the compost. The seeds they planted were growing well. It would be years before they got fruit off trees planted from seed, but things were looking good.

They removed some of their ships' plumbing to build bathrooms first in the women's compound and then for public use in the colony being built around the ship.

21

PYRAMD

A month after the Chinese ships landed on Vulcan, the colony ships landed on Pyramid. Four of the ships landed on the outskirts of the stone town the Martians had left around the central pyramid. One Russian and one USA mining ship landed near the mines prepared by the Martians. There were two ships in case something had happened to one of the mining ships. Again, one Russian and one USA ship landed near where the family suspected there were oil fields. These two ships had oil drilling and refinery kits on board. Three of the ships landed within two hundred miles of the pyramid city to be primarily farming colonies. The four other ships landed along the route between the stone city and the mines to act as relay points for resupply. The mining ships would provide minerals and the other ships would provide finished goods and food to the mining ships. That is not to say that the mining ships would not plant their own seeds from the stores and plants from their greenhouses.

The resupply ships would act like pony express stations: vehicles hauling metal up to two hundred miles one way, then trading those vehicles with vehicles with fully charged batteries to haul supplies back to the mines. The metals would eventually arrive in Pyramid City.

"Okay, my name is Karen and I need a set of volunteers. Are there any group of six women and one man that have mated up?"

"No? Okay, I need six women volunteers and one man. We don't think so, but this could be dangerous. If any others want to watch come on out near the pyramid. I have an experiment we need to do: enter the pyramid. Craig and family have been in the pyramid twice and everything worked fine. However, we braced the door to make sure it did not lock us in. It takes six women and one man to simultaneously press large buttons on the door. It should then open and allow access. Inside there are multiple training stations that will tell everyone the secrets of the Martians that built the city."

Ten women and twelve men stepped forward. To the men she said, "Okay, let's try this with one woman and six men."

She pointed out six men and one woman and they tried and failed to push in any of the buttons.

She then picked six women and one man from the remaining men and said, "Okay. We did not think that would work, but Craig was the only man in our group. We could only try it with our mix of six women and one man as specified by the Martians."

"Craig's family will stay out to make sure that you are not locked inside since we know we can open the door. We do not anticipate any problems, but we want to be overly cautious rather than take any risks. If that works out we will try some other groups one at a time. If everything works well, then groups can enter, view the videos of the Martians and then let others take their turn."

Are we ready?

The six women and one man followed instructions, lined up in a line and pressed their buttons. The door opened, the lights came on, and the group entered the door. They could be seen across the open space as they went to the far wall and then as instructed, pushed the buttons on a console and the video came on. The door remained open. All communications to the group inside were cut off while they were in the pyramid. Then Karen motioned that they should leave the pyramid. When they cleared the door, the door closed just as securely as it was in the beginning.

Then Karen picked six additional women and one man from the crowd that had not volunteered but were just there to watch. The door worked perfectly again. With the door still open and the group inside then she told the original group of six men and one woman to just walk in the door. The door closed before they could get there. "

"Okay, come back here and join the crowd. As soon as they backed off the door opened again." Then she tried another group of six women and one man. The door stayed open and allowed the second group. When the grouping with one woman and six men approached the door it closed again. Then another group of six women and one man and the door stayed open. There were now twenty-one people in the pyramid. She had told this last group to tell those inside to activate more than one training video. She could see that all three groups were watching three independent videos. She then motioned them to leave. The door stayed open until the last person left.

"Okay, let's try one more experiment. You, the first group, re-enter the pyramid by pressing the buttons again. Then stand in the doorway and we will see what happens when the grouping of six men and one woman tries to enter."

The floor started rising to force the first group from the door while the door closed again. When the men backed off, the door opened back up.

"Okay, I think that confirms it. There apparently no limit on how many groupings enter the pyramid and how many training videos are going, but the mix of women to men must remain at six women and one man. Don't play around, treat the pyramid as some strange and potentially dangerous. It is also very valuable as some of the information is new to us in Craig's family. I encourage you to use the videos, everyone should watch them, but let's voluntarily limit the people inside to no more than seven groups at a time and everyone take turns. I think you will have the rest of your life to see the videos."

Craig told the lumberjacks and carpenters near the city to get busy making doors and windows for the stone buildings left by the Martians.

It appeared that each apartment was made for six women and one man.

"Mechanics and technicians, get busy assembling the kits with some of the off road vehicles and helicopters first. We will figure out where to put manufacturing equipment later. Everyone else, start working to make gardens on the edge of the town. We will want to build fences around the gardens to protect them from animals before we plant anything. You have months of rations left on the ship. Live in the ship until you get apartments enclosed and cleaned."

"As soon as apartments get ready, start grouping together as seven member families with six women and one man per family and moving into the apartments. We will randomly select social security numbers of the men to decide who will move in first. If he does not have six women picked out to spend life with, he will be bypassed until voluntary groupings have moved in. For anyone that has not grouped into families, the computer will use your background information like a computer dating web site and select families that way. Everyone here was selected for health and intelligence, but voluntary families are the best. It would be unrealistic to think that these extended families will not change over time, but it is important that one man and six women be in each apartment. If a man wants to leave his women, he has to find a man to trade families. If a woman wants to join another family then she must find a woman from that family to trade with her. If a man dies his family would have to split up and join other families. If a woman died, the widows of another man might join the family that had lost a female member. Families should be trying to have children and stay together for the children. It is important for children to grow up with their birth father and mother around them. In a couple of generations the number of male versus female should balance out. In fact, historically there are more males than females born."

"It is important to use the barter system for trade."

"There is no cash or credit. Everyone is starting off totally broke except for their skills. There is no skill that pays better than another one.

I am not going to try to control your monitory system or your political system. For now, I would recommend that you start out by sharing with those that need it most. The miners and oil men are not spending as much time growing crops so they will need food from the rest of the colony. Their work will be harder on clothing than the rest of the colony so when you produce clothing they should get more than their share to replace what they ruin. You were all chosen with the idea you would have a good work ethic. You did not grow up spoiled with everything money could buy and you lasted two years in the training program."

"At some point families may deposit extra credits in a computer account that could be traded for other goods for the time they get sick or hurt. Medical is free, but the only way we can pay the doctor is with free food and clothing and making replacement bandages, scalpels and housing."

"I hate to use the word communism or socialism because I really believe in capitalism, but with no one owning anything yet, and everyone working for the good of the colony that is sort of what we have. But not in the sense that countries practiced communism on Earth. Those communists allowed themselves to be ruled by a few that became a form of royalty with the people living on the remainders after the rich took what they wanted. This also led to some lazy people just living off the ones that would work. There were severe shortages because of hoarding. We don't want that. To start with we want to start out with the spirit of cooperation, trust, and sharing. Money will come later. Later when the success of the colony is assured, maybe in a couple of generations and when we need to extend our civilization here, some people can go off and settle their own farms away from the ships. Right now you have the ships for power and you are totally dependent upon the nuclear reactors of the ships."

"Once the colony is well established future generations my stake claims on land or find new mineral deposits. No one should ever claim more land than they can care for. You have the laws and court decisions of the United States to fall back on in that future when capitalism starts again."

"We will leave you to work now and we will be visiting the outlying ships on Pyramid."

The farming communities acting as relays between city and mines and oil fields were already at work setting up stockades around their ships and some were at work preparing land for planting.

The family went on to the oil fields. The Russian and American ships were located twenty miles from the edge of what was determined to have oil. They had assembled an oil rig, but had not started using it yet.

Estera spoke first, "Before you start drilling for oil, you need to get your colony set up. That means a stockade fence to protect the colonists near the ship. It needs to be big enough to build log cabins and farming areas. The other colonies are best set up for farming, but your greenhouse has plants that need to be planted and your stores have seeds that need to be sowed. That means stripping acres of land of any indigenous plants. The stockade is to prevent a few pigs and cows, or whatever animals they are, from eating your plants before you can."

Jill said, "I agree wholeheartedly. You will have twenty years of nuclear power, but you will eventually have to have the oil. First thing is the stockade, then clear the land and plant the plants, then build some log cabins and then you can start drilling for oil. For training, try a fresh water well and test the ground water. To start with you will have to survive as an outpost colony, then you can drill for oil. Once you do find oil, you need to get the refineries set up to refine the oil. Until the other colonists can start producing pipe, you will have to build roads to use the oil tankers to haul refined products to Pyramid City. Yes, we named it and the planet because of the pyramid at the center of the city.".

Their next trip was to teleport to the mines which they gave some of the same spiel. Some of the experienced miners had already explored the Martian prepared mines.

"The veins are marvelous. We have coal mines, gold mines with monster veins of pure gold, silver mines, iron ore, copper, manganese, everything we need."

"My name is Karen and I am a hunter. You need to work together to build a stockade to protect this place. Cabins so you and your families can live outdoors with more space than you had on the ship."

The family continued with the rest of the admonitions and talks on future politics and then got on board SHIP and took off for Pangaea.

22

PANGAEA

They arrived a few days ahead of the landing on Pangaea. They broadcast to all twenty-two ships simultaneously.

"You are now approaching Pangaea and are below the speed of light. Your landing points are on the view screens and touch pads so you can see the exact spots where your ships will land. All locations are near a water source but out of the flood plain, we hope. Since we do not have a history of Pangaea we can only calculate a good guess. We have picked high spots. All ships will land in clearings near a forest. These trees are not Earth trees but can be treated as if they were. There are differences in the bark and leaves, but they are essentially the same trees you would find on Earth: Oak, Maple, Birch, Pine."

"We believe that this is the best planet of those we have found. It has everything needed for a successful permanent colony and a future human planet. There is one big continent so that every part of it will be accessible by land or coastal boats and ships. We named it Pangaea because the total land area is similar to Earth back when we think there was a single continent called Pangaea. Think of Asia, Africa, Australia, North and South America as one big continent. It will take generations to explore it."

"There is some minor wobble to the orbit that may be due to only having one continent so it is slightly out of balance like an automobile tire that is out of balance. We don't think this will be noticeable but buildings should be built sturdy in case of earthquakes from the wobble. A million years from now, the main continent could break up like it has on Earth. As a result of having only one continent it is impractical to sail all the way around the world to get from one coast to the next. For a few hundred years you will probably not have enough people to worry about visiting both coasts. There is only one mountain range that extends along one coast. The mineral resources are in the foothills of this mountain range so that is where the two mining ships will land. There is an area toward the poles that are covered with pools and ponds of crude petroleum that you can immediately access. We have done spot drilling and there is plentiful oil only one thousand feet below the pools. You could start pumping the oil from the pools immediately, but until you have your refinery and a pipeline or oil tankers to transport the oil, there is not much you can do with it immediately. Therefore the two petroleum ships with the pumps, refinery kits, oil drilling rig kits, will land close but not at the oil. The reason is that the oil is located in an extremely flat area where there are no mountains to block the wind. We were there when the winds exceeded seventy miles per hour for nearly twenty-four hours. However, there was little wind before and after the storm. Your colonies are located in a valley protected by high hills and dense forest that should be safe from the wind. You will have to commute to and from the oil fields."

"The other colony ships are located within extended commuting times between the oil fields and the mineral fields near the mountains. Since initially everything will be electrically powered and since the batteries will only work for about five hundred miles every colony ship is located less than two hundred miles from the next. You need to get the mining colonies working first to mine and smelt the ore for making pipe for the oil fields so that oil products will be available to all the villages. Copper for wiring is even more important initially."

"You have forests, Pangaea Buffalo for meat, edible fish in the steams and rivers, and even the oceans. The prairies are covered in primitive grains that can be made into flour for breads and other grain based food. It should be very good land for planting Earth grain crops that have been highly developed from similar primitive grain over centuries on Earth. The climate ranges from frigid near the poles to hot near the equator. This planet has very little tilt so the differences between winter and summer should be less. The tree rings we checked seem to confirm this, but you will be the first to live here year around."

"Since we have identified what we call Pangaea lions that are vaguely similar to African lions, we have included electric fence wire to protect your individual colonies. You will have to cut trees to use for fence poles. You need to set up the defensive wire first and build wooden gates where your individual computers will indicate. You have already seen videos of the wildlife we found on Pangaea. It seems there are a lot of animals related to cats which means most can climb trees and a wooden stockade."

"You should build a fence inside and outside the wire around your compound to keep people from getting too close to the wire. You will have to select teams to gather up dead animals that get too close to the fences. Hopefully the local wildlife will learn to stay away; the electric fence would also be lethal to humans so this can be a hazardous job."

"You should not waste time exploring, but immediately send out patrols of at least forty people to establish physical contact between ships. They can hunt along the way and have other groups of people to carry meat back to your villages. At no time have a group of less than ten armed people. I had a Pangaea lion stalking me on our first trip here. Craig had a tricky shot over my shoulder that wounded it, and then I finished it off. You have seen photos and videos of the lions."

"Some forests have monkey cats in the trees. They look like cats but swing in the branches grasping with their front paws. I am sure that we have not begun to find all the animals here. So be careful."

The twenty-one colony ships launched their GPS satellites all around the world plus spare satellites. The ships then landed within feet of their intended locations. The nearest forests were no closer than a half mile and no further than one mile. Because the ships were spread out for hundreds of miles there was no central area for multiple ships. With twenty-one ships they could communicate by radio, but would have to visit each ship.

Most of the ships were in groupings of two, with one grouping of three ships. That meant they were starting with ten colonies spread across a few hundred miles. It would take time visiting all of the separate colonies.

Jill teleported to the oil field colony of two ships. "You have to cut trees for the posts for the electrical wires first to make the colony secure from wild animals on the planet. Then you have to all work together to prepare acres of cleared dug up ground for the greenhouse plants and the seed planting for orchards. This is the north country so citrus will have to come from the southern colonies. Until you can get roads built you will have to use the dehydrated orange juice."

Esterea admonished them to get their fields prepared and planted. Sandy warned them about the wildlife and the fact that there may be more. Karen told them to only leave the compounds in larger armed groups and never go alone.

They went to the mineral deposits and made sure that they were setting up their compound properly and they were getting ready to mine the minerals needed to produce Impervium pipe for the oil fields. They would need hundreds of miles. They would need fifty miles of pipe just to get the crude to the refineries.

They had been traveling Pangaea for three weeks and the colonists had basically only gotten their electrical fences strung. They had sent patrols out to their nearest neighbors and brought back Pangaea bison for fresh meat for their village.

The family met on SHIP. "Girls, I know we are just started here, but we do need to check on the other planets. I am not that worried about Pyramid, because the pyramid should be busy teaching the colonists what they need to know. The continent where they are is apparently free of predators and they have plenty of semi-domesticated cows, pigs, and chickens. However, I want to go visit Vulcan."

Estera said, "I don't really care about them. Why are you wanting to visit them? They need my help?"

Jill said, "I agree, I would rather stay here where they are really spread out. There are twenty-one thousand earthmen here and they need to get their oil fields going and to do that they need to get their metal works going and they have to get their plants planted."

"Well, if we are arguing about staying here. I can hardly want to go and not stay and study this strange wildlife. Pangaea lions with arms and hands more like a monkey? Monkeys that look like cats? This is a very large land area, much more so than the other planets. I want to stay here and study the animals."

"Okay, Sandy, what about the dinosaurs on Vulcan?"

"They looked like early Earth dinosaurs, the wildlife here is unique." "I agree, we trained the colonists in the use of rifles and pistols, but few are hunters. If Sandy wants to study the wildlife, I think I should stay with her and make sure that when she goes out she has a full patrol with her."

"Okay, Dawn and Shelby. How about you two, do you have any reason to stay here for awhile longer?"

"Not me. Astral Navigation is my specialty. I programmed the courses to these planets and we got all of them here safely. I want to explore more of space."

"Shelby? What about you?"

"I am curious about studying the chemistry of a very young volcanic planet like Vulcan? I'm for going."

"Okay, Jill, Karen, Estera, and Sandy. Keep in mind that I can't control you, but I would like the four of you to stay with one village at a time so you are all together and remember that SHIP won't be here to save anyone."

"Dawn, Shelby, and I will be gone for at least a week visiting the Chinese on Vulcan. Why? Because, while I made the decision to dump them there, and I was the one suggesting we leave them on Earth or even shoot them down, I did have them sent to Vulcan as an all Chinese planet. I feel an obligation to check on them and see how they are surviving."

23

VERIFICATION

SHIP left in the morning, leaving four of the girls with the village near the mineral deposits. Dawn, Sandy, and Craig left for Vulcan. They had not made a trip direct from Pangaea to Vulcan before. They had found Vulcan on the way out from Earth, so this was a new course through a slightly different part of the second spiral of the Milky Way. During the voyage, they discovered four more planets that were positioned correctly to have life like Earth, but no long distance evidence of any life.

After four days they arrived at Vulcan. They first orbit Vulcan looking at the Chinese colonies. They verified that all of the GPS satellites were operational and that the standby satellites were still good and waiting to automatically start functioning when its neighbor failed.

Without landing they could see that the Chinese had finally started listening and had built barricades around their ships. They had cleared land and their plants looked healthy from space, but they could not really tell without direct personal inspection.

Craig teleported to the Chinese admiral's quarters. He was living in a four bedroom log cabin near the ship he came in on. SHIP had mapped out the rooms in detail and detected seven people living in the admiral's house. The admiral was in his living room as Craig appeared before him. The room was finished in finely carved wood furniture. The wood walls were finished very smoothly and sanded and varnished to a high shine. The walls were hung with priceless art from Earth that had been brought on their ship instead of things for the good of the colony.

"Welcome, Craig. See, we are surviving and thriving. He rang a dainty flowered bell and three girls came running into the room. What would you like, some dinosaur Bar B Que? A beer? We have used some of the local grass to brew a drinkable beer."

"I see you have your own private harem of six girls. Aren't you afraid some of your men might decide to take them away from you when the females on your planet far outnumber the men?"

"I have my own guards who have their own women now. Only one per guard, but when the other men can only visit the women's compound once a month, my guards are very appreciative of their station."

"I see that your gardens and fields have been planted and that your stockade fences have been finished."

"Yes. Once you stranded us here, I decided that we had better follow your directions to survive here. The local grains do not make good bread so we had to make sure our plantings were first rate. We are using the ships' processors to continue producing fertilizer and we get all the rain the plants need. We have rice fields that will be irrigated by pumping water from the river here to the rice fields. When the rice crop comes in we will save some of the grains to replant and plan on making rice wine with some of the crop."

"Don't you need to keep as much as possible for food instead of beer and wine?"

"You were correct in that dinosaur meat is quite good. Tastes like chicken. We have plenty to eat here, just a little short on the vegetables and fruits for now."

"I'm glad you like chicken. I plan on visiting your women's compound to see how they are doing."

"You mean that your six women are not sufficient and you want to sample ours? Our women were selected for their training in the arts of pleasuring men, but alas, over fifty percent are already pregnant." "No, I want to see that they are taken care of."

"We give them the best of everything. As you told me before, the continuation of the colony is contingent upon the health of our females."

"I saw from space that you have cleared the way for dirt roads to connect your ships. That was a good move, but what are you going to do for fuel for your trucks?"

"My men searched the computer and found out how to make diesel fuel from coal and we are busy setting that up now. We can use the ships reactors for electricity to process the coal to diesel. We have stripped off the armor from our armored personnel carriers to make them lighter weight so they do not get stuck as easily."

"Maybe you will be successful, but I am still going to visit the women's compound." Craig teleported to SHIP and Dawn teleported to the women's compound.

"My name is Dawn. I am from the ship that found this place and I am here to see how the women are doing on Vulcan." If it had been Craig, SHIP would have fed him the words in perfect Mandarin and he would hear their words as English.

At first no one spoke and just looked at her. Then one of the girls giggled and ran out of the room. A tall Chinese girl came into the room only a few seconds later. "I am Li Ming. You are called Dawn?"

"Yes. My name is Missus Dawn Decker. My unmarried name was Dawn Everly. I am married to Craig Decker, the commander of the ship that pioneered our way and provided many of the inventions that allowed our escape to the stars."

"You are here to check on us?"

"The women. It would not have been appropriate for Craig to come to the female compound so he sent me to see if you are comfortable and being taken care of."

"I see. And what would happen if we were being mistreated and unhappy?"

"Craig is all powerful. He was tempted to destroy your ships but relented by letting the Chinese escape Earth. We sent you to a planet all to yourselves to protect the other colonists that went to the stars in peace."

"And you think he could change our situation without us being punished?"

"Yes. I do think that. So will you tell me what is good and what is bad and what you would like done to improve your condition here?"

Li Ming paused in thought and finally decided to speak the truth. "The women here are prisoners in this compound. We are forced to whore ourselves with many men on a set schedule. Many of us have become pregnant from these liaisons and are still required to maintain our schedule of sex with different men each night. We are not allowed out of the compound, but come, let me show you around."

Dawn followed as Li Ming narrated. "This is our meeting room. It is where we can come to watch the videos. The only videos we have to watch are old television shows from the old Chinese government. We have heard from some of the men that there are unlimited videos from around the world and almost every book written. We are not allowed anything but government propaganda about how we women are performing an important function for the military. I do not see any need for military if we are truly on a separate planet with only four thousand other Chinese."

Dawn replied, "And you would like to have something besides Chinese government television and propaganda. I will put that first on my list that you have access to everything on the computer including educational television on this planet that Craig named Vulcan."

"That would be marvelous if you could make it happen, but education is not for women. We have been told all our lives that we are subjects, not people."

"That will be changing immediately. On the other colonies, women outnumber the men six to one."

"Does that mean that most women do not have to have sex with multiple men?"

"Yes, it means that many women wish there were more men. Some women choose to have sex with more than one man, but generally it is the men that cannot keep up with that many women."

"What about being told they must have children?"

"Now that is why there are so many women in the other colonies. To make these new planets successful, we need more population. More women, means more children in less time."

"I see what you mean, my name means "pretty and bright" in English. The other women look to me for leadership. I can see that our Chinese colony needs more women to have more children. With the few women here we cannot hope to even maintain our population let alone grow it. If this generation does not get everything done to set up a self sufficient industry, we will not have enough people to keep the systems going."

"That is correct. In the other colonies the women are critical for setting up this new civilization. Because there is a shortage of men each man is expected to have six wives if they can mutually decide to mate up that way. However, the women are not expected to be dependent upon the men because there are so few men. The women have duties just like the men: farming, making clothing, hunting for food, operating equipment, mining metals, producing oil products, repairing equipment, nursing, any skill at all. The men have a few jobs they are suited for because of their greater strength. They build buildings, fences, the heavy work of mining and drilling for oil. As far as intelligence all are basically equal. Men tend to be better operating and assembling equipment, but women are better at many other things. Theoretical physics, chemistry, even many engineering disciplines."

"We are fed well, our male visitors say our food is far better than theirs. We need more fruits and vegetables, but we have plenty of meat although it is like strange chicken. The slabs delivered to us are far bigger than any chicken I have heard of."

"Here is our courtyard. The compound is a large square with the only entrance the main door. The inside of the compound is open to the sun and weather. We have had some men smuggle in a few seeds for us to plant. We are mostly fluent in English and can read the instructions on the seed packets. In a few years, we hope that we will have fruit trees and bushes for some fresh food."

"Attached to our building is the medical center where the doctors are located. I understand that some of the men have been injured and that we are running low on some antibiotics. The doctors have gone out of their way to do what they can for the women. They seem to understand that we must be healthy to have many babies for the success of the colony."

"We have our own guards to keep the men out. The admiral did that correct. If we had male guards they would allow too many men to come into our compound. The only men allowed are those scheduled for sexual visits. They are limited to once a month unless they have done something noteworthy and then they get another visit."

"What is your biggest complaint except the videos?"

"For most it is that we are not allowed out of the compound to see for ourselves what it is like out there. We were military and know how to handle a gun or perform hand to hand combat. However, for some, it is that they cannot take time off for that monthly period or even when they are pregnant and feeling sick."

"I don't know how much I can help on the first of those two, but I think I can get you some time off. How about I try to make a deal with the admiral where you women can select a number of your women to get a day off. If you choose the same woman for several days, that is your option. I think that once a woman is five months pregnant they should be kept aside. As you said, with the population issue we need to make sure there are as few miscarriages as possible. I wish you were not in this situation, but when your country decided to ignore the rules and send mostly men, your fate was sealed. I'll see what I can do. I also think that you should have hours when you can do something constructive for the colony besides have sex and babies. Having many babies is essential for the survival of the colony, but not the only thing."

"Thank you Dawn Decker. I feel that you are being most honest with us. I know you are not to blame if you can achieve nothing. Women have always been second class in China."

Dawn brought her report back to Craig and Shelby. Craig went to the admiral with a dire forecast.

"Admiral. My wife, Dawn, was the one that visited in your women's compound and after discussion I have recommendations to help your colony survive.

1. The women need access to all of the videos on your ship especially those on Vulcan and the training videos unique to Vulcan.

2. The women need to be more than sex and baby machines. There are things that women do better than most men. They should have access to the gardens and fields. They can post their own guards to keep the men away while they work and surely you have enough control over your own men so that they do not try to interfere. Your colony needs clothing and your men are definitely not adept at making clothing. The women should have a shop built onto the compound for them to make the clothing. Communicate with them after they have had some time with the videos. They may find some other areas. They are human and I have found women to be as smart as men and while

men are better at some things women are better at others. You cannot afford to lose experts from your small population. If the women are not allowed to do more than vegetate they may start dying off too soon and your colony will die.

3. The women that are more than five months pregnant could possibly have a miscarriage and your colony would lose a child. They need to be taken out of the sex rotation to protect the colonies children. Keep in mind that you need more girl children. Girl children in China have been very underrated in the past, but you need women to go around for the male children in the next generation.

4. If the women are not happy, they will lose their health. I can understand why you do not want them to leave the compound where they could get hurt or wounded by the animals on Vulcan, but another thing is that you are treating them worse than whores. Women have their periods and some women find it painful and do not want to have sex. Within reason the women want to be able to select a few of their own to be temporarily taken out of the sexual routines for a day whenever the women's group decides.

5.   You want the women to get interested in science and research and development. With the time for watching the educational videos they may come up with new inventions I did not think of that would help your colony.

"Let me think on your demands. What would you do if I just ignore these demands? What would you do if I ignored your demands and punished the women for speaking with your female?"

"They are not demands; they are honest assessments of something you need to do for the success of your colony here on Vulcan. If you choose not to enact all of these suggestions, your colony will suffer from your bad decisions, just like they have suffered by coming to Vulcan except it might be fatal. If you follow these suggestions, it will help your colony thrive. I do not know what I would do if you punished the women. I have the power to destroy your whole colony. I could just kill you, but I think you might be more reasonable than your lowly troops. You would show your lack of intelligence. I think you will choose to carry out at least some of these suggestions."

"Well said, I will try all of your suggestions. The Chinese government made a gross error in the planning for this expedition. I did not help in our first conversations. I think I have learned that it is to my benefit to take your suggestions to heart. Thank you, Craig Decker. Will you be returning?"

"Yes we have to return to the other colonies but we will return here to Vulcan. I do not know a schedule, but we will return. Hopefully you will have good roads, good Earth crops, and maybe even some Earth animals. I suggest that if you don't have anyone trained in test tube animals that you have some of the women take on that training and that job. I'm sure you would enjoy some beef and pork with your dinosaur."

"Good idea, Craig Decker. I will hope we have a thriving colony in a few years."

Craig left the admiral and they were ready to leave Vulcan. "What are you thinking, Shelby?"

"Craig. I am thinking we should take a closer look at one or more of those apparently dead earth-like planets we saw on the way here."

"Before or after we visit Pyramid?"

Dawn answered, "I think that Pyramid is probably doing well without us. Yes, I want to visit them and see for myself, but a couple of those planets are actually closer than Pyramid. Let's take a closer look."

SHIP set out for the nearest dead planet. As they went into orbit they could plainly see the remains of cities and what were once orchards, but they found no infrared signatures signifying any large animal life. But something built the cities. They took several orbits and could find no evidence of a cataclysmic event. No super volcanoes, no big scar from an interplanetary body like wiped out Mars and Earth.

Craig commanded, "SHIP, what is the atmosphere like down there?

"Earthlike but high in oxygen and low in carbon dioxide. Perfectly breathable, but the plant life is not healthy, probably because the air is short on carbon dioxide that plants need to convert into growing."

"Okay, are we seeing cities down there?"

"Yes. Those were cities down there, but they have decayed." "Do you detect radiation or poisonous air?"

"The background radiation is ten times that of Earth, but still safe. Especially if you do not stay there long. If you want to visit, when I teleport you back I will not bring any radiation to the ship and I will repair any damage to yourself."

"Okay, give me some weapons, just in case, and teleport me down to what appears to be that open area that was surrounded by large buildings. I would like to see for myself and get some samples. Better give me some large Impervium sample boxes that will seal air tight for you to run tests on."

"This looks like old concrete I am standing on. Some of these things look like they may have been vehicles, because they were big enough to have carried people or things and what is left is in the streets. The buildings fell like the new your trade center except there is no evidence of metal girders. SHIP, teleport me to an area of small lower buildings. This looks like it might have been residential. Again there are shapes on the streets like they might have been vehicles at one time, but there is nothing recognizable as such other than the relative sizes and that they are in the street. I will send up some samples of whatever they were. I see nothing of value."

"SHIP, teleport me to the areas that looked like orchards outside the city."

"We need Estera to look at these trees. It may have been an orchard but hasn't had human care in a couple of hundred years at least. I am sending up some sample limbs and leaves, and some of the grass and brush growing up between trees. Shelby, get your kit and teleport down and let's take some water samples from the river down there." Craig walked to the river where Shelby appeared and took samples. She tested them on the spot and took some samples for SHIP to test."

While at the orchards they saw some miniature deer, small hog type animals, and what might be cows but only three feet high at their shoulders.

"SHIP, bring us back, first Shelby then bring me back."

"What does everyone think?"

Dawn said, "I think we need to go on to another planet and then on to Pyramid. We need to visit another planet to see if it is similar and then try to figure out what happened."

"I agree." Shelby responded, "The water had no algae at all. Nothing. Nada. That's not normal. It may be due to the lack of carbon dioxide in the atmosphere for the algae to feed off. That tells me there is no animal life."

The next planet was the same. SHIP had done some analysis and reported, "I found no evidence of animal life in the water or any of the samples. It appears that the buildings and vehicles may have been made with Impervium which turned out to not be impervious to everything. All the ingredients were present for Impervium, but the molecular bonds were broken. As a computer, the judgment as to what happened is beyond my programming. We need an archeologist or a climatologist to come back and study these planets."

Pyramid was doing great. Their civilization had so much handed to them on a silver platter that they could not fail. The birth rate was high. Whenever they needed meat they rounded up cattle, pigs, chickens. Their orchards were growing nicely. No fruit yet, but they did not expect to have fruit trees for a couple of years. They had gotten strawberries, grapes, raspberries, and other bushes to already produce. Their roads had been cleared, but there was still a lot of work to do.

Craig wanted to cut their visit short, "We need to get back to Pangaea, get Estera to study the plants on those dead planets. Get Jill to study the decayed

Impervium or whatever the metal was. As a geologist maybe she can help SHIP explain the high background radiation. I need to find someone to stay behind on Pangaea to be temporarily replaced with an archaeologist to study the missing civilizations on those dead planets.

"SHIP, can I change my crew?"

"As long as you do not exceed six wives. Once you add a new one, the old one can never return unless one of the originals dies or leaves voluntarily."

THE FAMILY

- Craig Decker – Captain
- Dawn Everly – astronavigation
- Jill Leary – Petrochemical engineering and Geology. Shelby Denton– Cheerleader – Chemistry
- Estera Shea— Skidmore – Botany Sandy Scofield – beach –Zoology
- Karen Martin aka She Who Wanders - Survivalist

FUTURE VOLUMES

GENERATIONS

SHIP discovers another earthlike planet, but when they inspect further they discover what was apparently a planet wide die off of everything. There were expansive cities lying in ruins. There was abandoned equipment from the cities to the farms. They discover that Impervium was not so impervious. The question is: what happened to this civilization? What happened to the Impervium that was supposed to be a new metal impervious to everything. SHIP and family decide to start a much broader search for traces of civilization in the stars.

COLLISION WITH ATLANTIS

Mankinds explorers meet the people from Atlantis. The ones they meet are the castoffs of the prime Atlantis society and they follow our explorers home. They are very scientifically advanced and ready to conquer mankind's worlds. Mankind fights guerrilla warfare against the invaders while Craig's descendants search for SHIP. They use the ship to visit

Earth again to see if mankind survived on Earth. They develop a different weapons technology that confuses the Atlanteans and peace is negotiated.

EXPLORATION CONTINUES.

First Contact with the real Atlantis survivors.

ABOUT THE AUTHOR

The Author spent over 39 years with the United States Air Force in the USA, Asia, and Europe. He had some part in the development of most of the new weapons system in development between 1979 and 1989. Some of those systems are just now being delivered. He taught classes in weapons system research and development and logistics management as a guest lecturer at the Air Force Institute of Technology and various conference rooms around the USA. Over 3000 current and future managers attended his class on R&D scheduling. He served on many brain storming teams to come up with unique solutions to military problems from shooting down space objects to moving "dud" bombs off an active runway.

He is now retired from both active duty and civil service. He is still active in writing, the local amateur radio club, towing the Shriner float in parades and going to almost weekly dances and generally enjoying himself.